WHAT *Was Lost*

THE HEALTH AND HAPPINESS SOCIETY

WHAT *Was Lost*

KATIE CROSS

THHS
PUBLISHING

WHAT
Was Lost

Chick Lit

Cover designed by Jenny Zemanek at www.seedlingsonline.com
Paperback interior by Atthis Arts LLC at www.atthisarts.com
Ebook productions E-books Done Right at www.ebooksdoneright.com

Published by THHS Publishing.

ISBN 978-1-946508-21-8

Visit the author at www.kcrosschicklit.com to learn more about *The Health and Happiness Society*.

For all my readers—the best is yet to come.

Grief

Snow flurries drifted to the ground below a slate sky.

Ahead of me lay my brother's coffin, adorned with crimson, white, and emerald flowers. Their delicate strands and bright color against such a bleak backdrop pricked my heart like a pincushion.

The backdrop of a city filled the horizon behind his grave. Most of it was obscured by newly fallen snow and heavy clouds. Next to me stood one of my best friends, Rachelle. She reached over and took my hand, squeezing it gently. The gesture—from someone who wasn't outwardly affectionate in the first place—meant a lot.

Oh, how I needed it.

The gentle sound of my sister-in-law weeping filled the tepid air. Not many people lingered at the graveside, most of them my brother's friends that I'd gone to school with. Must have been eons ago. Decades, actually. The passage of time on their faces felt surreal. They had wrinkles and graying hair just like me—although my hairdresser Janae helped me keep my blondish color looking natural, even if I was fifty-one.

Jerry had been a quiet man in a quieter life. He lived in a perfectly normal house, on a perfectly normal street, with a perfectly normal job as an accountant. He'd been perfectly happy with normal. Nothing outstanding had ever happened to him—until his third heart attack. While his heart hadn't been working well for a while, I still felt robbed. He was taken too early.

Like all the others.

We stared at the coffin as if we didn't know what to do. Part of me felt numb. The same part that, deep inside, couldn't believe I was here. Again.

Jerry's pastor climbed out of a car near the entrance to the cemetery and headed across the crinkly grass. Even I felt relief.

Someone else was in charge.

The pastor positioned himself at the head of Jerry's beautiful mahogany coffin. "Thank you, ladies and gentleman, for your attendance today."

His soft-spoken voice punctuated the air, but the rest of his words drifted in the wind of my thoughts. They moved in and out, fluid and fleeting. Rachelle tugged on my hand and leaned closer.

"Are you all right, Mira?"

"Fine," I whispered.

She opened her mouth to protest, seemed to think better of it, and gazed forward again. My phone buzzed in my pocket. Lexie, no doubt. Maybe Bitsy checking on me. Tears welled up in my eyes for the first time that day.

My fingertips grew cold as we waited for the preacher to finish his quiet, steady monologue. Once he concluded, the queue of people seemed to float back. The pastor wandered off to greet my sister-in-law, clasped her hands, murmured a few words, and turned to someone else. I watched him go, wondering what it would be like to come in and out of funerals so easily. So unattached.

"Mira?"

My sister-in-law's trembling voice caught my attention. I turned to find her at my side and embraced her. She felt fragile in my arms, like a cracked eggshell. She'd always felt frail. Someone I instinctively wanted to protect. It must have been why Jerry fell in love with her eight years ago—they had nothing else in common.

"Are you going to be okay for the rest of the week?" I asked, pulling back.

Charlotte nodded, swallowing hard. Tears glazed her eyes like a new piece of pottery. I recognized the look. She would be okay for the rest of the day, probably even the month. With death, time was the real enemy. Eventually, you couldn't hide from the fact that you had to live the rest of your life without them at your side.

"Yes," she said. "My brother Franklin and I will be leaving for Canada next week. I just . . . I can't . . ."

"Tolerate the idea of Christmas without Jerry singing carols and getting drunk on eggnog?" I asked with a wry smile.

She half sobbed and clung to my arms. "How have you done it? I-I can barely breathe. Your babies, and y-your parents, a-and Bill, and now . . . and you're . . ."

The words she didn't say lingered in the air.

You're all alone now.

"One breath at a time." I tightened my grip on her. "I promise, you'll get through. Sometimes that might be the most you can focus on, but eventually those breaths add up, and time passes."

Charlotte's baby-blue eyes were red-rimmed and swollen, smeared with makeup that she'd attempted despite me advising otherwise. Despite my love for a good doll-up session, a funeral was no place for mascara.

A morsel of resolve seemed to strengthen her. I could see it in her eyes.

"Okay," she said. "Okay."

Her brow wrinkled, forming near-perfect crease lines just above her penciled eyebrows. She was the only woman I'd ever met who knew makeup better than I did.

"What about you?" she asked, mopping her face. "What's going to happen to you now?"

The urge to laugh almost overwhelmed me, but my throat was too tight. Wasn't *that* the question of the century? Jerry's death had left more than just a brother-sized hole in my heart. It had wiped out my last living relative. There was no one left. No one for me to rely on if things got ugly.

Rachelle's hand tightened around mine, and I realized I'd forgotten she was there.

"I'll be just fine," I said to Charlotte. Although my voice had some lift to it, the words felt wooden coming out of my mouth. "I always am."

Tears pooled in her eyes. She reached out, taking my free hand, and squeezed it. "I'm going to miss you, Mira. Jerry loved you so much. I hated it at first. You were his favorite and always meant the world to him. You never let him down, even through all these health issues and scares. I know it wasn't easy, all this driving and taking care of me and him."

The tears sparkled in her eyes now. One of them ran down her cheek, looking chilly in the frigid winter air. I squeezed her hand, unable to speak while the quiet crowd milled around us. People with unfamiliar faces started to line up behind her.

"I love you, too, Charlotte. You were the best thing that ever happened to him."

Charlotte nodded once. She managed a wan smile at Rachelle, then looked back at me.

"You're so strong, Mira. So strong. I draw strength from you. Thank you."

My heart hiccupped in my chest. A joke, surely. I wasn't strong. Living one breath at a time hadn't been a choice. Life didn't *ask* if I wanted to keep my family.

I knew that I would never see Charlotte again. Once she went back to Canada, she would have no reason to return. They had married in their mid-forties—kids had been out of the question. The cold feeling in my chest only grew.

Orphan, it whispered. *You are an orphan.*

Even at fifty-one, I knew it was true.

"You should go," I said to Charlotte. Tears stung my eyes. I didn't know if I could actually say goodbye. The thought of turning around and leaving Charlotte and Jerry was almost more than I could bear. Jerry wouldn't have wanted it that way, but Charlotte wasn't the go-it-alone-type and I would never leave the shop.

Charlotte gave me one last embrace, pressed a salty kiss to my cheek, and turned around. When I couldn't see her soulful eyes anymore, I was glad. Breath came easier then. I stepped back a couple of paces. Rachelle followed, never letting go. The crowd seemed to envelop Charlotte. She fell into their collective embrace.

"Do you want to go talk to Jerry's friends?" Rachelle asked. Her breath puffed out in front of her.

"Not really."

"The meeting after?"

"Definitely not."

"Then let's go home."

Silence stretched between us for several beats. Neither of us moved. There was a dinner afterwards for family and close friends, but the thought of talking to total strangers about my brother, a man they knew so differently than I did, made me sick to my stomach. Jerry would want me to go home and have a stiff drink.

Or an ice-cold Pepsi. With some tiramisu. Or maybe even some French fries. Bitsy would kill me for thinking about eating while mourning.

But surely grief earned me a pass in the calorie department, even from Bitsy.

Jerry's coffin caught my eye as I turned to go. In such a toneless, gray world, the splash of color from the flowers almost felt like a joke. Maybe the heavens knew exactly how ugly I felt inside, so they sent this awful gloom as a sign. Like something was about to burst in my chest. A dam that I'd been holding back for years and years.

I was Mira. The politically correct, sweetly naive, not-too-confident-but-could-handle-herself Southern belle. The owner of Mira's Sewing and Vac. A widow. The woman who adored Pepsi and wild makeup.

But maybe, now that Jerry had left, maybe I wouldn't be. Maybe, like the clouds, I would just break. Spill frost and ice and bitter cold all over everything and everyone.

With a deep breath, I shoved back the desperate thoughts and squeezed Rachelle's hand.

No. I would never. Could never.

"Yeah." I nodded. "Let's go home."

Whatever that meant now.

Mira, it's Lexie. I didn't think you'd answer, so I wanted to leave a message. I'm so sorry I couldn't make it to Jerry's funeral—came down with something and I'm puking my guts out. But know that I love you. I'm there with you in spirit, and I'll check in with you when you get back. By the way, I sent you a package of my favorite brownies, two thingamajigs of your favorite eyeshadow that you can't buy there anymore, and maybe far too many other treats that I shall not name in case of Bitsy. Don't tell Bitsy?

Megan here, Mira. I'm so sorry about your brother and that I couldn't be there to invade your house and fix you a western omelet after the funeral. You've been through so much, but you got this, girl power. Let me know how I can help.

Oh, and in those moments when you feel like you don't got this? Call me. I'm always here.

Belonging

My bag landed on the wooden floor with a *thud.*

Silence permeated my house. Too quiet. But it had always felt that way, even before Bill died. And once he was gone, the hush settled in like it had decided to stay.

The late November air followed me inside with a rush of cold. I left my bag at the bottom of the stairs and tweaked the thermostat as I headed for the kitchen. Seconds later, the distant whir of the furnace kicked on. Comfort. Like the pulse of a beating heart.

Despite the stillness, I drew some comfort from my own space, no matter how big it felt. A hint of Mama's favorite potpourri on the air. Persimmon, mixed with pomegranate. A strange combination, but she adored it. I couldn't seem to part with it.

I stopped in the middle of the room and sniffed.

Lemon.

Tears filled my eyes as I glanced at my perfectly buffed wooden floor and a sink that sparkled with the light scent of bleach.

Bitsy had come over and cleaned my house.

"Thanks, Bits," I murmured.

With five bedrooms, a kitchen, a couple of living rooms, and plenty of bathrooms to clean, I only lived in a small part of the bottom floor and an upstairs bedroom. I surveyed the fridge with my head tilted to the side. Half a carton of milk. A lump of hard butter. Noodles made out of sweet potatoes—something that Bitsy had told me I had to try. I still hadn't tried them.

Toast it was.

My phone rang just as I reached for the bread, butter, and the last two eggs. At least I could snazz it up and make it French toast. I propped the phone on my shoulder.

"Hello?"

"Mira!"

Sweet Lexie's bright voice rang through the phone line. The sound brought a little cheer to the empty kitchen and warmed my heart. Of *course* she would be the first to call and check on me. Lexie wouldn't expect me to be strong. She wouldn't care if I fell into a wallowing mess of tears. Although that sounded appealing, the rest of me just wanted to sleep.

Bless all of them, but they took care of me.

I pushed the ingredients onto the counter, managing to infuse real delight into my voice. "Hey, Lex!"

"What's going on over there?"

"Just walked in, honey. Going to make some dinner."

"Anything good?"

"French toast."

She groaned. "That sounds sooo good. Bitsy pulled me into the no-bread challenge. I regret every second of saying yes."

"I heard about it. Didn't join."

"How are you?"

Overwhelmed. Exhausted. Not sure what to do next.

"Hanging in there."

"I'm so sorry again, Mira."

"Thanks, honey."

"Anything I can do?"

"Bring my brother back from the dead?"

"Yeah," she snorted, half in amusement. "I'll grab Dad while I'm at it. He and I have some talking to do."

A grin flittered to my lips. I grabbed a frying pan and set it on the stovetop. "Indeed. Bitsy came and cleaned my house, so unless you want to restock my fridge, I think I'll be okay."

"Well, you know where to find me the moment you need me. Speaking of Bitsy, have you heard from her?"

"Ah, no. Just got back."

"Dang. I can't get ahold of her."

My brow furrowed. "I'll probably see her really soon." I leaned against the counter. "Want me to have her call?"

"Just had a question about next week's meeting. I'm supposed to coordinate it, and we're talking about the big Christmas party Rachelle is planning."

"Oh. Right. I'd forgotten all about it."

"No worries. You have a lot on your mind. Thanks, Mira. Oh, gotta go. Bradley is calling."

"Sure. Talk later, honey."

My enthusiasm to fix dinner waned after I hung up. I turned to crack an egg but stopped. The options weren't all that appetizing, after all, and I wasn't that hungry. An ice-cold Pepsi, however, would do the trick. The way the bubbles fizzled between my teeth always gave me a little thrill, and I hadn't had one in months now.

I chucked the toast back into the fridge and glanced at the clock. 8:30. Bitsy was probably putting the girls to bed, so calling would be pointless. I'd call her later.

My eyes roved the empty kitchen. After Bill died, I'd expected to tap into my inner messy girl that had always driven him crazy. But I'd been so used to being neat for him that it seemed wrong to tap into my authentic side.

"You know what, Bill?" I said to the empty air—because I always did. Because it was so much easier than not talking to anyone. "I think I'll refresh my lipstick and just go check on the shop. That's what you would do, isn't it?"

Relief flooded me as I grabbed my purse, my car keys, and my phone, and headed off to the shop.

Where I *really* belonged.

Mira's Sewing and Vac waited for me in all her beautiful, dark, Christmas-decked glory.

Shadows cloaked the ten-shop strip mall that had been my second home for the last twenty-five years. Only the pale, anemic glow of a street light illuminated the empty parking lot. I parked in front of my store, only two shops away from the far end. My keys jangled when I shoved them into my purse, opened the door, and headed inside.

A crisp breeze sent leaves scuttling across the parking lot ahead of me like old bones. I shivered when the crisp air pierced through my coat and chilled my skin. My breath billowed in front of me as I approached the main door. Vague, lumpy shadows as familiar to me as the veins on the back of my hand haunted the inside.

Lights sprang to life when I flicked the switch on. Then I turned and shut the door behind me, locking it with a firm *snick*. I stopped, closed my eyes, and inhaled deeply.

Home.

Brand-new sewing machines flanked me on the right, spread out on high, thin tables. They were new, glossy. Behind them sat the used section. Well-loved sewing machines of various ages populated those tables. Less glamor, but lower prices. Along the wall behind them ran rows upon rows of thread. Gigantic spools for professional sergers, smaller ones for home-sewing systems, and more. The rainbow of colors was my pride and joy—no other store had a selection like mine.

Some of the thread was imported from Europe, even.

To the left were vacuums, lined up like shiny new bobbins. The new and used sections were barely separate—inventory was low. Common, for this time of year.

As if being back at Mira's Sewing and Vac imbued me with magic, a spark of life bloomed in my veins.

"It's because it was your favorite place, Bill," I said as I gathered the mail off the floor. Bill had so deeply loved the store that I'd often referred to it as *the other woman*.

His voice slipped easily through my mind. *I know.*

It always did here. As if his friendly ghost inhabited these walls.

My nose wrinkled when I stopped at the cash register and sorted through the mail. Two light-pink makeup compacts and a shiny lip gloss stuck out of the pencil bowl. I resisted the urge to check my reflection. What did it matter?

An envelope grabbed my attention. A new shipment of vacuums had come in yesterday. No doubt James, the owner of the Italian restaurant next door, had signed for it on my behalf.

The shop had always smelled musty, no matter how many times we had the carpet cleaned or scrubbed the walls. No number of essential oils, potpourri combinations, or cleaners had worked it out. Over the years, however, it had come to be familiar. Comforting. After a while, Bill had started to smell the same way. Maybe both of us had. When I could smell the shop, I could smell Bill.

Enough to keep me company on the darkest nights.

I yanked off my coat, tossed it onto the back of a chair, and opened the fridge. Diet Pepsi—the regular was hidden in the back in case

Bitsy came around—as well as delicious pastries from the Frosting Cottage, leftovers from James, and a half carton of ice cream from *Ice Cream Delights* down the row. I grabbed an apple and a box of fettucine alfredo James had sent over a couple of days before, and shut the fridge.

The television flared to life as I flicked it on, letting the sound of a TV show host fill the empty space. When I settled onto the couch on the other side of the room, my aching heart finally gave a contented sigh. I whizzed through the channels until I found a cheesy Christmas romance.

Must you torture me in death? Bill asked.

"Yes," I said, popping my lips as I twirled the pasta on my fork. "Just what I hoped for."

The cushions sighed beneath me as I sank into them. I grimaced. Time for a new couch, but . . . I *still* couldn't bring myself to do it. Bill adored this couch. So had I, at one point. When things were good, we had snuggled up to movies on it after work.

A commercial for a Black Friday sale flickered on the screen. I bit back a groan. Of course. The holidays were coming up like a speedboat. Leave it to Jerry to die around the most family-oriented time of the year. Not to mention all I had to do to get ready for the Black Friday sale and my annual Christmas Eve Extravaganza. Last year, it had generated in one day more than double my revenue on my best month.

My eyes slid to a free calendar tacked on the wall. Thanksgiving was only a week away.

My thoughts roamed to Bitsy and her girls. What was I going to get them this year? Bitsy wanted that KitchenAid, but Jim had said something about getting it for her . . .

I checked my phone again and frowned. Nine-thirty, and I still hadn't heard from her. Unusual, especially after I'd been traveling. I opened my phone and sent her a quick text.

> *Made it back. Just at the shop for a while.*
> *Give me a call.*

A Christmas jingle played in the background during a commercial break.

Bill and I had spent several holidays in the shop—mostly after the miscarriages. The empty home was always too big, then. At the shop, Christmas lights burned bright and cheery. A fresh wreath on the back of the door smelled like evergreen. Customers flowed in and out, looking for presents, filling the void. Bill dressed up as Santa Claus, just for the fun of it.

If Jerry had lived, I would have seen him this Christmas. I would have driven to his house, watched him get drunk on eggnog, and woken up in the morning to the warmth of my small family. Charlotte always made really thick pieces of French toast for breakfast, dripping with maple syrup, golden eggs, and sizzling sausage.

This year. This Christmas it would be just one person.

Me.

"No, I won't be alone for Christmas," I said out loud just to emphasize how silly it sounded. I wouldn't be alone for Christmas! Any of the Health and Happiness girls would invite me over. Bitsy was probably already planning on it, even though this would be her first Christmas with Jim and the girls. Besides, there was the Christmas party Rachelle was hosting.

With another quick shake of my head, I grabbed my phone, sent Bitsy another text message telling her to just call me tomorrow, and sank back into the couch just as the romantic comedy returned from commercial break.

The bell on the shop door chimed the next day around noon.

A man entered wearing a pair of black slacks and a button-up white shirt without a tie. Young, probably thirty-five. I'd never seen him before. Men of his age—and quite *attractive* appearance—rarely stopped by Mira's Sewing and Vac. Unless they came in looking for a present for their wife, but this guy didn't look the part. His wife seemed like the type to drink mocktails every day at noon and go out to lunch with her friends after a pedicure.

A week had passed since I'd sold anything more than thread and bobbins, which was an abysmal new record. Bill would have run some ads, but they never paid out anymore.

"Hello," I called with a little wave. "Can I help you find something?"

He smiled in a charming, white-toothed way. "I'm here to speak with the shop owner. Are you Mirabelle Montgomery?"

"Mira, please. Yes, I am."

My metaphorical hackles rose. Anyone who called me *Mirabelle* was someone to suspect. There was something a little too suave about his loose blond hair and the way his piercing blue eyes seem to look right through mine. His stance was a little too . . . easygoing, as if he'd trained for it.

He stuck out a hand.

"My name is Tadd Williams. It's good to meet you, Mira. I've heard a lot about you from the other shop owners in the area. All good things, of course."

Why was he talking to the other shop owners?

After I accepted his handshake, his hand dropped to his side. He glanced around, something like reluctant admiration in his eyes. It certainly wasn't disgust, which I knew how to spot in new customers. A few leaks over the years had led to ballooning stains and crumbling tiles in the ceiling, but the overall charming facade hadn't faded. It was still as warm and cozy a shop as ever before.

"Good to meet you, Tadd," I said. "Is there something you'd like to talk about?"

He smiled. "Yes, actually. I'm here to see how you like running a business here."

"Here?"

"In this strip mall."

For a long beat, I stared at him, not sure what to say. He let the silence ride, as if he were used to this kind of thing. With a smile like that, he probably was.

"It's . . . wonderful."

His gaze tapered. "Really?"

"Of course. Heaven on earth."

"The structure was built over fifty years ago."

"Tread carefully," I said with the saccharine smile Mama used to give to the crotchety neighbor that chased our cat with a rake. "So was I."

A flash of something appeared in his gaze. Amusement, perhaps.

A gleam of a challenge. I may not have been as naturally gifted in sales as Bill, but even I recognized another salesman when I saw one.

"A young age at any rate," he said, "but doomsday for real-estate prospects."

"Real estate?"

He reached into his pocket and extended a card. I accepted it reluctantly. *Platinum Developers.* The back of it glossed a bright silver, reflecting my startled expression. Tadd motioned around us with a twirl of his hand.

"My company is interested in buying this strip mall. I'm going around to talk with the store owners to see about your experiences here."

Why would you want to buy this place? I almost asked, but bit it back. It may not have youth on its side, but it had charm. Experience. Wisdom. No new real-estate agent or developer could mimic that.

"Oh?"

He nodded, taking my shocked expression in stride. "Yes. We'd like to bring new life to this part of town."

"And new profits."

God don't like ugly, Mama would have said about my sass. I almost apologized but stopped myself. Normally I wasn't so blunt. Today, with Jerry at the forefront of my mind, blunt felt good. Mama would roll over in her grave, but she could use a little exercise.

Tadd's easy smile appeared again, annoyingly nonplussed, before fading into an earnest expression.

"This neighborhood is tired. We've had our eyes on it for a while. With downtown growing, expansion and traffic here has slowed. I'm sure you've seen and experienced the results of that firsthand, like most of the other shop owners."

I pressed my lips together and extended my arm to give his card back. "Some businesses can stand on their own, traffic notwithstanding. It's the advantage of age, you see. I have very loyal customers."

"I'm glad to hear that," he said, and seemed to mean it. "Unfortunately, of the nine other stores here, few can say the same. Crime has risen, and housing has been suffering. That means traffic here is at an all-time low."

Why would he possibly care about that?

"What does that have to do with Platinum Development?" I bounced the card. He acted as if he didn't see it.

"We want to help the community."

"Right."

His eyebrows rose in genuine surprise. To his credit, he said nothing, just regarded me in silent question, as if he couldn't believe I would doubt him.

"A development company?" I said, feeling as if I were sinking deeper into a hole of my own digging. "I find it hard to believe that your motivations would be so angelic. You want to develop it, I'm assuming?"

"Ah . . . yes."

What he *didn't* say rang in the air. *More like pulverize it,* I thought. The idea of this strip mall turned to rubble made my stomach churn. No. No way he could just come in here, upend lives, and erase memories.

"There are already stores, restaurants, and plenty of mini malls here," I said. Just south of the shop lay a more industrial part of town, but where I stood, there was still commercial property. "It hardly needs developing."

"Developing has many definitions. In not-very-distant history, this used to be the most active part of the town, probably back when you and your husband started here?"

The lingering question and simple insertion of *your husband* immediately cued me in: he'd done his homework. Likely a guy that wasn't used to losing, or changing his plan.

I already didn't like the feel of this.

"This is sounding a lot like you taking my business away from me," I said.

Negotiating had been Bill's area of expertise. While Bill worked out contracts and big sales, I decorated, ran the register, and created long-standing relationships. Even though I'd been running this on my own for years, I still would have preferred him to handle the legal matters. The shop had been on the brink of ruin more than once, unfortunately. But not once since Bill died.

Or maybe I'd just flirted with it for a long time.

Tadd shook his head. "Not at all. Your business is your own, wherever you want to take it. What we're interested in is the real estate in this area."

"You *do* want my store."

His even expression remained steady. "I want to discuss your experience here, as well as an offer that could bring you money, take a lacking piece of real estate off your hands, and open up better investment opportunities for your future."

"Again, you want—"

"To set you free." Tadd leaned forward, eyes bright. Despite myself, I couldn't help but stop. "Free to do whatever you want. Retire. Buy a new house. Get out from under the weight of running a business on your own."

"You don't know anything about me," I snapped.

His words sank in, anyway. Perhaps they wouldn't have if some corner of me hadn't thought about them before. If I, in the deepest parts of my longest nights, hadn't daydreamed about what it would be like to be free of the shop. To travel.

Without me? Bill asked. His whisper, spoken so softly I almost didn't hear it, pierced my heart.

"Never," I murmured.

"I know that Mira's Sewing and Vac has been open for twenty-five years," Tadd said, pulling me from my thoughts. "In all that time, you haven't expanded into any other local franchises, which makes me wonder where your financials are."

His eyebrows rose slightly, but he asked no questions. I let the silent assumption slide. Underneath my skin, a fire burned. No. We couldn't expand while drowning in debt from all the doctors, could we? I drew myself up a little taller, straightening my shoulders.

"That really isn't your business, is it?"

"Not if you don't want it to be."

"We didn't want to expand, thank you very much."

"Listen, Mira, I can see your skepticism. In fact, I appreciate a woman this honest. I get it. It's hard to believe that a development company would have pure motives. That's why I'd love to sit down and explain what we're thinking, what our plan is, and why. I think once you see where we're coming from, this won't seem so scary."

"I never said it was scary."

Another awkward silence. Something welled up inside my chest. Hot. Stinging. Like a whip ready to lash. I tamped it down. Residual emotions from Jerry's funeral, surely.

"Listen, Tadd, you're a really nice guy and probably have a substantial resume to prove it. But this is *my* store. My husband and I started it twenty-five years ago. I'm not going anywhere."

"You're on a ten-year lease, correct?"

Eureka! I'd forgotten about that. Now *there* was a way to get out of this silly notion of a development company coming in and . . . doing something. I propped my hands on my hips.

"Better believe it, honey. Only three years into it, and I've never broken any part of the agreement or been late on a payment. Can't break that."

He nodded slightly and dragged his bottom lip through his teeth. The bell rang on my door as someone stepped inside. Relieved, I waved to a young girl named Harriet who'd been coming in for craft supplies to make something for her father for Christmas.

"Back here, honey," I said. "I have everything you need." When I turned to Tadd again, his expression had resumed the bright friendliness of his initial approach. "Maybe later. I have customers to deal with. Besides, plenty of people have tried to buy this place before. They never do. It always falls apart at the last minute. I appreciate you personally stopping by, but it would be a waste of time for me to worry about it now. Have a happy Thanksgiving!"

My cheery, fixed smile seemed to do the trick in nudging him out. He regarded me for a moment, so I straightened my shoulders and met his gaze with a tenacity I didn't usually have. Then he smiled, and I couldn't help but notice that it *was* charming. Maybe even kind.

Crazy yankees.

"It was really good to meet you, Mira," he said with a hand lifted in farewell. "I look forward to working together. Let me know if there's a time of day, or a number I can call you at. I'm available to answer any questions you have at any time. And I'm serious about discussing our plans."

He strode away with the same confidence he'd brought in. Once outside, he headed to the right. My eyes followed him until Harriet's sweet voice pulled me out of my reverie.

"Hello, Miss Montgomery. I'm so excited to see the acrylic paints!" I rushed to help her.

"Wonderful! I have a special order for you right here."

The Hard Stuff

That night, I went to a place I tried my hardest to forget existed.

Bill always used the attic for storage. After he died, I rarely ventured up there. The open, sprawling space felt so . . . wasted. We'd bought this house for the six kids we planned on having. Living out our marriage with none of them meant we had few belongings to keep, even after twenty years.

The winter sun had drifted low in the sky when I stepped into the dusty space. Pale light shone through the round windows on either side of the attic. Dust motes drifted in the air, swirling around as I carefully moved across the cracked floor, past old cardboard boxes, a lampshade with hideous mustard tassels hanging off the bottom, and a collection of old photos I'd rather the world didn't see. A wooden crib that my father had given me loomed unused in the far corner. Next to it stood a mannequin I used in the store for a while to display projects when I ran the sewing club.

I shuffled by with a little pain in my chest. The last time I had been up here was a year after Bill died. When I couldn't stand to see his stuff anymore, I'd boxed it up and brought it upstairs.

At the back of the room, I spotted what I'd come for. An old, tattered cardboard box labeled in black sharpie that said *shop forms*. I grabbed a chair and pulled it close, then sat down with the box. Yellow, brittle papers waited inside.

The papers rustled as I shuffled through them, glancing briefly at words, dates, names. The dates ranged back anywhere from twenty-five to thirty years ago. A volley of memories overwhelmed me. Bill's college transcript from the year we had met on campus—all B's and C's. Receipts from a carpet cleaner. Paperwork about an obscure sewing machine. A birthday card from Jerry that I read twice, then tucked aside to take downstairs. Bill kept everything. His scratchy writing across the top of an invoice, noting the date and time of payment, gave me a nostalgic feeling.

Several leather-bound books filled the bottom of the box. I yanked them out and tossed them aside.

Journals.

Searching through the shop paperwork was like drifting through old scrapbooks, albeit ones that were less organized. A large yellow envelope tucked into the very bottom of the box caught my eye. I tilted my head to the side and freed it.

"Hello," I murmured. "What are you doing here?"

The envelope was thick, but only toward the bottom, as if it were filled with something oblong and small. When I reached inside, a handful of old photographs came out. Black and white, sepia-toned, a few dull color photos at the top. My heart nearly stopped when I recognized Jerry's face among the images.

Young Jerry.

The pictures were from my childhood, my parents' childhood even, and a few glimpses of our teenage years.

"My goodness," I murmured.

I sifted through the pictures, wanting to laugh and cry at the same time. What were these doing at the bottom of this box? Why were they *here* of all places? Nestled in the pictures were old receipts, postcards from different states when my mom and dad took road trips. So many little knickknacks of paper and time. Seeing Jerry's young, healthy face again, so soon after his death, left a gaping hole in my chest.

Did life continue after this? How could a person just be . . . erased? Most importantly—what had I come up here for?

At the very bottom of the envelope waited several pieces of folded, lined paper. My throat tightened. I knew what those were. For a long time, I just stared at them.

Bubbling rage surged in my chest. The same thing I'd felt when Mom and Dad died in the car accident. The exact wrath that had filled my heart when Bill died, leaving me *almost* utterly alone. The anger that attempted to overwhelm me at Jerry's funeral.

The papers flopped open, revealing their secrets.

My own, clean cursive handwriting filled the pages. Numbers ran along the left side of the paper. Written off to the right in neat, even strokes was a list. I had written it before I graduated high school. In fact, Jerry and I had mapped out what the rest of my life would look like. We were still young enough to be innocently naive, to think we could actually control what would happen.

How little we knew.

To confront the list I'd created when I thought everything was possible was silly. Why experience more pain? Why put myself through it? The knot that had been sitting on top of my heart since Jerry died bloomed into a flower of fire.

Still—I couldn't stop myself. As if the words grabbed my eyes and forced me to see them, I began to read.

Mira's Life List

1. Become an expert seamstress.
2. Move to New York to become a fashion designer.
3. Go to beauty school.
4. Marry someone ridiculously wealthy.
5. Go on a safari in Africa.
6. Open up a bookstore.
7. Become a lawyer.
8. Learn how to fly my own plane.
9. Win a year's worth of Pepsi from the local grocery store.
10. Run a marathon.
11. Go swimming in Hawaii.
12. Kiss during a rainstorm. Doesn't matter who, but a husband is preferred.

I snorted.

In fact, I *had* kissed someone during a rainstorm. A guy named Tommy Jones, who had been as neutral as his name. The kiss itself wasn't great. Cold. Raindrops hit my eyes and made my mascara run. Mascara that had, at the time, cost an exorbitant amount and shouldn't have been wasted. By the time we made it to shelter, hail pelted my shoulders like wet, stinging needles.

Still, I couldn't help a dry laugh at the list. Even at eighteen, I had clearly loved Pepsi—my whole family had. Further proof that it ran in my veins. Proof enough to show Bitsy that it deserved to stay with me—judgment free—during this rough time.

13. Have six children.
14. Homeschool all six children.
15. Learn how to make really good meatloaf. Not the kind that Mom makes, but don't ever tell her that.
16. Literally have a white picket fence.
17. Go on a long, pointless cruise with my husband. The kind where you don't really do anything but eat. Just make sure that the cruise line offers Pepsi, or plan to take my own.

This time, tears bubbled up in my eyes. *Six children.* Maybe my nerve endings were raw from losing Jerry, or maybe it was the full weight of the truth, but none of those things had happened.

The heart of my life list had been wrenched away. Taken. Lost in the pain of health issues, miscarriages, stillbirths, and financial ruin.

I continued to read through blurry eyes, perusing more than reading. We did have a white picket fence. We did have a really big house. We did, technically, have five children. Except none of them had lived. None of them had even seen full term. What did it matter? Whether or not I accomplished all of these things didn't make my life meaningful . . .

...did it?

I stuffed the list in my back pocket, slammed the lid on top of the box, and straightened. My hips creaked from the fast motion, and I grimaced. Goodness, I could barely even *read* about adventures anymore. Only a week away from the gym for Jerry's funeral, and I could already feel myself weakening.

The floor groaned as I worked my way back to the attic entrance. I would carefully climb down the ladder, tuck it back together, and push it into the attic again. Once it closed, I'd brush my hands off, walk downstairs, and forget the list. Visualizing it made it easier to forget all the things left undone.

Too late, I thought. *It's too late.*

Because fifty-one years of life that I'd planned on living but never did was nothing I wanted to dwell on. Missed chances. Lost opportunities. I could barely breathe through the pain in my chest. What had I accomplished? Had Jerry accomplished what he wanted?

What about Bill?

Pictures of Bill flashed through my mind. I remembered this feeling of reliving old grief once new grief washed over me. When Bill died, my parents' death replayed itself every single day. Sometimes, their memories weighed on me so heavily I wasn't sure I would make it through the hour. My heart was as creaky as my hips. It wasn't supposed to be this way.

This ending had never been on my list.

I made my way downstairs, yanked open the fridge, and cracked open a cold Pepsi I'd brought from my stash at the store. Let Bitsy say whatever she wanted. For me, this was the hard stuff.

It was definitely time for the hard stuff.

People dressed in bright colors, muted by heavy coats and frosty breath, streamed past my car.

I stared out the front window at the aged steeple of my church, depressed by the wet, stained stones. Wind gusted past, ushering people inside. Several dead leaves clung to the wet sidewalk, flapping in the temperamental weather. I sighed. Why had I put on pantyhose?

There was nothing in me that wanted to go inside.

Warmth, eventually some coffee, and familiar faces would greet me. I'd hug everyone—the way I always did—and paste a smile on my face. Just like normal. We'd talk about God and Jesus and the meaning of Christmas and how to be a good neighbor. There was a chance I'd feel better after.

Or worse.

Still . . . I couldn't force my body out of the car.

For some reason, my legs wouldn't move. Every time I commanded my hand to reach for the doorknob, it stayed put, as if weighed down. My heart felt as heavy as lead. Jerry hated church. Hated religion. It had been Mama's only dying regret, I had always imagined, that her son hadn't connected with God. With such an empty chasm in my chest, I could understand why.

Sometimes, it just seemed easier to let go.

My engine whirred quietly as two teenage girls tripped by, arms linked, giggling as they splashed through puddles while dashing inside. I leaned back in the seat with a sigh.

"Just . . . go. Go, Mira. 5, 4, 3, 2, 1 . . . go!"

Nothing budged.

I sighed again.

"Not today," I murmured, reaching for the gear shift. "I can't. I'm sorry. I don't even know who I'm talking to, but I can't go to church this week. Next time, Mama. I swear."

Just as I reached to pull the gear shift back, a noise sounded behind me. A creaky Honda—just like the one I drove in 1984—chugged into the parking space next to me. The slow, jerky movement of the car infuriated another driver, who laid on the horn two more times. Based on the strange angle of the other car, it was immediately clear that the Honda had snuck into the parking spot first. I glanced over to see an old woman behind the driver's seat, oxygen tubing strapped to her face.

She flipped a middle finger to the other car in her rearview mirror.

Gladys Rainier, the grumpy old widow who frightened most of the children—and adults—in our congregation. I hadn't seen her in years. In fact, I hadn't thought she could leave her house. Although I couldn't hear, it didn't take a lot of imagination to know what she was mumbled at the honking car. After jamming her car into park, and with excruciating slowness, she opened her door, stood, and straightened her bent body. Through my car windows, I could just make out her shout.

"Go to hell!" she called, shaking a fist. "You don't belong at church if you're barking at an old crippled lady!"

I held back a snort of laughter and put my car into reverse. If she didn't care, I didn't either.

"Amen, sister," I muttered as I slowly backed away. "You tell 'em."

A chill ruffled my hair, thanks to a recently fallen snow, as I stepped out of Mira's Sewing and Vac on Monday morning. Ice crystals sparkled on the sidewalk, which was slick with patches of ice. Fog filled the horizon with the impending scent of more snow. The lack of shoppers personified the bleak day.

Even with the lack of traffic, shop owners prepared for Black Friday deals. Puppies yipped from the pet store when the door opened a few spots to the left. I waved to Sheila, the owner, who waved back.

The scent of basil and melted cheese wafted toward me from James's Italian Restaurant. I peered around the edge of the window. No customers for the usual lunchtime rush. Red-and-white checkered tablecloths filled square wooden tables. Vases of fresh flowers, bundles of silverware, and upside-down glasses waited for patrons.

Like me, he had lost his partner. His wife had died over twelve years before, leaving behind him and a teenage daughter, Jacqueline. She left for college four years ago, and James started serving breakfast.

He stood behind the bar now, a white towel slung over his left shoulder, a dirty apron tied around his waist. He was a thin man despite working every day with pasta—obviously he had better genetic arithmetic than me. *Looking* at his pasta made me gain ten pounds.

With a soft touch, I rapped on his window with my knuckles. He glanced up, saw me there, and waved. I beckoned him out and stepped back.

He joined me outside on the sidewalk, shrugging an old black jacket over his long, flannel shirt. His hands shook with a permanent tremor, the soft brown skin worn with age and kitchen utensil use. Curls of white filled his thick, tightly wound hair, giving way to full lips and chocolate brown eyes. He smiled, and it filled his entire face.

"Mirabelle," he said softly. "I haven't seen you in a week."

My heart clenched like a fist. I hadn't told him about Jerry's death—just that I'd be out of town. Even now, I didn't want to say the words. A world without Jerry—*my* world without Jerry—felt far too lonely.

"Yes, yes. I'm good. Thanks for getting those packages for me."

"Always."

"Did you get a visitor yesterday?"

He shook his head, tsking under his breath. "I know *you* must have," he said. "I did too."

"Tadd something?"

"The one."

Relief swept through me. Hadn't dreamed it, anyway, and I hadn't been singled out. "What do you think?" I asked.

"I think he has a lot of ideas. But so have other people. This place isn't going anywhere."

His certain tone, the steady confidence, settled something inside me. My shoulders eased down.

"You're right. What options would he have, anyway?"

James shrugged, breath puffing out in front of him. "If Charles would sell? Buy out our leases. Or own it until the leases expired. Find a loophole and take the leases away. Probably *something*."

All options that sent a knife into my throat. "Would . . . would you sell if he offered to buy out your lease?"

He scoffed. "Can't believe you'd even ask me that. What do you think?"

I grinned. "Thought I'd give you a chance in case you wanted to surprise me."

"It's not really up to us, though. Is it?"

We fell silent, our gazes drifting to the other shops down the row. What if a majority of owners were willing to give up their leases? Would Charles cave? Could we fight something like that in court? The questions piled up in my head, creating a slippery slope.

Perhaps I was asking them too early, anyway.

"What do you think everyone else is going to do?" I asked, fighting off a shiver. A gust of wind whistled past, sending an old newspaper scuttling by. Sirens blared from the neighborhood over.

"I think Sarah will sell eventually." He nodded to the thrift shop on my right. "She's too young not to be tempted. Tyler won't give up the nail salon anytime soon, I bet."

I sent him a sidelong glance. "You're talking as if this is inevitable. What if we don't sell? What if no one sells their leases? The developer can't do anything about that."

He pushed his lips to one side of his face as if in thought, then shoved his hands into his pockets.

"Not inevitable," he said. "Just thinking out loud."

"Maybe we should try to hold some kind of meeting or something for shop owners? You know, before the holidays kick off. There's always more traffic then, and if people are getting customers . . ."

My thoughts trailed off, but I didn't know why I couldn't finish the sentence. James made a humming sound deep in his throat. We had entire conversations where he didn't say a single word, but I walked away feeling as if he'd heard everything.

A bell tinkled behind me. Sarah shuffled out of the thrift store next to mine, wearing a long robe that sashayed around her skinny ankles. She held a cup of what appeared to be steaming coffee in one hand. Her bright red hair frizzed out around her face in bounteous curls that nearly drowned her pale skin.

"I think I know why you're out here talking," she said, eyes wide.

"I bet you do," said James.

"Hello Sarah," I said. "How are you?"

She gave a little shrug with one shoulder. Health issues had plagued her ever since she first moved in two years ago. She proclaimed herself perpetually unmarried, because she didn't feel like taking care of anyone but her parakeets. The occasional, temporary boyfriend popped in and out. Still, I knew she was lonely. There were days she'd come over to my shop and talk for over two hours, even during open hours.

"I suppose Tadd visited you as well?" I asked.

"I think he came to me first," she grumbled. "Guys like that can smell weakness."

James tilted his head back and laughed, a hearty, full-belly sound. Sarah gave a nervous chuckle but shifted back a step. She slid me a telling glance. We'd have to talk after James was gone.

"You think this'll happen?" she asked, frowning into her coffee. A hint of sparkle behind her caught my eye. Banners hung in the thrift store window, along with bright crimson and emerald lettering proclaiming holiday deals.

"Nah." James shook his head. "Lots of people have tried buying this place."

Although none of them came to us individually, I wanted to add, but seeing the tension in Sarah's face, I decided not to.

Her brow furrowed. "I don't like this. I'm not saying I'd sell my lease if they offered. I mean, it's not like he gave me a price or anything. He just tried to sell me some mumbo-jumbo about caring about the community and wanting to improve it. Improve it with what?" She spread her hands. "A brand-new mall? *That's* just what this nasty place needs."

This time, I tilted my head back and laughed. "That was exactly what I thought!"

James hummed in his throat again.

"Look," Sarah said. "Here's the problem: I don't know how to say *no*. If he were to make me a good deal, I'd probably take it. Business isn't the same as the first six months when I opened, and I have medical bills."

She visibly flinched when I put a hand on her shoulder and then quickly withdrew.

"This isn't going to go anywhere, Sarah. Nothing to worry about, all right? James and I have been here almost thirty years. Plenty of people have tried to buy Charles out before, and it never happens. He's stubborn."

Sarah nodded, but I could tell her heart wasn't in it. "Maybe," she said. "I'll just see how this plays out."

My mind wandered to Bitsy. She still hadn't returned my calls or text messages, and I'd been home for two full days. I might close the shop early and go check on her.

"Whatever happens," James said. "This restaurant has been my life, and it's my retirement. Nothing is going to happen that I'm not happy with, and it would take a lot to make me happy if a developer really wants to *improve our community*."

The resolve in James's voice strengthened my own. *If* Tadd posed a problem, we'd weather it together. Just like I would have with Bill.

No one will take my store, Bill whispered.

"I know," I murmured. I wouldn't lose his memory.

Not to a developer.

The news flickered on the television set in my kitchen while I stood at the counter, chewing my bottom lip, my phone pressed to my ear.

"C'mon, Bitsy," I murmured, glancing at the clock. Seven in the evening. She should be home making dinner by now. The phone continued to ring.

Finally, her voice said, "This is Bitsy Walker. Please leave a message, and I will get back to you as soon as I can. If you're calling for Bitsy's Maid Services, I'm sorry to say that we aren't accepting new clients at this time. Please—"

I shut the phone off, then slumped against the counter. Ten minutes. She'd call back in ten minutes.

While the TV droned in the background, I tapped into my favorite new game—Candy Killer—and started to play. The bright candies, destructive explosions, and happy characters allowed me a moment's reprieve. Something about destroying the candies and winning the level gave me deep satisfaction at the end of the day.

The bombs pleased me most.

My eyes darted to the TV. The news. I hated the news. Not only did it depress me, but all of the anchors looked the same. Why couldn't they have a happy news hour where they talked about the good things people did?

A series of explosions flashed across the screen on my game. I'd won the level. "Take that." I set the phone aside, satisfied, and turned to the counter.

A bag from the Sandwich and Soup Deli rustled when I reached into it. My empty fridge chugged out cold breath. After ditching church yesterday, I'd opened the store just to have somewhere to go. Fifteen bottles of Pepsi lined my counter. I'd stocked up again at the deli—the first dramatic backslide from my healthy diet in at least a year. The bill had been well over $40. But I'd comforted myself knowing that I wouldn't have to go to the grocery store and I'd supported a small business.

We had to band together these days.

I changed the channel to a romance movie on a ranch somewhere and dove into the sandwich. Something uneasy churned inside me.

Where was Bitsy?

Had she said *no new clients*? I couldn't remember the last time Bitsy had turned down work.

A shiver of surprise moved through me. That message had been new—from today. At least she was still alive. Not only alive, but obviously doing very well. Perhaps she was busy at work.

That was it.

"Good for you, Bitsy," I said between bites, then grabbed a banana pepper that had fallen to the counter. Bitsy deserved the prosperity, heaven knew. No doubt her number of clients had something to do with Jim helping her out with the business. For being an ex-military man, he knew his way around people. Still, I felt a niggle of worry.

I flipped over to the Home Shopping Network channel. An excited thrill zipped through me. Jewelry! My favorite segment.

That would shut my paranoia up.

"Bits and baubles," I murmured. "Nothing cheers a girl up like jewelry. Pretty is as pretty does, Mama always said."

After sipping the last of my Pepsi and finishing half my sandwich, I rolled the rest back into the crinkly paper and stuffed it into the fridge. The quiet house settled around me with low creaks as I walked to my bedroom. I left the television on, the volume turned down, just for a little noise.

This empty house was too quiet.

I fell asleep midway through destroying candies, without removing my makeup, and while forcing thoughts of Jerry, and church, and Bitsy out of my head.

My Happy Ending

When I walked into a French bakery for lunch the next day, the scent of croissants, butter, and fruit compote lay thick on the air. People bustled down a narrow aisle between tables. I found solace in the hubbub.

A familiar cry rang over the crowd.

"Mira! I'm over here."

A slender woman stood in the back, waving for me. I scooted through rows of tables and chairs, packed full with the lunch crowd, and headed toward the right corner. My old best friend Jackie Greene, whom I'd known since I was five, always sat in the back of everything. Store. Restaurant. Movie theater. She was slight in frame, attractive, and quiet, and seemed as if she wanted to fade into the wallpaper.

Seeing her was a relief.

"So good to see you again!" I said, pulling her into a hug. She wasn't usually a hugger but made an exception for me. I clung to her for a second, wondering whether I felt she needed the hug, or I did. "It's been far too long since we've gone to lunch."

When she pulled away, a familiar smile lit up her face and bright blue eyes. "I agree," she said. "We need to do this more often."

Back here, the sounds of the milling bakery weren't quite so encompassing. A waitress strode by wearing a black apron, black pants, and a white shirt. She smiled as she passed, dropping a menu in front of me with practiced dexterity.

"Be right with you!" she chirped.

Jackie leaned forward, propping her chin in one hand. "So . . . what's going on? How are you? Is the store doing okay? Why has it been so long? I feel like once Lexie moved out, both of us got busy."

She finished the barrage of questions with a smile, setting me at ease. Was she upset that so much of my attention had slipped to the Health and Happiness Society the past couple of years? No. Jackie had her own life. Her own distractions. Besides, if there was anyone I could talk to, it was Jackie. She always had my back, even though we only spoke every few months now.

"I'm . . . hanging in there, I guess," I said.

Her gaze melted into concern.

"Jerry? Mira, I'm so sorry. He was such a good man, and I'll always remember him as the brother I never had."

A whole heap of . . . *something* ugly sat on my chest. Put there, no doubt, by Tadd Williams and his charming smile. Oh, this lunch with Jackie would be a rant all right.

"Yes, Jerry," I said with a wry smile. "He's always stirring up trouble, even in death."

"Do you want to talk about it?"

"There's so much to say," I said, a little breathless. Speaking to *someone* about it would be such a relief. "I—"

The chime of a call on her phone stopped me. Her eyes widened as she held up a finger.

"Just a second. I have to grab this."

"Of course."

Jackie canted her body to the side, pressing the phone against her far ear as she murmured a soft, "Tell me!"

Strained silence passed. I fidgeted with my spoon and fork and averted my gaze. Should I tell her about Jerry first? Or Tadd? Or my emptier-than-ever-house?

After a squeal, a few more murmured responses, and a quick dab at her eyes, Jackie pulled the phone away from her face and turned back to the table. She pressed both hands to her cheeks, which flushed a becoming shade of pink. My shoulders straightened.

"Jackie . . . are you okay?"

She sucked in a sharp breath, and then a massive smile wreathed her face. "Yes, I'm really, really good. I just . . ."

She trailed off, looking to the side, and sniffled. Her profile was near-perfect. Not only did she have petite shoulders and a graceful, arching neck like a swan, but she was quite lovely. There was something Audrey Hepburn-esque about her that I deeply envied, and deeply loved. She had tendrils of gray and blonde swept up into an elegant bun near the top of her head, and she wore a string of pearls around her neck for a simple lunch date.

Despite their differences, I could see so much of Lexie in her.

"Are you sure everything's okay?" I asked. "You seem . . ."

Distracted.

Something sharp caught my stomach, a feeling that was familiar. The kind of panic that surfaced whenever I thought something was wrong with someone. The kind of panic that came after losing *everyone.*

Would I lose her, too?

No. No, she looked entirely too pleased to be dying.

Still, one never knew.

She waved an errant hand through the air. "Yes, yes. I promise, everything is just fine," she said, beaming. "I have some news that I really shouldn't tell you, but I don't know how I can stop myself. And I'm sorry I interrupted you, but I think I'm going to explode if I don't tell someone."

The words rushed out of her like a freight train. I swallowed hard. The joy in her gaze didn't comfort me. I felt the urge to brace myself. Like I was barreling down the tracks at full speed, burning the simmering coals of rage, and didn't know how to stop.

I swallowed hard and reached for a Pepsi that hadn't come yet. "Oh?"

Jackie chewed on her bottom lip. Hesitancy filled her expression, maybe even a little uncertainty. Right then, I knew what she was going to say. The words weren't needed.

"Lexie's pregnant," she blurted out.

My out-of-control train slammed right into that same old brick wall, like a punch to the spine. I stared at her, stunned.

"Pregnant?"

"Oh, Mira!" Tears filled her eyes. "I just *had* to tell you. Lexie will forgive me—I know she will. Or you can just act like you don't know or something . . . I'm going to be a grandma. Again! She just got out of the doctor's office, and they confirmed it with a blood test!"

A wooden smile came to my face of its own volition. In truth, I *was* happy for Jackie. I was ecstatic for Lexie, most of all. She would be such a wonderful mother. But deep, deep in my chest came the same sinking, disastrous, horrible, lost chasm. The one that engulfed me with every loss. The sticky, tenacious darkness that only bred rage and memories.

Every negative pregnancy test.

Every grave I'd ever wept over.

Every quiet evening at home, alone.

Where is my happy ending? I thought. The question whisked my breath away.

Shame rushed up to chastise me, and it sounded like Bill. *Why does it have to be about you? Why can't you just be happy for Jackie?* I shoved all those thoughts away when I realized I'd left a long silence.

Jackie stared at me in a mixture of jubilation and confusion.

Putting on a good show was a forte of mine. I had perfected the art of acting happy for others, even when I was dying inside, years ago. My soul could wither, but my smile would remain. Mama's favorite prayer ran through my mind. *Lord, fill my mouth with worthwhile stuff, and nudge me when I've said enough.*

I forced out a little squeal.

"Jackie! Oh, Jackie! That is so wonderful!"

Jackie beamed, seeming relieved.

"It really is. I was so happy when Kenzie had her baby, of course. But this means bigger things for me and Lexie. You know how much I've worried about her."

"Yes." I laughed, even though it sounded strangled. "Remember when you wanted to put Lexie on that diet of cucumber water and grapefruit?"

She preened. "I still think it would have helped."

"Regardless," I said, waving that aside as I desperately grabbed for a small glass of water. Maybe it would quench the desert in my throat. "Now she's pregnant, and you get to be a grandma again."

"She's alive." Jackie patted her hair away from her face. "She's living her life in ways I'm not sure her father *ever* did. I'm just so proud of her. And relieved. I think that this will be my chance to really bond with Lexie. We've never seen eye-to-eye the way she did with her dad."

She trailed off as the waitress approached, and I realized I hadn't even looked at the menu. Funny how it felt like the world had stopped. As if there were a new gravity that tilted things onto a different axis even though the news had nothing to do with me.

Not really.

The waitress pulled in a deep breath, looking a little harried, and smiled. "Sorry about the wait," she said. "What can I get you?"

Jackie scanned the menu, and I realized that she had come for the same reason I did. She wanted a friend to talk to. To spill all her most exciting news—and some of her pain. Every grandbaby Jackie had was a grandbaby her deceased husband would never know. The Health and Happiness Society hadn't come between us—*life* had. Once Kenzie had her little girl, Jackie and I had drifted away.

Now I could see why.

I jerked out of my thoughts to find Jackie and the waitress staring at me. My eyes darted to the menu. "Oh, sorry. Caprese salad, please. No. Wait . . ."

A hundred delicious options populated the page, all far less healthy—and more immediately satisfying—than salad. Screw good-girl foods.

Time for hardball.

"Make that a chicken carbonara with a Pepsi and an extra side of bread."

When she left, Jackie's eyes latched onto mine. She smiled in a half-hopeful way. I braced myself, waiting for condemnation of my food choice.

"Do you think you can keep it from Lexie?" she asked. "I know I really shouldn't have told you. But I just had to!"

With one long, relieved breath, I reached across the table and grabbed her hand, then squeezed it. "You have nothing to apologize for," I said. "You absolutely should have told me. Of course I'm not going to tell Lexie! Besides, I doubt she can keep it from the Health and Happiness Society for long, anyway. Bitsy has a nose for change like a hound. Especially if Lexie's pregnancies were anything like yours."

Jackie grimaced. "Good point. They were pretty awful. Kenzie's wasn't so bad, but maybe Lexie's will be. At the very least, she's going to have a real challenge navigating the cravings of pregnancy with her . . . issues."

She flicked the word off her tongue, like she was trying to throw it away. A piece of garbage that she didn't really care about. The muscles at the back of my neck tightened. Jackie meant well, but she'd never understood food addiction, despite her husband dying from extreme obesity.

Sometimes I wondered if she chose *not* to catch on.

Maybe she thought it was easier to pretend those things didn't exist—that her husband and daughter didn't have them—than to acknowledge them.

I let it go.

"Are you hoping for a girl or a boy?" I asked, leaning back again.

"Girl," she said with definitive confidence. "Definitely a girl. Lexie deserves to raise herself."

Lexie hadn't been easy for Jackie. The two of them were far too different—and yet so similar.

"Besides," she continued, "if Lexie has a girl, Kenzie can give her the hand-me-downs."

"Good point. That saves a lot of money."

"They need it. Stereotypical poor college students for now. Lexie said she plans to tell everyone in the Health and Happiness Society at the Christmas party this year. By then, she'll be well out of the first trimester. Much safer to . . ."

She stopped. Her gaze softened for a moment and met mine. A lump grew in my throat. How well I knew the ugliness of early lost pregnancies.

And late ones.

The boiling rage continued to bubble deep, deep inside.

"When is she due?" I asked.

Stay cool, I told myself. *Just get through lunch. Then you can feel all you want. Just get through lunch.*

The waitress returned with unsweetened iced tea and Pepsi. The ice cubes clinked quietly against the edge of the glass when I snatched it off the table and gulped three times. If Jackie noticed, she gave no sign.

"July, I think?" she said. "She just took the pregnancy test earlier this week, so she's *fresh* pregnant. She's guessing she's about seven weeks."

I grimaced. "She won't like being pregnant in the summer, I'm sure."

Three of my five pregnancies had been in the summer, and with all of them, I'd only made it four months.

Jackie laughed a little. "No, I think not."

"Tell me all your grandma plans," I said after another refreshing sip of Pepsi. "Tell me everything. This could be a fabulous opportunity for you to forge a new bond with Lexie."

"Of course I have plans!" she cried, laughing. "Not only for a new nursery, time off for my job, and ways to teach Lexie how to be a mom, but getting those two grandbabies together. Especially on the holidays. Won't it be wonderful to have a reason to *really* celebrate Christmas again?"

I swallowed hard.

"Wonderful."

Jackie grinned and reached into her purse. "Look at these nursery ideas. I have so many quilt ideas, I can't even populate them yet. Doesn't that little giraffe just scream Lexie?"

"Definitely."

Jackie's plans unraveled slowly, encompassing custom-bought cribs and a stroller that only had three wheels instead of four—*the better to exercise with,* she explained. The chicken carbonara came as Jackie launched into a story about her other granddaughter, and we fell into old memories with a few laughs.

Beneath the surface simmered thoughts of Jerry. Long after I left the restaurant, I realized I hadn't said a word about him after all.

A tangle of white Christmas lights sat like a ball on Bitsy's porch that evening.

They illuminated the worn wooden boards with a gentle glow. Night had just fallen, leaving a belt of stars in the sky and my breath frosting in front of me. Warm lights shone from inside, where I caught a hint of movement in the kitchen. I pulled my jacket tighter around me and started up the sidewalk in relief.

She *was* alive.

Jim sat on the porch, muttering as he wrestled with the light ball. Something about *Lana* and *Christmas in July* came from under his breath. I fought off a giggle. When he heard the crunch of salt under my feet, he looked up.

"Oh, hey there, Mira. Haven't seen you in a couple of days. Where've you been?"

"I've been around."

He cleared his throat. "Oh, yeah. Your brother's funeral. I'm really sorry."

I managed a wan smile. "Me too. Bitsy doing okay? Seems like she's been busy."

"Really busy. She's, uh, just inside if you need her."

His gaze dropped back to the lights. The sound of the girls singing carols came through the closed door. Did I detect a hint of gingerbread on the air? Bitsy loved gingerbread. *The ginger balances out the bread part,* she told me once. *Especially if you use stevia. But only during the holidays.*

"You can go on in." He jerked his head toward the door. "She'd love to see you, I'm sure."

"Thanks."

The sound of *The Grinch* played on the television when I stepped inside, enveloped by the scent of gingerbread permeating the entire house.

"Hellooo?" I called.

Two warm, pajama-clad bodies threw themselves against my legs with happy squeals. Lizzy and Lana, Bitsy's daughters, held me tight. For a moment, I could almost pretend they were mine. I soaked up every second of their touch.

"Mira!" Lana cried, pulling away. "Where have you been? We missed you. It's like you haven't been here in days and days and *days*."

"I know! Are you twenty years old now?"

"No!"

"Are you graduating high school yet?"

"No," Lana said with a laugh. "You know I'm still in elementary school, silly Mira."

"Oh, right. You just look so grown up now. It feels like it's been so long."

Lizzy gently put her arms around my waist and smiled. She'd lost a tooth on the bottom, leaving an adorable black gap in her grin. I rubbed her back and wished I could bottle her up to take her home.

"Looks like someone had a visit from the tooth fairy," I said. "What'd you get for it?"

"She left a whole dollar," Lizzy said, casting a sidelong glance at her sister. "I hid it in a special place. Mom says if I earn enough money, I can start a savings account!"

"You're well on your way. Are you going to spend any of it on Christmas presents?"

Lizzy tilted her head to the side, as if contemplating my suggestion. "No," she finally said. "I'm going to save it. I want to go to Hawaii with my dad, but he said I have to pay for part of it."

"A wise father. It will mean more to you that way."

Lizzy didn't seem convinced, but she went back to the couch and sat next to Lana. They focused on the movie again. A freshly decorated Christmas tree illuminated the room from the far corner. The green boughs were lush but appeared plasticky. Globe-like ornaments littered the couch and the floor, near coils of tinsel on the ground. Everything else in the room was neat and straight, but to see *any* chaos in Bitsy's house was . . . unusual. She had come a long way in relaxing her control on things ever since her ex-husband Daniel moved back into town. Little signs of continued progress popped up all the time, but an unfinished project?

Strange.

"Hey there, stranger," Bitsy said.

I whirled around to find Bitsy standing in the doorway between the living room and the kitchen, arms folded across her chest. She wore an apron, a pair of sweats, and a worn concert t-shirt. Her comfortable clothes—at such an early time in the evening—meant she must not be feeling well.

"You're alive!" I said.

"Long time no see," Bitsy said with a weary smile. "I'm sorry I haven't been over yet."

"You cleaned my house! You didn't have to do that."

"Of course I did! Your brother died, Mira. You need some TLC. C'mon. I made gingerbread."

She waved me into the kitchen. I followed like an obedient puppy.

"Your Christmas tree looks really nice," I said, feeling awkward.

For the last five years, she had invited me over every time they put the tree up. It was a tradition I had looked forward to.

She must have forgotten.

Bitsy sighed with a curled upper lip. "It's fake, which kind of breaks my heart, but it's much easier to clean up. Economical. Jim had it in his garage, so we brought it over here earlier today."

"Win-win," I said.

The sound of Jim's big boots clunking along the porch filled the background while I settled into a stool at the island. She leaned against the counter, arms folded across her chest lips pressed into a line. Her gaze darted to her notebook, which usually detailed her to-do list but held a stack of opened letters. She tucked one underneath the rest.

Maybe Daniel had been acting up again. He had a habit of pressing all of her buttons and distracting her from everyone else.

Bitsy was . . . tense.

Her eyebrows lifted. "How are things since you returned?" she asked, fighting off a yawn. "Are you doing okay?"

"Hanging in there. I guess." I sighed, thinking about my conversation with Jackie. "The shock hasn't worn off yet. Or maybe it has and I've just mourned so much that it doesn't last long."

Her whole body slumped to the side as she ran a hand over her face and fought off another yawn.

"Possibly," she murmured.

"You okay, Bits?"

"Sorry, I haven't listened to your voicemails yet. This week has been really busy. And . . ."

She trailed away, gazing into the distance. She shook her head and straightened.

"Yes. No. I don't know, Mira. I just—"

"Hey, Bits." Jim rapped on the window above the sink with a gloved hand. He held up a length of lights and pointed to the side. "How far over do you want the lights to go?"

"Use them all up. Try to keep it symmetrical?"

Jim lifted one eyebrow, then disappeared. She smirked when she turned back around.

"He's never put up Christmas lights. Can you believe that? He's been deployed five out of the last ten Christmases, but still. Seems a little ridiculous for a man of his age. Anyway, I just received—"

The phone rang. Bitsy glanced at it, frowned, and held up a finger.

"So sorry, Mira. Let me just grab this really quick. I have this client . . ."

"Sure," I said, but before I got the word out, she had already left the kitchen. The distant, fuzzy sound of her murmur came from down the hall. "Yes," she said. "I did receive the paper today and—"

Her bedroom door shut, sealing off the rest of her words. I peered into the living room.

"Enjoying the show?" I asked.

Lizzy nodded. Lana waved a hand. I shuffled to the ornaments, picked one off the floor, and put it on the closest bough. Bright lights reflected off the shiny exterior, casting a glow on my shirt. Would I even get my Christmas tree out this year?

Probably not.

A craving for Pepsi made my tongue tingle, but I stuffed it away. There was still one in my car from when I'd stopped at the gas station earlier. I'd drink it later. While playing Candy Killer.

Maybe I should get this back under control again.

After picking up the rest of the ornaments, setting them on the tree, coiling the tinsel, and stuffing it all back in the storage container, I sat on the couch.

Five minutes passed.

I made my way back into the kitchen. A haphazard mess covered the counters. Nothing extensive—remnants from a gingerbread recipe, no doubt, but enough to put her on edge. I filled the sink with warm water and suds. Fifteen minutes after I finished her dishes, swept, and wiped down her counters, Bitsy reappeared.

"So sorry, Mira," she said, pushing the hair out of her eyes. "I didn't mean to take so long."

Stress dimmed her eyes.

"Do you want to talk?" I asked. "You seem . . ."

She shook her head with a sharp back and forth. "No. I mean . . . yes. Not really. At least, not tonight."

Opening up had never been easy for her. She continued with a long exhale.

"My father and stepmother are coming over for Thanksgiving, and I'm not too happy about it. Having them over, and Jim and his daughter Cora and . . . it's just a lot right now with all these clients and my landlord—"

She cut off.

My heart gave a flutter. Thanksgiving. I had totally forgotten. For the past four years, I'd spent it with Bitsy.

"Not excited about your dad?" I asked.

Her brow wrinkled. "My stepmother is nice, but . . ."

"Controlling?"

"A bit, yes. I filled up with clients so I've been working a lot. I didn't plan on putting up the tree tonight, but Jim was so excited."

She slumped into a stool in the kitchen and yawned with a wave of her hand. "Keep going," she said. "I want to hear what's going on."

The burning need to talk had faded. In fact, I couldn't remember where I'd left off, or what I wanted to say. Before I could ask how self-care was going, Jim rapped on the window again. Bitsy clenched her teeth and sucked in a sharp breath but turned around with an even expression.

"Yes?"

"Need some help with the ladder," he said. "Ground's uneven."

Before she could refuse, I broke in. "Go ahead," I said. "I need to get going anyway. We can talk later."

As if on cue, Lana shrieked. Lizzy shouted back, and seconds later I heard a loud *thud*. Bitsy stalked to the living room, calling over her shoulder, "I'm sorry, Mira. It's been a really bad day. Can you come over tomorrow, maybe?"

"Sure, honey. No worries. I'll see you for the meeting?"

"Oh. Right. Yes, the meeting. Of course."

With the sound of the girls still fighting behind me, I stepped onto the porch. Jim looked like a glowing scarecrow dressed in Christmas lights. The once-massive ball had become a stream that illuminated the porch—and his face.

"Is she coming?" he asked. "The ladder's not very steady. Her ground is really uneven over here."

"She's on her way. The girls were getting into a fighting match."

"Ah."

"Do you want me to help?"

"I'm okay to wait. Thanks."

He nodded once as I shuffled down the stairs, clutching the banister to keep from falling.

"Have a good night, Mira. Good to see you."

I waved and headed for my Cadillac. The frigid air burned my nostrils with every breath. My car chugged to life, then roared. Chilly air blasted my face. I grabbed my drink, took a swig, and pulled into the street.

On the way home, I stopped for a hamburger, fries, and a milkshake. An ad for a free turkey for Thanksgiving played on the radio, opening a pit deep into my stomach.

With the meal, I bought another Pepsi.

A sullen gray sky hovered over me when I walked back into the shop an hour after leaving Bitsy's. Despite the late hour, I couldn't help myself.

Frost crawled along the window in delicate tendrils. James had shoveled the snow in front of his door and mine into fluffy white piles in front of the parking stalls.

My keys jangled as I unlocked the door and pushed inside. Shadows greeted me. Sewing machines, vacuums, spools of thread, swaths of fabric, and quilting blocks. All of my old friends waited in stoic silence.

You're always safe here, Bill said, as if he greeted me at the door. *Even if your best friend is acting weird.*

"She wasn't acting weird. Just tired."

Why are you here? It's late.

"I needed to think."

You can't think at home?

"Too quiet."

As I stepped inside, something crinkled beneath my foot. A piece of paper lay on the floor, as if someone had slipped it under the door. I scowled.

Community Meeting

December 5th

> Do you long for a safer community? Do you want more jobs, more prosperity, and more safety for your children?
>
> Come to the community rec center to talk with local developer Tadd Williams about how you can change the fate of this neighborhood.
>
> Dinner will be served.

I snatched the paper off the ground and balled it up in my fist. Safer community? More jobs?

Was he *kidding*?

This was a strip mall—not a casino. He had a lot of nerve putting this under my door, considering the way we'd parted. Not to mention the fact that he planned on serving dinner. *Dinner.* What happened to light refreshments, anyway?

Who was he trying to impress?

And why?

I flicked the lights on with a *humph*, then slung my purse onto the desk and pitched the paper right into the garbage.

You're overreacting, Mira.

I put my fingers on my temples and let out a long sigh. "I'm not."

You should go. I would go if I could, and you know it. It's foolish to leave the enemy unstudied.

My eyes wandered to the empty desk. I could picture him hunched over a vacuum, pieces scattered around him like grains of sand. He always wore a headlamp with a magnifying glass. When he worked, he hummed. I could prattle about anything—he enjoyed the lack of silence.

He can never take what we built here, Mira. He won't.

"I know," I whispered, stamping back the rage. "I won't let him."

I trust you.

I settled into the old couch, grabbed my phone, and started destroying candy with relief. My thoughts drifted to Bitsy and what she didn't say. When I was caught in a web of grief, my emotional sensitivity went way off kilter. Maybe I'd imagined tension in her eyes. The underlying current of *something* not said. What could be haunting her?

My fingers itched to call her, but for some reason, I couldn't.

Instead, I fell asleep on the couch to the sound of Bill humming his favorite song in the back of my head.

Snow fell, melted, and iced the next evening.

Slush tinged with dirt was piled high on the sides of the road. Water raced down the streets, seeming to drive the cold all the way into my bones. My fingers and knuckles were stiff when I pulled up to Bitsy's house, rimmed with lights.

"Just a meeting with all your best friends."

The idea of venting my thoughts about Jerry, the holidays without family, and Tadd's subtle strategy that *obviously* wouldn't work gave me a moment of relief. The girls always had my back. They listened.

They always did.

"Can't mention Lexie," I chanted under my breath with each step. "Can*not* mention Lexie."

Buttery light spilled onto the damp grass when I walked up the porch. Lizzy and Lana's half-hysterical shrieks sounded through the tinsel-lined windows. The door opened as I reached for it, and both girls threw themselves into my arms.

"Mira!"

"You're back!"

"To see my favorites?" I cried. "You betcha!"

Both tore away, yelling at manic speeds with only a few intelligible snippets here and there. A Christmas pageant. Cookies in their classroom. Extra gingerbread for the meeting tonight.

"It's sooooo yummy, Mira," Lizzy said, twirling in a circle. "And look! My skirt makes a bell!"

"Beautiful, honey. Did you say gingerbread for tonight?"

Lana nodded. "For the Health and Happiness Society meeting, silly. Isn't that why you're here?"

"Of course."

Bitsy rarely provided an *actual* treat at the weekly meeting. Some form of healthy recipe, or a new cookbook, or a snack that was low calorie but high vitamin, sure. On occasion, in the summer, she did have iced tea lightly sweetened with stevia.

"Oh my goodness!" I said. "You're so busy. When will you have time to write your list for Santa?"

Lana dug into her pocket, pulling out a warped paper. "Keep it with me all the time," she said proudly. "Just in case. I don't want Santa to miss anything. Besides, Daddy is really rich. I can get whatever I want for Christmas this year."

My eyes widened. "It can't be that easy."

Before she could respond, I reached out and started to tickle her. She giggled and darted away. Lizzy followed. By the time they disappeared, I spotted Bitsy in the kitchen, phone pressed to her ear. She ran a hand through her hair. Paperwork was scattered across the table in front of her, complete with a checkbook, old receipts, and what appeared to be last year's tax records.

I sat on the couch and leaned back to study the Christmas tree. Maybe, one of these days, I would turn on a Christmas movie at work. One of Bill's favorites, like *Holiday Inn* or the original *Miracle on 34th Street*.

Or maybe *The Grinch*.

Rachelle breezed through the door, water droplets in her dark hair. She shook them off and headed for the couch.

"Hey, Mira!"

The smell of sugar and fresh bread followed her. She wore a red shirt with flashing Christmas lights, and her hair was pulled out of her face with clips. At her side dangled a brown paper sack.

"Did you bring something good?" I whispered. She cast a glance at the kitchen. Bitsy hadn't turned around.

"Oh, yeah. You know I got the goods, sister."

Her hand dove into the bag and extracted a beautiful cinnamon roll with green frosting. Red sprinkles decorated the fluffy icing with merry little Santa Clauses, mistletoe, and what appeared to be reindeer. I almost squealed.

Now *that* made me feel like Christmas.

"Please tell me this is for us to share?" I whispered.

She shook her head and gently stuffed it back in the bag. "For you to take home! Hurry, put it in your purse."

"God bless you, honey."

"What's going on with Bitsy?" Rachelle asked. "I've texted her several times this week but haven't heard back."

"You too?"

"I thought she was dead. When I stopped by to check on the girls, she was talking on the phone and couldn't get off. I stayed for twenty minutes but eventually left without talking to her."

"Not sure," I said, feeling squirmy. "She has been acting a little . . . distracted this week. She's always stressed around the holidays."

"Probably more with the Health and Happiness Society Christmas party coming up."

I'd completely forgotten about that.

"How about you, Mira?" she asked before I could reply. "How are you doing? Sorry I haven't kept up with you this week. The Thanksgiving rush—"

"Don't worry about it."

She frowned. "I could have at least texted."

"Where is Megan?" I asked. "She hasn't responded on the group chat in a while either. I texted her, too, but never heard back."

"Don't know. Every time I've tried to get ahold of her the past week, it goes straight to voicemail. Lexie tried texting her mom. She said Megan was fine and would call later. Things are getting funky around here. Anyway, back to you. How are you really doing?"

I paused, waiting for something to prevent us from speaking. As if the universe had actively conspired against me recently. This time, Rachelle just stared at me, waiting.

Hallelujah.

The words rushed to the tip of my tongue in a landslide.

"Oh, it's been . . . it's been really *hard*. I—"

"Sorry!" Bitsy barreled into the room, wide-eyed and frazzled. "So sorry about that. Things have been crazy at . . . ah . . . work and then with Jim and . . . but anyway."

Bitsy set her open laptop on its usual spot on the coffee table.

"Let's get started. Megan and Lexie are probably waiting. Rachelle, there's a tray of gingerbread slices in the kitchen. Would you grab it, please?"

"Wait, Bitsy. We—"

Lexie popped up on the screen, cutting Rachelle off. Her face was pale, her lips pinched, but she managed a smile. Something inside of me cracked—how badly I wanted to ask how she was doing! I forced it back and waved.

"Hi Lexie!"

"You don't look so good," Bitsy said as she sat next to Rachelle.

"Not feeling so great," Lexie croaked.

Bitsy's eyes narrowed, but she said nothing.

Megan popped onto the screen. "Sorry," she said with a grimace. "I didn't mean to be late."

"We're all a little bit late today," Bitsy said.

I wasn't late, I wanted to say but refrained. No reason to get grumpy.

"Megan, why are you so tan?" Rachelle asked. "Isn't it December in the Rocky Mountains, too?"

A conspiratorial grin crossed Megan's face. She tilted her head to one side. "It just so happens that I returned from a trip last night."

Lexie frowned. "Is that where you've been?"

"Yeah, sorry about that," Megan drawled. "It was really unexpected and fast. I meant to tell you but forgot."

Rachelle leaned forward. "Why are you smiling like that?"

Megan's grin broadened.

Lexie's eyes widened. Her face brightened. "No. Freaking. Way."

Megan lifted one hand. Something sparkled in the dim light of the video chat. A ring.

"What is that?" Rachelle hissed.

Lexie laughed.

Bitsy paled.

"That is definitely a ring!" Lexie cried. "Engagement or wedding? OMG, Megan! It's gorgeous. It's simple! It's . . . so . . . *you*."

Megan held it closer to the computer screen, where a single glittering stone sparkled in the light. Although Megan was anything but traditional, it was clear *that* was a wedding ring.

"You *eloped*?" Rachelle screeched.

"It happened so fast!" Megan said, apology evident in her tone. "Justin posed the idea and . . . I loved it! We didn't even tell my parents. We took off with the twins and acted like it was a big vacation. Then . . . we got married on the beach. It was pretty amazing. No drama of a traditional wedding, and we could do whatever we wanted."

She trailed away, glancing from one face to the next, wide-eyed.

"You're a freaking rock star, Megan," Rachelle cried, breaking the silence. "Way to do what felt best for you!"

"If what you wanted was a small wedding with just your brothers, I'm so happy you did that," Bitsy said. "Congratulations!"

"Looks good on my part," I added, forcing a smile. "Beautiful ring, Megan. Just beautiful. I'm so happy for you!"

All of us seemed to hold our breath, waiting for Lexie. A beat three seconds long filled the room. Megan stared intently at the computer screen until Lexie declared with a squeal, "It's perfection!"

Rachelle cat-called, Bitsy clapped, and I shouted "Congratulations!" For a brief moment, I remembered Bill. The feeling of first love, the newness of life together, when everything seemed sublime and surreal.

"Not to steal your thunder or anything, but can I go next?" Rachelle asked, raising a timid hand. "I have big news too."

Bitsy nodded.

"I'm buying the Frosting Cottage bakery."

Rachelle sucked in a sharp breath, then glanced around to see all of our reactions. I blinked.

What?

The Frosting Cottage had found its ground once Rachelle had turned things around for my good friend, Sophia. But Rachelle didn't know the first thing about owning a small business. The heart and soul it could take out of the work. The taxes, the bills, the electricity, the stress, the frustration of customer relations and dealing with leases. Not to mention that buying it meant Sophia wouldn't be there.

Was she leaving too?

"Wow," Bitsy stammered. "That *is* big news. When did this happen?"

"Today," Rachelle said as she bounced in her seat. "I decided today. Sophia approached me about it a few weeks ago, but that's a lot to take on, and I don't even have my degree yet. I had to think it over."

"Where is Sophia going?" I asked.

"Moving back to her hometown to take care of her parents. She *could* keep the Frosting Cottage as an investment, but she doesn't want roots here."

Because she'd never come back, probably.

"Congratulations, Rachelle!" Megan said, holding up a fist. "You'll kill it. Frosting power."

"Good grief," Lexie said. "I wasn't going to share my good news for a while, but now I have to, since it's a trend."

Bitsy spread her hands. "By all means."

"I'm pregnant!"

Audible gasps tore through the room from everyone except me. Lexie giggled, eyes shining. "Wow! Even better than I expected, and I had high expectations!"

"You're what?" Megan screeched.

"You didn't tell me?" Rachelle cried.

"Oh, dear," Bitsy murmured.

"Just found out myself," Lexie said, holding up a hand. "I swear."

I conjured up the brightest smile I could manage and called, "Lexie, I'm so happy for you. You're going to be a wonderful mother."

"When are you due?" Megan asked. "I could make it out for the birth!"

"You better," Lexie said. "Between all of you, I think I'll have all the doulas that I need to get me through. The four of you will just have to fight over who's going to feed me fudge brownies between contractions."

They dissolved into giggles.

"Goodness," Bitsy said. "This is quite the day."

"What about you, Bitsy?" Lexie asked. "Any good news?"

Bitsy cleared her throat, her face pale. "Ah . . . no. No, just normal . . . ah . . . normal stuff."

"Something wrong?" I asked.

"It's just that . . . I mean . . . no. Nothing is wrong." She forced a smile.

Megan frowned.

"Busy with Thanksgiving and changes at work, that's all. Let's talk about the article I found! *Cultural responses to expectations of thinness among women.*"

She reached for a pile of papers and handed them to Rachelle and me. My mind spun as Bitsy's voice trailed into the background, talking about *changing size standards* and *the new anorexia.*

Elopement. New beginnings. Babies. A secret Bitsy wouldn't tell. Although I tried to stuff the thoughts away, they surfaced again and again.

No grandbabies for Mira.

No marriage prospects.

No new beginnings.

I felt the coming changes in the Health and Happiness Society like an icicle in my heart. I thought it would leap out of my chest and clatter onto the floor. So much goodness. So much . . . new. How could we weather it? These girls were smack dab in the middle of life. Where time became precious and everything else demanding.

The flood of thoughts about Jerry that I'd been longing to express flittered away. I couldn't even recall them when I tried. Instead, I couldn't help but feel sheer panic.

Was the Health and Happiness Society going away too?

I can do this, I thought, swallowing back tears. *I can do this. I can get through this meeting without crying.*

One steady thought pulled me through, banishing my tears as I pretended to shuffle through the article, reviewing the spots Bitsy had highlighted.

The store.

I didn't have a husband, babies, or a new business to distract me, but I had the store. An ice-cold Pepsi waited in the fridge next to handmade butternut squash ravioli and grilled asparagus from James.

No tears.

I could do this.

Thanksgiving

Thanksgiving Day rolled around with the scent of pumpkin in the air.

At first, I stared at my bedroom ceiling with a glassy, unblinking gaze, half in the world of dreams, half in the chilly reality of home. Not a sound stirred in the quiet house. I strained to hear.

Why hasn't Bill gotten up to make the turkey? came the unbidden thought. I let it roll through my mind like a wave, waiting for him to respond to my mental cry.

He didn't.

With a scowl, I frowned.

"Hello? Why aren't you telling me Happy Thanksgiving?"

Silence.

Right. Bill was gone.

I rubbed a hand over my face. I'd officially lost my mind. Maybe I'd cracked and everyone else was sane except for me. I was talking to my dead husband and panicking because he hadn't spoken back.

"Bonkers," I muttered and shoved the covers off.

If Bill were alive, he would have been down in the kitchen already, baster in hand, knuckle-deep in stuffing while the Thanksgiving Day Parade played in the background. For some reason, he always sang "The Star-Spangled Banner" while he stuffed the turkey.

Freedom to stuff my own turkey, he said. *Good stuff.*

Never made sense to me, but a lot of Bill didn't.

A quick glance at my phone verified my greatest worry—no word from Bitsy or Rachelle. Aside from a group text from Megan wishing everyone a Happy Turkey Day, nothing. I racked my mind again, torn. Should I call Bitsy? Go over? Make my usual pie just in case?

No. There was so much going on for all of them.

With a sigh, I climbed out of bed. I'd head to the store. Black Friday was just around the corner. That would give me something to do.

If nothing else, I always had candy to blow up.

I stopped at the cemetery.

Before walking toward the wrought iron fence, I pinched off a piece of the thick cinnamon roll that Rachelle had given me, tore it free, and sank my teeth into the bread. Cinnamon burst into my mouth. The frosting dissolved on my tongue and trickled down my throat in a sweet river. I hadn't tasted anything so good since Bill died.

Sometimes, I thought I couldn't taste at all anymore.

"God bless you, Rachelle," I murmured. One last bite and I slipped through the gate.

Everything lay in quiet serenity. Another family talked amongst themselves on the other side of the snowy space. A bouquet of white flowers covered what appeared to be a fresh grave.

After Bill died, I couldn't bring myself to visit him much. Pretending he was on vacation seemed so much easier. Besides, he wouldn't stay here as a ghost.

He'd probably reside in the fridge.

Coming to the cemetery now felt anything but natural. Still, the brisk air roused me from the post-meeting stupor I'd stumbled around my house in. I crouched next to his headstone and laid my usual offering near his name: a small bundle of Twizzlers.

"Brought your favorite." I dusted snow off the top of his simple headstone. "Just like always."

Once I'd lost him, I realized just how unprepared we'd been for death—despite facing it so many times. Bill had always seemed invincible. A silly thought considering he'd been overweight most of his life and on a CPAP at night. He'd certainly tipped back a few too many beers as he'd aged. I wished I could hold onto a piece of that naiveté. It seemed so much better than knowing more than everyone else.

"This always feels weird." My nose scrunched. I glanced around, but the other family had left. "I'm going to just keep talking in the hopes that I stop feeling so dumb."

I tucked aside a piece of grass that had drifted over his name, then straightened. Snow littered the ground in a patchy array, intermixed with piles of slush and mud. A couple of graves were ringed by fake flowers, filling the space where a surviving spouse's death date would eventually be inscribed. Widows roamed the city, just like me.

"I wish you were actually here," I said. "There's a lot going on with my friends and Jerry dying and . . . and the store."

My thoughts trailed away until a cold gust of wind sent a shiver through me.

"Why aren't you talking to me today?" I growled.

Because I'm busy, he said, voice bright. The way it always had been after he slapped on aftershave following his ritual cold shower every morning. Relief flowed through me like a serger tearing through silk.

"You're not busy. You're dead."

Shows how much you know. Bitsy may be expecting you. Like an unspoken rule, or something.

"She might *not* be expecting me," I muttered. "And she's already stressed. Not sure I want to sign onto that today."

True.

"Besides . . . I'm not even sure . . . I . . ."

Just spill it.

"Something is going on there, and she's closed herself off again. You know there's no opening her back up."

That's not what's really bothering you.

It wasn't. But I couldn't touch the dark spot in my mind. It encased a bubbling, frenetic turmoil. Hid my flashes of rage. It was the darkness that moved like liquid underneath all this fury. Instead of letting myself see what was really there, I shook my head.

"I'm not going to invite myself to Bitsy's."

There's always Rachelle.

"Rachelle's having dinner with her mom, William, and his grandmother. That would be just as awkward. No one *asked* me to go, Bill. I'm just supposed to show up?"

Erasmus does it all the time.

"Erasmus is a weird man."

Great lawyer, though. Rachelle could use a maternal influence, even when her mother is *around.*

"I'm not maternal, Bill. All of our children died."

Silence rode in the wake of my comment. He would never have

said that. Nor would I have said it to him. He'd suffered with guilt over all our losses, even though it hadn't been his fault. If he were here, he'd have told me to buck up. Make a damn turkey if I wanted one.

Why are you here? he asked.

"Because I never come."

We talk all the time.

"But . . ."

You think I'm just a figment of your imagination.

"You're dead, Bill. You *are* a figment of my imagination."

I wasn't always.

I pressed my lips together, rubbing them until they felt warm. What I wouldn't give to actually talk to him for five more minutes. To tell him the way I felt about Tadd and all the changes in the Health and Happiness Society. I'd tell him about how Jerry's death had affected me. Not just because I'd lost all of my family, but because it brought back grief from when he died.

But he wasn't here. Couldn't help me. No amount of wishing would bring him back. If it would have, I'd have had him back in my arms years ago.

"I'm back on the Pepsi."

There are worse vices.

"You had undiagnosed diabetes when you died, they said. There probably aren't *many* worse vices."

Don't think that way. You're always predicting the worst.

"Because it's always happening. Don't you remember? None of this was in the plan, Bill." My voice hardened. "None of this was the life we were supposed to live. You're dead. You're gone. I'm here and I'm . . ."

Stuck. Lost.

A whistle of wind replied.

Although I hadn't said what I wanted to say, and I wasn't really sure I could, I felt better.

With my hands tucked into my pockets, I slipped through the cemetery and back to the Cadillac. Snow fell in fat flakes that melted on my car. Tires hissed as they drove by. I hadn't heard them inside the cemetery. As if it were a different world.

Sometimes, it felt like it was.

By noon the next day, the rush of Black Friday had been more than I'd expected—but still somehow underwhelming.

Aside from a couple of deeply discounted sewing machines and thirty spools of thread, nothing significant had flown off the shelves. In fact, the parking lot remained depressingly empty.

When the bell tinkled on the door and a voice rang out from the front, I glanced up.

"Mira?"

My brow dropped into a scowl.

"Tadd."

Tadd strolled in, hands in his pockets, all casual ease. The wind had tousled his blond locks and brightened his eyes. He *would* be attractive, the slime.

"Happy Holidays!" he cried.

"You celebrate Black Friday as a holiday?"

"In general, no. But I never know how to be politically correct anymore, so I figured generic is safest."

With grudging respect, I admitted he was right. He stopped across the register from me. I attempted my sweetest smile. *If you don't have something nice to say, then hush it,* Mama would have said.

"So?" I asked. "Are you here for more snooping?"

"Never snooping. But I did want to talk to you more about my company's plans for this space."

"You're a stubborn little thing, aren't you?"

"I've been known to get what I set my sights on."

"Bet you never said that to your wife."

He grinned. "You'd be right."

A smile twitched at the corners of my mouth, but I refused to give in. Instead, I cleared my throat, noticing he carried a bundle of papers.

"You'll never convince me that this sale is going to happen, Tadd. There have been plenty of people interested before, but they moved on to downtown after a while. Charles can be stubborn."

His eyes sparkled with a mischievous glint. "Maybe. But they weren't me."

With a flick of his wrist, he unrolled the papers on the counter between us. A plethora of photos, words, and blueprints. I blinked, attempting to make sense of the chaos.

"What is this?" I asked.

"Plans for the strip mall."

Amidst the blue-and-white lines, a familiar image coalesced of a much taller, more intricate building. The schematics were broken into words, figures, and numbers I didn't understand.

"I don't speak engineer."

He laughed. "You don't have to. That's my job. Do you see these over here?"

Several photographs stuck out. Chic new developments with outdoor escalators, marble floors, and newly paved parking lots. Flower boxes lined a row of similar windows and doors, like townhouses only . . . different.

"What are they?"

"There's a movement to rehabilitate old buildings into something better. A way for big cities to make best use of space that would otherwise be forgotten or wasted. In this picture, you can see they took this strip mall with fifty different retail spaces and turned it into a housing development. Over here? A medical center."

I blinked. The before and after pictures were startling. A crumbling, sad exterior with blank windows—like gaping empty eyes—lay next to a bright, polished new building. Although subtle, I could just make out the vague similarities between the two. Same building. Very different aesthetic.

"Oh."

Tadd punched one hand against the other as he stared at the pictures, a hungry light in his eyes.

"Platinum Development wants to prove this is possible on a micro level. Instead of turning a 50,000 or 100,000 square foot property into something else, we want to turn this strip mall into a neighborhood development."

"Apartments?" I asked.

"Both. Housing *and* retail space. Things people actually need. Pharmacies, banks, small grocery stores, you name it."

He hadn't been kidding when he'd said they wanted to change the neighborhood. If I could decipher anything from the blueprints, multiple levels were planned on *top* of the current strip mall.

"What exactly do you mean?" I asked, staring at him with a narrowed gaze. I couldn't peg it, but I felt as if there was something he wasn't saying.

"We want to revitalize the neighborhood."

"You already said that."

"It bears repeating. This is one of the more difficult neighborhoods in the area. Which is surprising, considering its close proximity to the college and the prosperous new downtown."

My thoughts flickered to Rachelle. The Frosting Cottage was one of those new retail spaces that had afforded the city so much new revenue and life. He certainly wasn't wrong. Downtown had blossomed over the last three to four years, and had significantly contributed to the . . . *generic* decline in traffic to our little strip mall.

Nothing I hadn't weathered before.

"What does that have to do with me?" I asked.

"My company wants to take advantage of the location. Not only that, but we want to decrease crime, provide better housing, and offer greater access to the things that everybody needs. You've been here long enough to know that this neighborhood is struggling. What if we could provide medical care more locally? What if we had more stores to supply jobs to local residents?"

"You're a salesman. You're trained to say things the right way. What aren't you telling me?"

A flicker of a smile appeared on his lips.

"Skeptical one, aren't you?"

"My mama raised me to find common sense first, and my dad was a car salesman. I know all the tricks."

He held up his hands. "I'm definitely not here to trick anybody."

I shoved the papers back at him.

"Great. But that doesn't change the fact that the sale is not going to happen."

A crease formed between his brows—the first sign of anything but ease and amusement.

"Why not?"

I sputtered to a stop, even though my mind raced. *Because this neighborhood isn't suited for it. Because we all have leases. Because . . .*

"It's not in my plan."

The words rushed out of my mouth. Until I heard them myself, I didn't even know they were there. Tadd's gaze narrowed.

"Your plan?"

"That's right. It's not in my ten-year plan."

This time, *he* stumbled for words. I didn't blame him. They'd failed me as well.

"I see," he finally said.

"Do you?"

Shock overcame him this time, one of the most genuine responses I could have expected.

Go get 'em, tiger, Bill said.

My spine straightened. "My husband and I watched this strip mall grow. We invested our lives into successfully running this business. I won't be kicked out because someone wants to . . . you want . . . to be out with the old and in with the new."

"That's—"

"Bill, Jerry, and my parents have died, and I don't have any babies to hold, and everyone else is moving on, and I spent yesterday all alone in this store, but you can be damn certain I'm not letting go of *this* place."

Tadd opened his mouth, then closed it again. His brow wrinkled. For what felt like a short eternity, we stared at each other. Blood pumped through my body, whistling past my ears. Would he leave? Would he laugh?

Never underestimate the power of a hissy fit, Mama would have said.

Tadd pulled his bottom lip through his teeth, sucked in a deep breath, and said, "I get it."

A pause stretched. I waited for more. "That's it?" I asked.

"You don't want to lose your business."

"No." My chin tilted up. "And I won't."

He half smiled. "You won't."

"What?"

"Owning a business is like having a home, isn't it?"

"Sometimes."

"Home is where you take it. It isn't restricted to certain buildings or locales or even workers. You can create a whole *new* home." His eyes darted to the ceiling and then back to me. "One that doesn't need repairs."

My nostrils flared. It was one thing for *me* to notice the failings of Mira's Sewing and Vac, but for him to point them out?

As if he read my mind—or the fury in my eyes—he held up both hands in a gesture of surrender. "Look, I'm not here to get anyone angry. I just wanted you to know all of your options before this proceeds. I want you to be in the best place possible at the end of it, just like the rest of this community."

"There will be no *end*," I muttered between clenched teeth.

He sighed. "Mira, final negotiations are underway. Platinum Development is acquiring this strip mall from Charles with a contingency on the leases. I'm sorry that upsets you."

His words rang hollow in my chest. Wrath rose up in my throat, hot and stinging. He sauntered back a step, as if he saw the fire and all the brimstone that burned behind it. For a moment, I could hardly believe him. Charles sell?

Contingency?

What did all this mean?

"You don't trust me, and that's just fine," he said before I could speak. "I wouldn't expect you to. At least know that we plan on improving the community. This isn't just about revenue and sales and taxes."

The space between us likely saved his sweet little life. My hands were clenched at my side. My jaw tightened like a ball of rubber bands. It had been a long time since I'd had such a visceral reaction to a total stranger. I normally loved everyone I met.

"Get out."

"Fair enough," he said. He rolled up the papers—that I'd only glanced at for less than half a minute—and met my gaze. "I'll keep that in mind as we move forward. I'm sorry that it's not in your plans, Mira, but we *will* continue to work on this."

My glare lost strength by the time he disappeared out the front door, taking my easy day with him. If they really were at this stage, and Charles was letting it go, then why play the nice guy?

Why do the community meeting?
Something wasn't adding up.

Walk Away

Lucky's Irish Pub welcomed me with the smell of corned beef, fried potatoes, and foamy beer.

Slush lay thick on the sidewalk when I shut the door behind me, squishing between my toes in my old rain boots. Pat O'Malley bustled behind the counter. He was a round, barrel-chested man with kind eyes and a quick smile. Gray dusted his temples, which didn't have much hair these days.

Aside from a few casual dates that I'd accepted to stave off the gnawing loneliness, I'd never seen him anywhere *but* behind the counter. A white towel was draped over his shoulder. Food dotted a black apron. From a slit in the wall, a plate appeared, followed by a cry of, "Two cows, make 'em cry with twins, sea dust, and keep off the grass."

Only three patrons filled the pub on this dreary Saturday night. A tired-looking waitress leaned against the bar with a hand propped under her jaw. Her gaze focused on the television hanging above us. Pat slid the plate down the bar. An older gentleman with rheumy eyes caught the plate, held up a hand, and picked up the first of two hamburgers. Pat resumed wiping the bar without missing a beat.

The sound of clattering dishes rang in the background when I approached. Pat glanced up at me.

"Hey, Mira," he cried, grinning. "What brings you here? Haven't seen you in a while."

I set my floral bag on top of the bar, then slid into one of the stools. The way my legs dangled off the ground made me feel like a little girl.

"Got some Pepsi?"

"Balloon water with sand," he said, winking. "Coming right up."

When he returned, I grabbed a straw and plunked it inside the foamy brown drink. The Pepsi soothed my ruffled chest when I took a long pull.

"Just wanted to see how you were doing," I said. "Now that Lexie is gone, we never see each other anymore."

He nodded once. "True."

"So? How've you been?"

He shrugged. I saw myself in his wrinkled face. The weariness in his drawn eyes. The fatigue of the constant cycling of days. There was nothing so broken as living the same life every day.

"Not so bad," he said. "Just doing the thing, you know?"

"I do know. You got a minute?"

He raised one eyebrow. "Need to gab?"

"Desperately."

"Janice," he called to the waitress. She sighed, blinked, and looked at him with half-lidded eyes and a yawn. "Give me twenty. Keep Marco on the rocks, eh?"

The old man waved again.

Pat put both hands on the counter beneath him and nodded once at me. "Lucky day for you. I haven't given free therapy for anyone today. Go for it."

I leaned forward. Instead of telling him about Tadd Williams, or the strange feeling of the Health and Happiness Society moving on without me, I blurted, "What's your purpose without your wife?"

Once I heard the question, I understood how deeply, how badly, it had been burning inside of me. I held my breath, as if the fate of the rest of my life hinged on his answer.

In some ways, it did.

Pat tilted his head. He had a thick jaw and broad, bulky shoulders, like a bulldog. But there was a softness in his gaze that I saw often, as if he were really an overgrown kitten.

"My purpose without Ingrid?"

"What do you wake up for?"

He twirled a finger. "The pub. Why?"

"Is that enough?"

"Sure. Has been so far. She's been gone ten years."

I leaned back, my heart sinking in my chest. That hadn't been the answer I'd wanted. I didn't know what was. Pat lowered his voice. "You all right, Mira? You going through something?"

"I don't know why I'm asking. I just . . . I feel . . ."

"Lonely?"

"Lost."

He braced both arms on the bar again and rested his bulky upper body on top of them. For a moment, we stared hard at each other.

"You aren't thinking of doing something stupid, are you?" he asked.

"No, nothing like that. I'm not suicidal."

"Good."

"I'm just done. You know? At least, I think I am. I'm tired of waking up in my big house. I'm tired of eating healthy. I'm tired of people *leaving*. Pat, I'm floundering. I have been for years."

"You lost a spouse."

"Seven years ago!"

"It happens."

"Well, floundering is overrated. Do you ever feel that way? Do you ever get tired of living the same life? We don't have the blueprint everyone else does, right? No kids. No family left. So, what about us? What if our businesses go under? What if we die? What happens to all of our belongings? Don't we get to leave a legacy, too?"

He straightened, his eyebrows high on his meaty forehead. "Of course we do. It's just different."

"Who gets your pub when you die?"

He shifted, as if he had an itch between his shoulders. "My nephew, I guess. Brother's kid. Kind of worthless, but someone."

Someone rang through my head.

I didn't have that.

Was it Bitsy's job to take care of me? No. Nor Rachelle's. Nor Lexie's. Nor Megan's. Did the responsibility of caring for myself fall on my shoulders now? Yes. My shoulders.

My shoulders alone.

"I suppose it's all on me, then."

He rolled his eyes. "God doesn't work like that. You'll be taken care of."

I snorted. "Right."

My pastor would have slapped me silly for even insinuating it, but I couldn't help but wonder. Everyone else had left, or moved on. What if God did that too?

I looked away so I didn't have to meet his gaze. "What if I just walked away?"

"What?"

My voice lowered. I didn't even know myself, as if these words came from a different body. "What would happen if I walked away from everything Bill and I created. Just . . . left everything I am?"

"Can you do that?" he asked. "I mean . . . walk away from yourself?"

"I don't know."

"Why would you *want* to?"

"Because this isn't how it was supposed to be! I had a plan."

He leaned forward. "Listen, Mira. I get it, all right? Your mind is spinning. The holidays are coming up. That always sucks. Sometimes, I still feel lost too. But it fades over time. I like my restaurant, I like my patrons, and I like waking up every day."

This won't fade, I thought. *It's too powerful. It's a beast inside of me. There's something locked up. Something I'm afraid to see. Afraid to touch. Afraid I'll burn from the inside out if I set it free.*

Pat reached out and put a heavy hand on top of mine.

"The question is can you wait it out? Let time work her magic?"

Tears filled my eyes. I didn't even try to blink them away. They dribbled down my cheek.

He didn't understand. Time'd had plenty of years to work her magic, but life kept taking. Just as I caught up, someone else vanished.

"No," I whispered. "I don't think I can."

He squeezed my hand. No one in the Health and Happiness Society would know how to handle this.

Not even Bitsy.

"It's going to be okay, Mira. Whatever it is that's bothering you, it always goes away. Sometimes you have to chase it. Grief doesn't last forever."

"Thanks, Pat."

"Anytime. We may not have our spouses, but we gotta stick together."

With a final sniffle, I wiped the tears off my cheeks with my fingers and forced a smile. Pat let his hand drop.

"What are you doing for the holidays?" I asked with a sniffle.

"Nephew."

"Oh, right. Hope it's fun!"

A half-hearted chuckle rolled out of him. "He's a laugh when he's drunk, and on the holidays, he's always drunk. His wife cooks really good, and his kids are funny. It's better than being home alone, anyway, or cooking food for people who hate everything. Why does Christmas bring out all the grumps? How about you? You spending it with Lexie? Or your brother, down in the city?"

My throat tightened. "Not this year," I said. "Not sure what I'll do yet."

"You'll figure something out."

I smiled. "Thanks again. I needed someone to talk to. It's been . . . hard to find someone who understands."

He spread his hands. "You know me. It's what I do."

"Thanks."

I slid off the bar stool and headed toward the door, the sound of ESPN ringing in the background. The bell sang again as I slipped outside and headed through the puddles. Darkness had long since fallen, sweeping the world in a wintry cloak. I lived only a half mile away, but it felt like further. Stretching my legs felt good. I hadn't worked out since before Jerry's funeral.

Later, as I lay on the couch, staring at the shifting shadows on the ceiling, I couldn't help but wonder if I was the only one asking these questions.

Did James ever feel lonely while he ran his store without his wife? Did he fear what the future would bring? But then, James had kids.

Had Bill thought about it?

Jerry?

Mom?

With these thoughts whirling around my head, I pulled out my phone and started Candy Killer. An hour later, I fell asleep while the Home Shopping Network droned in the background.

I dreamt of Jerry.

"Hey Mira, it's Rachelle. It's Sunday. Sorry I missed you. You must be at church. I wanted to check in and see how you were doing. We didn't get a chance to finish our conversation at the meeting,

and I've been worried about you. Are you going to be at the meeting this week? Bitsy turned it over to me. We're going to talk about the big Christmas party. I could use your help. Hope things are well. Call back? Bye."

"Mira, Bitsy here. Sorry about the last meeting. Things weren't all that organized but should be next week. Rachelle is taking over the meeting on Tuesday, 7:00. See you there. Bring Christmas party ideas. Oh, and are you available to babysit the girls so Jim and I can go on a date next week? We want to Christmas shop. Just let me know. Thanks!"

Tuesday evening, I stared at my phone with shaking hands.

Sending a text message certainly wasn't the most dramatic thing I'd ever done, but I felt as if it was.

Of all the many friendships I'd experienced, the Health and Happiness Society were the women I had stuck with the longest. I'd first met Bitsy at a meeting for a dieting group. Not long after, we'd started our own and created such a beautiful thing. These women knew me best.

Or did they?

Sorry, I can't make it to the meeting tonight, the text said. *A few things came up, but have fun! Send me the article for the week.*

Bright. Cheery. Apologetic from the beginning. Vague, but innocuous. Typical Mira. I couldn't conjure anything better to prevent questions. If they called to ask why I wasn't there—or what had come up—I wouldn't have an answer. I didn't know why I couldn't face them.

The thought of sitting in Bitsy's Christmas-laden house, hearing their happy updates, jolliness in the air, sent spikes of pain through my chest.

Before I could overthink it, my thumb pressed *send.*

While I waited for their responses, my heart banged like a drum. So many thoughts whirled through my head, I could barely comprehend them. Would they be angry with me?

Only a few minutes passed before the first chime. Rachelle, as I'd expected.

Let us know if you need anything.

Take care! Megan wrote.

I waited fifteen minutes. Then twenty. *I'm sure Bitsy will take extensive notes on the discussion,* Lexie eventually replied.

Nothing from Bitsy.

Finally, I sent back a smiley face and set the phone aside. While I drew in a deep, shaky breath, my gaze roamed my house. Empty. Clean, of course.

So I didn't have to face them now.

Didn't have to help plan a happy Christmas party that would tear me to pieces inside.

But what now?

Candy Killer. Pepsi. Home Shopping Network. A small dinner that didn't involve a lot of clean-up. The self-care arithmetic of the night I most wanted.

"Yes," I murmured, wondering why I felt so empty inside. "I guess that's it."

The Widows Club

The numbers on the sixth page of my fourth-quarter tax form blurred together for the tenth time.

My eyes almost crossed from the effort of staring at the figures, wishing they'd just sort themselves out or drip off the page or fly to an accountant that I could afford. I muttered a curse, then followed it with a request for forgiveness. A splitting headache pulsed in my brain when I rubbed my temples. After Bill died, I'd done a crash course in running the financials of the business. Normally I didn't mind the paperwork.

Tonight, it felt like death.

Even though Christmas carols rang on the air through the radio, I felt no Christmas spirit. I shoved away from the desk and toward the refrigerator. A plethora of water bottles and brand-new Pepsis waited inside. This time, I grabbed the water bottle and sipped.

So bland.

A clock with a needle for hands and buttons and thread for numbers ticked above the door. Ten minutes past six.

Closing time.

Call Erasmus, Bill said when I returned to the desk. I could almost picture him standing over my right shoulder, peering at the mess of forms. Erasmus had taken care of things for the first six months after Bill's death when it overwhelmed me.

"Erasmus has nothing to do with this."

He's my estate lawyer. And my friend. He can help you.

"Erasmus doesn't have friends."

He had me.

"I don't need him. I just need to finish this."

Deciding to put the taxes on hold again, I grabbed my jacket off the back of a chair, shoved my keys in my pocket, and headed for the front door. Two customers walked into James's restaurant as I flipped off the lights and locked the door behind me. At least *he* was seeing traffic. Things had been abysmal since Black Friday.

Once I sat in my car, I paused. Where was I going? A sinking realization filled my chest.

Nowhere.

Normally, I'd head over to Bitsy's house—assuming she wasn't cleaning somewhere. I thought of the Frosting Cottage, but Rachelle was bound to be busy with Sophia moving and selling her the business. Besides, it would just be awkward since I didn't show up at the meeting.

Wouldn't it?

With a sigh, I pushed the keys into the ignition and cranked the car on. I knew where I needed to go. I just hadn't been there in weeks.

The sparkling tinsel and window paint decorating the front of my gym came into view ten minutes later. My bag sat in the back, as if begging to be used. Now that Rachelle had scaled back her workouts and Lexie was gone, I came by myself.

For several minutes, I watched people walk in and out. No workout machine, class, or television show motivated me to get out of the warm car and into the snowy night. Although destroying candies and racking up points *did* have a certain mindless appeal, the idea of being around people in a brightly lit environment didn't.

I thought of Jerry and drove away, allowing the car to take me wherever it wanted to.

After weaving in and out of traffic for fifteen minutes, I found myself in front of Bitsy's house. Snow had started to fall in gentle flakes. Soft curls of slate clouds filled the sky, mere wisps against the fading light. I stopped across the street and sighed.

Maybe I'd been imagining this whole thing.

My imagination—which had probably overtaken reality—could have conjured up a dream. Lexie wasn't pregnant. Rachelle wasn't buying a business. Megan wasn't married. Bitsy wasn't hiding . . . *something*. For a moment, I could almost sink into the hope. It quickly faded.

No, I hadn't imagined any of that.

That was real.

Inside Bitsy's house, the girls darted back and forth in front of the window, and then Lana darted outside. Skidding on the porch, she ran as fast as her thin legs would carry her over to Jim's house, threw open the door, and dashed inside. Lizzy followed soon after.

"Well," I said a with a sigh. "Good for you, cute little family."

Despite the pain in my heart, I meant it.

Within seconds, I threw the car into gear and tore down the slushy road, feeling a sense of invincibility in running away. Ten minutes later, my car stopped again. This time at church.

A single light illuminated the far side of the building. Pastor Burke's office. I sat with my hands in my lap. Yet another place I hadn't attended recently. Church had always been a reprieve. A sanctuary. But now? It felt like more work. Jerry hated church and religion.

"Mama always said he was a godless heathen, didn't she?" I murmured, thinking about his grave and the bottle of whiskey Charlotte had buried him with.

Visiting Pastor Burke couldn't hurt. He certainly wouldn't turn me away, and he knew how to listen.

Just as I set my foot outside, a rustle of movement at the main doors caught my eye. Two women hobbled out, holding on to each other. One was relying on a cane while the other seemed to gab at an incomprehensible speed.

"Gladys?" I whispered, staring at the bent woman with the cane. Gladys was well over eighty and had been a widow for almost thirty years. Her biting tongue ensured *everyone* in church knew her.

In fact, the prayer circle often prayed for her.

I stood half in, half out of my car until Gladys broke me from my frozen shock. "Well?" she snapped. "What are you doing just standing there with your mouth open?"

They were only a couple of steps away now, headed toward a rusty Oldsmobile under the street light. An oxygen tank trailed behind them. Gladys's thin eyebrows narrowed over her eyes.

I cleared my throat as I sheepishly extracted myself from the car. Both of them stared with unabashed curiosity.

"Ah . . . just deciding whether I want to talk to Pastor Burke," I said.

Gladys rolled her eyes. "Don't waste your time. Nothing he can do for you." Her eyes gleamed as she appraised me, head tilted back. "Come to my house. Poker game tonight."

"We could use another player," her friend said. Stella, if I remembered right. Another lost soul Pastor Burke was constantly trying to get in touch with.

My eyebrows rose halfway up my hairline. "Poker game?"

"I'm not dead yet," Gladys muttered.

"Oh, I didn't—"

"There's always time for gambling," she said. "After you put on a few more years, you don't even care how much money you lose."

I seriously doubted it.

Stella jerked her head to the side, motioning toward the Oldsmobile. "Come on. Follow us over. You look like you need a good, stiff drink. We have lots of those."

Before I could refuse, they shuffled to the car. I fumbled over my own thoughts. Were they serious? They didn't even know my name, even though Gladys had once yelled at me in the ladies' room for wearing the wrong kind of pantyhose.

Poker? A good, stiff drink?

Hadn't this lady just walked out of *church*?

Before I could extract myself from my surprise, Stella drove away, her brake lights illuminating the night. She stopped three inches from the back of my car. The passenger window rolled down.

"Well?" Gladys bellowed. "Are you a chicken, or are you a woman?"

The window rolled back up. Stella peeled out of the slushy parking lot. I glanced at the church and the disappearing Oldsmobile, then ducked back into my Cadillac.

I followed close behind them.

Gladys' house was a small thing tucked into a dark neighborhood.

I shuddered as I passed several battered homes, most boarded up, so small they'd fit in my attic. When I pulled up to the sidewalk, I parked and blinked. Did I want to be here? Was I really so desperate? This wasn't something I would normally do.

Which was probably the reason I should do it.

I'd seen Gladys at church a few times, but we'd never really interacted. When she came, she sat in the back, cracking dark jokes about the people crying through the sermons. They weren't even *funny* jokes, but she'd always laughed.

Sometimes uproariously.

Robin's-egg blue paint splotched the outside of her little shack, which perched next to a muddy yard with no grass. The driveway filled with dead weeds wasn't even big enough to park a car in.

When I convinced myself to step outside, Gladys and Stella were already hobbling toward the house, oxygen tank in tow. I joined them at the walkway and followed them through her creaky chain-link gate.

"Maude will be here in a minute," Gladys called over her shoulder. "Then we can start."

"I ordered takeout," Stella said. "Won't come for another hour though."

"O-okay."

Only one neighbor had strings of Christmas lights draped around their house, illuminating the air with a festive feeling. Gladys's house looked like a tomb. Dark, cold, dead. They waved me inside.

I froze. I had two choices.

Leave and go back to my empty house that probably looked just as stark and lonely. Or, I could stay.

I stepped inside.

The stale smell of burnt coffee filled the house. The whir of an oxygen machine activated as Gladys shuffled past, jabbing a red button with her crooked finger. She sank onto a couch, panting. Stella grabbed a pillow from the other side and put it behind Gladys's back.

"Thanks, Stell," Gladys gasped.

Stella turned to me with a blank expression. "How do you take it?"

"My coffee?"

Gladys snorted. "Want coffee? Go to Starbucks."

"On the rocks, or straight?" Stella asked.

Several seconds passed before I comprehended that they were talking about alcohol. Stella pulled out an amber-colored jar from a nearby cupboard and held it up.

Whiskey.

My mouth dropped. "Whiskey?"

Stella giggled as she fondled the jar against her cheek. "Who's going to stop us?"

"We're just pickling ourselves from the inside out," Gladys said, barking a hoarse laugh while Stella stared at me.

"I don't, ah, drink whiskey," I said.

Gladys jerked a thumb toward the kitchen. "Coffee's in there."

"I'm not that thirsty, thanks." I glanced behind me. Stella had shut the front door. The room felt claustrophobically small. How did Gladys live here? Where did she sleep?

"Maybe . . . maybe I should just go? I'm terrible at poker and—"

"We aren't going to eat you," Gladys said. "But if you want to go, you're welcome to. Maude will be here any minute now, though, and—"

"I'm not a minute late, Gladys Gardner, so don't you dare tell me I am."

The front door slammed open. I jumped, gasped, and whirled around. A woman in her early sixties stood there in a gray cardigan, a string of pearls, and a pair of freshly pressed black slacks beneath a pure white pea coat. High-heel shoes shone against the worn wooden floor, which hadn't seen a buffing in probably decades.

Her eyes darted right to me. They narrowed. "Who are you?"

"Mira."

"She's going to play with us tonight," Stella said. Two glasses clinked together as she pulled them from a cupboard. "We found her poking around outside the church after we spoke with Pastor Rogers."

"Burke," I mumbled.

"Whoever."

"And I wasn't poking around. I—"

"A whore again?" Maude asked.

"What?" I screeched.

Gladys tilted her head back and laughed. "I brought whores to the game before. They're normally my favorites."

Maude advanced farther into the room. "She has a habit of collecting the lost."

"I'm not lost," I said.

The words came out small. Pitiful, even. The only thing that kept me from bolting was sheer curiosity. Did these women really get together to play poker and drink whiskey?

Why?

Maude set aside a Gucci handbag on the threadbare couch and sank into one of the cushions without hesitation. If I looked out of place here, she positively radiated it. She reached into her bag and tossed a new set of poker cards onto a folding table in the middle of the room.

"I brought the cards."

Stella had pulled two folding chairs out of a nearby closet and set them around the outside of the table.

"Sit," she said, shoving one at me. It slid across the floor with a rattle and stopped a few inches short.

Maude's eyes flickered to mine. "You scared?"

"Not *scared*, I'm just . . ."

"Bad at poker?"

"Sure."

The cards slid out of the box and into her hand. "Good. So is Stella. That'll even this out."

Stella nodded before tipping back a shot.

The strangeness of the situation compelled me to bend my knees and sink into the chair. Gladys reached into a drawer next to her and pulled out a pipe. Within seconds, she was puffing away, bluish smoke leaking from the top of the pipe. Attached to her nose was a clear plastic tube of oxygen. My mouth almost dropped open again.

"It's not a cigarette," she said. "Pipe tobacco is totally different. No danger here."

I had serious doubts about that.

Stella caught my eye and motioned to Gladys's right, where a fire extinguisher sat on the floor. She winked. I looked away.

Maude had shuffled the cards four times and started dealing. Stella settled on the chair across from me, whiskey bottle at her side. Only then did I notice a subtle, light layer of dog hair gracing her shoulders. Were those shoulder pads underneath her pink sweater?

"Texas tonight?" Stella asked.

"Five-card stud," Gladys said.

At first, I stared at the pile of cards accruing in front of me without any idea of how to proceed. How should I tell them I didn't know how to play poker?

"I don't—"

"You'll learn," Maude said. "Pick up the cards, and organize them by suit."

"But—"

"You were wandering around the church parking lot for a reason, right?" Gladys asked.

My reply stalled. "Uh . . . I wasn't *wandering*. Just was in my . . . yes. I-I guess I was there for a reason."

"Your husband is dead."

"Yes."

"You don't have kids."

"N-no. I—"

"Me either."

Buried in Gladys's rheumy eyes was something I thought I recognized but couldn't name.

"No children?"

"None." She straightened up. "I knew the look in your eyes the moment I saw you in the parking lot."

Stella slid a shot of whiskey across the table toward me. Amber liquid sloshed over the sides in thin dribbles. "That'll help," she said.

"I can't drink that."

"You can," Stella said. "You won't. There's a difference."

"It's fine, Stella," Gladys said as she pulled her cards off the table one at a time. "Take it yourself."

Stella eagerly complied. I leaned forward, shoving the cards away from me and into the middle of the table. No one said a word.

"What do you mean, you knew the look in my eyes?" I demanded. "That doesn't make any sense."

Gladys peered at me over her cards. "Desperation? Sheer terror? Maybe a little resentment bubbling under the surface? Over all, you're a woman made of wrath and scorn right now. We've all been there."

Words failed me. Gladys reached into her drawer again and extracted a pair of sunglasses. She slid them over her eyes. Stella fidgeted with a cross around her neck, rubbing it against her bottom lip while she studied her cards. Maude remained as stony as a statue, but her eyes flickered to me, then to Gladys, then back to me.

"What do you mean *wrath and scorn*?" I asked.

Stella looked at me from across the table. "Widow?"

"Yes."

"How long?"

"Seven years."

Beneath the slight haze of whiskey in her eyes, I saw a sliver of interest.

"You?" I asked, glancing at all of them. Stella tossed down her cards, folding the hand to Gladys, who cackled.

Maude sighed and gave in. "Twenty years."

Stella raised a hand. "Eighteen."

"Thirty-four," Gladys said.

"*All* of you are childless?"

"Just me," Gladys said. "Only child. No siblings. Parents long gone before my husband."

Maude glanced up with an expression of amusement as she finished dealing out the next round of cards. "My third husband drove his car into a lake. The other two were heart attacks, but I'd divorced them long before."

"I'm sorry about your third."

"I wasn't."

I pushed the new cards away again.

"A fitting end," Maude said. "He was happy with the way he went. Better than the alternative."

"Dying peacefully at home?" I asked.

"Alzheimer's."

"Oh. Sorry."

"What about yours?" Stella asked.

"Stroke," I said. "Followed by multi-organ failure, a couple of heart attacks, and a pulmonary embolism."

"Grief," Stella said. "The good Lord pushed him down and kicked him while he was there."

My heart almost stopped. She had almost taken those words directly from my brain. I couldn't count the number of times I'd thought that myself. Bill's death had been unnecessarily severe. He'd fallen apart for a week, forcing me to make decisions I'd never thought I'd have to make. Only Jerry had been there to help me.

Now Jerry was gone.

"Still better than Alzheimer's," Maude muttered.

"You work?" Stella asked.

"I run a sewing store. It's not far from here, actually."

Maude's sharp gaze met mine again. "Mira's Sewing and Vac?"

"You know it?"

"Seen it. Sounds awful," Gladys said.

Stella rolled her eyes. Maude glared. Heat rippled through me again. What did Gladys know about me anyway?

"I enjo—"

The words faltered. For some reason, I couldn't say, *I enjoy it.*

Stella motioned to the three of them with a jerk of her head. "We get together once a month to play poker, let loose, and stop being the women that people expect us to be."

"Something about losing your spouse breaks open a different part of you," Maude said, eyes narrowed on her cards. "In some ways, you stop giving a damn. But you need to give a damn because others expect it. None of that here. Do whatever you want. If you want to smoke while wearing oxygen? Smoke. If you want to eat takeout against the advice of your doctor? Do it. If you want to be angry? Be angry. Only rule here is this: don't push anything off anymore. Not goals. Not time. Not emotions."

"Don't push anything off? That doesn't make sense."

"Oh," Gladys murmured, cackling, "she's angry, all right."

Her words rang through my head. Stella peered at me, then reared back, as if she saw something in my expression. Something *I* didn't even know was there.

"You *are* angry," she murmured. "Why?"

The thought struck me that she had no idea what she was asking. No idea the demons I could unleash. The vents of rage that could open and spill bloody magma right from the middle of my heart all over this place. My breath caught with the power of my own helplessness. If I let it out, it could destroy them.

Her question forced me to reckon with it for the first time.

Why *was* I angry?

"I don't have any family left," I said. The words came out on their own even though my throat almost closed up. Even Gladys seemed to stare at me from behind her glasses. "My only brother just died. My husband is gone. Parents are gone. All my babies . . . gone."

No pity, no condolences, no patting of my hand. They waited, as if they knew what would come next.

"I'm tired of being alone. I'm tired of not being young anymore. I'm tired of weight staying like it's found a new permanent residence. I'm tired of being afraid. I'm tired of thinking about what will happen when I die. I'm tired of worrying *how* I will die or who will care. I'm tired of people moving on with their lives when I can't. I'm tired of being nice. I'm tired of Bitsy judging my food. I'm tired of Lexie living the life I was supposed to have. I'm tired of Megan being brave and Rachelle starting fresh. Without everything that was *supposed* to happen in my life, what is the point?"

My fist banged the table with the last four words. Fury scalded my veins, so freeing and hot I felt like I could fly.

Stella slid me another shot of whiskey.

"Here."

I grabbed it, threw my head back, and tossed it down my throat. It burned like a thousand fires all the way down. While I coughed and sputtered, Gladys leaned forward.

"Sounds like it's time to walk away, isn't it?"

My eyes watered as I met her gaze. *Walk away.* Wasn't that what I'd been doing my whole life? Planning, losing, realigning? Figuring out a way to survive until the next loss, the next tragedy, the next thing? Find a new dream, lose it, recalibrate. New friends when my current ones cycled on. New schedule. New car. New patio awning *just* to have something change.

Isn't that what widows had to do?

"To hell with rules and expectations," Maude said, eyebrows lifted halfway up her forehead. "Do whatever *you* want, Mira. Sounds like it might be the first time you've done it. That's what it means when you don't hold back."

A thousand memories raced through my mind. Bitsy conducting the first meeting. Lexie's bright gaze on her wedding day. Rachelle's fearful expression the first time she stood outside the Frosting Cottage. Megan cooking breakfast at my house when she stayed during a visit. Sophia tearing up when I agreed to help her for free. Jackie dropping off bolts of fabric to make a quilt for her daughter.

"You know what?" I said. "I think you're right."

Stella grinned.

Maude pressed her lips together.

Gladys pulled her sunglasses off and jabbed them at me. "To hell with that. I *know* we're right. I haven't been living this life for thirty years without learning a thing or two."

I slammed the shot glass back down.

"To new beginnings."

Megan Style

I woke the next morning before the sun rose.

Frost covered the window panes in my bathroom in spirals and whorls. The chilly bathroom tile radiated cold into the bones of my feet. I shivered and grabbed a fresh towel. The store wouldn't open for at least four more hours. So why was I up so early?

Why did energy buzz through my veins?

Why did I feel as if I'd just been handed a new life?

Because you're starting fresh? Bill ventured. For a brief moment, I thought I saw him standing at the sink, shaving cream lathering his jaw and littering the counter in white flecks. I stared at the empty spot with deep longing.

"I'm not—"

My rebuttal died, taking Bill's memory with it.

I *was* starting fresh. The decision had been made at Gladys's house. I'd outgrown the Health and Happiness Society. Or maybe they had outgrown *me*. The idea of continuing felt impossible.

To walk away?

To be . . . Mira? Unfettered by past losses. Unchained by the fear of losing *more* . . .

Nothing about that felt wrong.

"It's not like the girls need me anymore, anyway," I murmured and cranked the hot water on.

Steam roused the last of my sleepy stupor. When I emerged, all traces of doubt were gone. By the time I rubbed my hair dry, my eyes caught sight of something on the edge of my dresser.

The bucket list I'd found in the attic.

I stumbled toward it, as if drawn by an invisible string. The handwriting was a fresher version of the chicken scratch I had now, a testament to a time when I was younger and not so hurried. My eyes skimmed the list, which went on for several pages. My gaze stopped on one item that I hadn't seen before.

Rescue a kitten.

Bill had been allergic to cats—not to mention a staunch advocate against felinekind. But Bill wasn't here now. Getting a cat would break an unspoken, staunch rule in our home. If I was starting over, scaling back my involvement in the Health and Happiness Society, I needed to start somewhere.

Wasn't *this* the moment for drastic measures?

The midlife unraveling everyone always spoke of?

To hell with rules and expectations, Maude had said last night. *Do whatever you want, Mira.*

I set the list aside and reached for my bra. "I'm getting a cat, Bill. Right now. I'm tired of being alone, and I'm tired of thinking it would be fun. This is happening Megan-style. No plans, just action."

There were so many cats.

Most were trapped in solitary cages, only occasionally rooming together. Sleeping, meowing, pacing, yawning. Their worlds were small. Although it was well-kept, the humane society felt like a horrific place to get stuck, with its anemic lights and prison-like tile floor. The kind of place no one escaped. I immediately realized my mistake in coming alone. No one would stop me from adopting *all* of them.

The temptation fought a heavy war in my heart.

"These are our kittens over here," Daphne said as she escorted me down a hall lined with cat cages. She probably wasn't older than twenty, with dreadlocks, glittering diamond earrings, and a button-up polo. As we walked down the corridor, she reached out to greet each animal with a warm smile and a loving word. Many shrank back, either indifferent or jaded. I knew exactly how they felt.

"We keep the kittens housed together so they're socialized before they go to their new families," Daphne continued. "We currently have five kittens. As you can see, many of them are still quite young."

We stopped at a larger cage with black, white, and brown kittens. They tumbled over each other in a haphazard mess, or slept tucked in balls, pink noses hidden beneath their tiny tails. I wanted to scoop them all in my arms and snuggle them.

I squealed under my breath.

"They're adorable!"

She laughed. "Did you have something that you're looking for in particular?"

"I don't have any expectations. Just wanted to see what you had. I'd like a companion. Something easy. Not quite as intense as a dog."

She nodded knowingly, and I wondered if she heard this kind of thing all the time. The longer I stared at the kittens, the more Tadd the developer filled my mind. I turned away without holding any of them.

"Do you have any . . . older cats? Cats that have been here for a long time, or are old and need a little extra help?"

Her expression softened. "Yes, we do. Come with me. I'll show you."

We walked deeper into the room. Many of the cages we passed were empty until we got to the back. Three cages waited there. They were larger than the rest, with soft bedding and cats inside asleep, tails twitching.

"We give them a quieter environment because they've been here over a year and are over twelve years old, which is considered senior-citizen status. Sadie, on the top, is fifteen years old. She's geriatric now. Her owner surrendered her when they were moving and didn't want to take her with them. She wasn't getting along with their new puppy, so they brought her here."

I frowned. "That's horrible."

She shrugged. "There are a lot of reasons people surrender their animals. But, in the end, it's good they have a safe place here."

Sadie, an elegant black-and-white feline with a luxurious tail, stared at me through slitted yellow eyes. Judgment and condemnation oozed out of her gaze. This was a girl who had been around the block, who knew what it was like to lose.

"Is she grumpy?" I asked.

Daphne nodded with a laugh. "We've all tried to befriend her, but she's not too interested. We have to draw straws for who's going to clean her cage."

"I'll take her."

The words rushed out of me in a breathless moment. But as soon as they were out, I knew I meant them. Adopting her was the right thing to do. No one should die alone, not even an ornery old cat in a rescue shelter.

"Really?"

"Really."

"Okay," she drawled, as if she were afraid that I was going to change my mind. "I can—"

I pointed to the next cage. "Who is this?"

"That? Oh, that's Malcolm."

Malcolm was a calico cat. He stopped licking his paw to stare at me. Black and brown spots mingled on a backdrop of white fur that looked silky. He was skinny, unlike Sadie, who had rolls to spare. Instead of condemnation, he looked at me with utter curiosity.

"How old?"

"Thirteen. Came from—"

"I'll take him."

Her eyes widened. "Both?"

"And the third. Geriatric also?"

"Y-y-yes. That's Marilyn. She's the oldest here. Looks a little rough but has the sweetest temperament. She's seventeen."

Marilyn didn't even stir. One of her ears was hacked off on the corner, and her lip appeared to have a scar. The longer I stared at her, the more I knew I had to do it. They needed a home to die in with freedom and grace.

"All of them." I nodded once. "I want them all."

"It's really unusual. I'm not sure . . ." She trailed off.

I lifted an eyebrow. "These cats deserve better than dying in a shelter, don't you think?"

"O-of course."

"I can give them that. Being an old cat lady has always had an appeal to me, anyway."

Daphne blinked twice, as if she wasn't sure whether I was serious, then shook her head. "O-okay. Well . . . I'll just . . . I'll just get the paperwork started right now. Let me check with my manager. I mean . . . no one is going to believe this. Proof that Christmas really does bring miracles, I guess?"

"It has very little to do with Christmas," I said, hooking a finger around a bar on Malcolm's cage. "And everything to do with death."

Daphne spun on her heels, calling someone's name. I stood there, staring at my three new companions and wondering what it would be like to have a cat in the house. No—three cats. Would it feel less empty? They might despise each other. There would be cat hair. Possibly territory issues. Pee. Cat litter. Would Sadie or Malcolm or Marilyn even care about *me*?

Did it matter?

"You and me, my friends," I whispered. "It's going to be you and me. You may not live long, but in my world, not many people do."

Sadie closed her eyes and fell back to sleep. Malcolm yawned. Marilyn didn't even stir.

I spun on my heels and marched toward the office.

I told you this wasn't going to go well.

"It's fine," I snapped at Bill. "It's . . . just . . . be quiet."

Three cat carriers, four vials of medicine, three different types of specialized cat food, two containers of litter, and three beds—somewhat matted with fur—filled my kitchen table the next day. I scoured the paperwork in front of me, wondering if maybe I had lost my mind. Adopting three cats would be a sure sign of it. Who knew cats were so expensive to keep alive long enough for a graceful death?

"Who had diabetes?" I muttered, glancing toward the living room. Malcolm stood on top of the couch, staring out the front window. Sadie had slinked away and disappeared the moment I set her free. Marilyn had strolled over to the couch, jumped up, and curled into a ball as if she couldn't have cared less.

Hardly what I expected, but at least they weren't yowling.

While I wrestled with the covered litter box in the laundry room, and attempted to find a spot where each cat could have their own meals—they had to be fed separately, apparently—Malcolm disappeared, and Sadie reappeared, but only briefly. They flitted around like shadows.

They're going to get hair everywhere, Bill said. I could see him standing at the sink, hands on his hips, nose scrunched in disgust as I walked past him carrying the packet of informational flyers the shelter had given me.

"So did you."

Not like this!

"You aren't even here."

You really think there's some kind of glory in becoming an old cat lady?

"No one said anything about glory. They needed a home. Just like . . ."

The words trailed away. *Just like the children you never let me adopt.* I didn't have the heart to voice the words, even after his death. Bill disappeared.

I tossed the papers on the table and sank into a chair with a sigh. Marilyn stirred, stretched her legs, and fell back to sleep. In the distance, I thought I heard something clatter.

I acted like I hadn't.

Just as I sorted through what medications belonged to what cat, and when they had to be administered, my phone buzzed with a new text from Bitsy.

> *Details from the last meeting have been emailed to you. This week's meeting will be your turn. I have a few suggested articles you may want to review for possible discussion topics. Let me know if you want them.*

My throat went dry. In my mind, I'd already cut the strings. The Health and Happiness Society and I had a clean break. In fact, I'd almost deleted the app off my phone. For two solid minutes, I stared at the screen.

What now?

I'd forgotten that the girls weren't in my head. They didn't know I was moving on, that our time together had come to a close. Just the thought of telling them made acid rise in my chest. I closed my eyes.

The *last* thing I wanted to do was run one of the meetings.

No, I wouldn't go back. My mind was firm on that much. This was about me now, not them. New life. Walking away. Starting over. Different Mira. Cat lady Mira, in fact.

I chewed on my bottom lip. Somewhere upstairs, a cat meowed. Malcolm, perhaps? It would take a while for me to sort out their voices. I eyed Marilyn, who lay like a dead pillow on the couch. Assuming they all *had* voices.

My thumb hovered over the conversation. Three new replies popped up.

Rachelle: *Sweet! I love it when Mira conducts. Best. Snacks. Ever.*

Megan: *Can we discuss the best time for our flights to come in for the Christmas party? I'm looking to book ASAP. Mira, you better be ready, cause we're coming to your place again!*

Lexie: *I just threw up from excitement AND pregnancy. Because guess what? The semester ends on December 10th. Bradley and I will be driving out December 11th. We'll be there in just over three weeks!*

My heart skipped a beat. Three weeks! I hadn't seen that much of Lexie in . . .

Like a sinking weight, my heart dropped into my stomach. I wouldn't see her this time either. "They'll leave," I whispered. "They'll move on. They'll forget me. It's better to break away now."

Bitsy was already wrapped up in something. Megan, Lexie, Rachelle. They'd all keep hitting benchmarks long since denied me. The hot current in my chest swirled like embers.

Only rule here is this, Maude had said. *Just don't push anything off anymore. Not goals. Not time. Not emotions.*

It was just too risky to go back to old friendships.

Good Lord willing and the creek don't rise, Mama would have said.

With a trembling hand, I navigated out of the text conversation, pulled up the main screen, and after fiddling for several minutes, managed to delete the app. Once I was sure it was gone, I turned the phone all the way off.

Then I set it aside and stood up.

"All right, kitties," I said. "Let's refresh my lipstick and get you squared away, then. After that, I'll show you how to play Candy Killer and where the Pepsi is kept—although you won't need any of that."

"I hate being in public."

Sarah fidgeted with a floral dress with buttons running down the front in an uneven line. It sagged off her thin shoulders, several sizes too large, even underneath her bulky wool jacket. With her pale face and her hair pulled back in a tattered ponytail, she looked years too young to be here.

A cold winter wind brushed by, sending flurries past my car. The heat kicked on with a burp, chugging out a slow trickle of cool air. I stared at the community rec center with a feeling of disbelief.

Had I *really* insisted that Sarah come with me to the community meeting Tadd and his business were holding?

Yes. I had.

I shouldn't even give Tadd the time of day. Wouldn't that just encourage his idea that his takeover would actually happen? Because it wouldn't.

Sarah rubbed her hands together and blew into them. The tips of her fingers had a bluish tint. "It's so cold!"

I grabbed my purse off the floor behind her seat. "C'mon," I said. "Let's get this over with."

She glanced at me. "You really don't like Tadd, do you?"

"Do you?"

She shrugged. "He's a really nice guy."

"He wants to take over the mini mall. Put us out of business."

"I mean, you could open the store somewhere else, right?"

"Let's go."

I pushed into the cold winter air, dismissing her comment as youthful naiveté. Move the store? Open somewhere else? Start over without Bill?

"Is James coming?" Sarah asked as we stepped into the building.

Signs with the Platinum Development logo directed us toward the back and to the right.

"Not sure. He texted me something about a catering engagement. He's horrible with technology."

Ten seconds later, we stepped into a broad room. Tables ringed the edges, covered with svelte, navy blue tablecloths and silver square accents. Poster boards lined the tables, alternating with clipboards, cups filled with complimentary pens—that looked quite expensive—and flyers. Food burdened a table in the middle of the room, overflowing with steaming dishes, white plates, and bundles of silverware. Waiters clad in black and white stood behind the table. People milled around everywhere, at least sixty strong. "No wonder he ordered dinner," I murmured. Who wouldn't come to this?

Tadd stood in the middle of the room, laughing with an elderly couple.

Oh, he was good.

"Geez," Sarah whispered. She advanced, as if pulled in by a magnet. "This is so nice!"

A white projector filled one wall, alternating graphic illustrations of what could only be Platinum Development's plans for the strip mall. In the picture, a building several stories high sat on top of the shops—only the shops were completely redesigned. A pharmacy, medical clinic, clothing shop, and gas station were a few of the stores along the bottom. What appeared to be decks and porches on top likely indicated apartments.

Could they do residential *and* commercial?

"Good ideas!" Sarah cried, eyes bright. "The closest pharmacy is twenty minutes away."

I cleared my throat. She curbed her excitement with a click of her teeth. When I counted three doors over from the left, I scowled. The projection showed Mira's Sewing and Vac as a coffee shop. Of all the heartless designs. All of this for a strip mall that hadn't seen its glory days since the new downtown moved in?

There had to be an angle.

"There are a lot of people here," Sarah said under her breath, turning to me with wide eyes. "I mean, I expected ten, tops. Most of them people like yo—us. To protest, of course."

My eyes narrowed on a familiar figure in the back. I nudged Sarah with an elbow, almost knocking her to the side. "Look." I tilted my head. "There's James."

"James?"

He caught my glance and waved, then beckoned me over. We slipped along the edges, passing 3D displays, blueprints, and a drink station with every possible soda. I ignored the Pepsi.

Tainted.

"James?" I asked, surveying his dirty apron and careful eye on the food. The sweet scent of apricot chicken and creamy fettuccine filled the air. I knew those smells.

"You came," he said, seeming pleased.

"*You* are catering?" Sarah asked, jaw agape. "But isn't that . . . I mean . . . isn't Tadd supposed to be the enemy?"

James nodded. "Yep. But the enemy has money."

Rough times had come to this area of town—and James had felt it as much as me. Of course he wouldn't turn down a catering job. And how *strategic* of Tadd to offer it to him.

"Great turnout," Sarah said, smiling nervously. "Right?"

James nodded. "More than I expected."

"Triple what I thought," I said, glancing behind me again. James nodded to the other side of the room. Another army of poster boards and displays, only this time people were standing next to them. Each display represented a store, apparently, that would be moving into the strip mall.

"Tadd knows what he's doing," James said. "Looks like he already has contracts with all those stores to go into the strip mall if they acquire it."

"If?" Sarah muttered. "More like when."

I fought off the urge to shoot her a dirty look. Instead, I sucked in a sharp breath, purposefully glancing over Tadd when I saw him look our direction.

"Get some food," James said. "Take all you want. He had me catering for one hundred people."

"What will you do with the leftovers?" I asked.

"He said it'll go to the homeless shelter."

Of course.

My appetite wouldn't tolerate eating here—not even if James had fixed it. Tadd appeared in front of us as if by magic. Sarah squeaked and stepped back, but Tadd acted as if he hadn't noticed by turning to me first.

"Mira, so pleased to see you here."

My Southern roots forced me to smile. "Thanks for the invite," I said through clenched teeth. He wore an elegant, but not overstated, white button-up shirt with a subtle mustard tie.

"I hope you've been able to look around," he said, waving a hand. "We set this up for anyone in the neighborhood but planned for individual meetings for the shop owners."

"How kind."

Tadd motioned to a man on the other side of the room. His black hair grayed at the temples, and he had a strong jaw, tan skin, and a bright white smile.

"That's Troy Endicott, the owner of Platinum Developers. I thought you might like to meet him." Tadd's gaze met mine like two cars slamming into each other. "It would be a good opportunity to learn more about his vision for serving the community with his resources."

Sarah piped up. "Everything seems to be going really fast. I mean, we just met you a few weeks ago. Why?"

Tadd smiled. To my horror, I could tell it put her at ease. Hard enough for even *me* to do.

"Why wait?"

"Does Platinum have something to prove?" I asked.

"Definitely."

His lack of hesitation or apology silenced me. James excused himself to assist a server, leaving me feeling abandoned.

"Really cool that you hired James for the catering," Sarah said. "He makes the best cream sauce."

"I agree! Quality is a top priority for us."

"Can you tell us how long this will take?" Sarah asked. "I mean, if the picture is any indication, the renovations will be extensive."

I jabbed her in the ribs. She cleared her throat.

"Sorry, I mean *would* take. If this, you know, ah, goes through and . . . whatever."

Tadd, unruffled as ever, launched into a detailed explanation with words like *immediate construction* and *renovation from the inside out* and *tight timelines*.

I couldn't help a niggling thought that lingered in the back of my mind. *Residential and commercial.* What must have been minutes later, Tadd cleared his throat. Sarah had moved toward the food table, leaving the two of us alone.

"I'm really pleased you came, Mira."

"Oh, uh, thanks. I was, you know, in the area and thought I'd stop by on my way home."

"You live on this side of town?"

My cheeks flared. The rec center was well over twenty minutes away from where I lived.

"Quite the turnout," I said. "You certainly know how to draw people in."

He shrugged, glancing over the milling crowd. "Food will typically do it, but that really wasn't the point. I think most people can appreciate and understand what we're trying to do."

"Shred dreams and destroy businesses?"

The words slipped out before I could stop them. Even if I could have taken them back, I wouldn't. Saying exactly what I was thinking, and expressing the emotion that came with it, felt way too good. The corners of his lips twitched, but he didn't smile.

"I'm not surprised you have that perspective, but no. That's not the goal of Platinum Developers. Can I introduce you to Troy? I think if you just—"

"I really need to get going."

My phone dinged right then, as if I had planned it. I glanced down to see a text message from Bitsy. *You okay?* I shoved it into my pocket.

"Of course. Thank you for coming."

His graciousness made my teeth clench as I strode across the room to Sarah, who was holding a breadstick in a napkin and speaking with two women in pencil skirts and shiny buns. Margot and Lacy Davis, two of the three attorneys at Davis, Davis, and Winthrop. Their office was several doors down from mine.

"Lacy, Margot, good to see you," I said.

"We were just talking about all these ideas," Lacy said, gesturing around. "Maybe it wouldn't be so bad if Platinum bought the strip mall. I mean, new housing is definitely needed. And we aren't far from the college. With the new bus route the city would provide, students could get to class within fifteen minutes. Plus, a younger vibe might help. Everything here looks . . . tired."

Margot's brow furrowed. "Perhaps," she said carefully. "Assuming that's their true goal."

"My thoughts exactly," I muttered. "Sarah, let's go."

"Really? James said that he had desser—"

"Yep. Now."

"Okay, bye!"

She gave a timid wave over her shoulders to the two sisters as I hooked an arm through hers and dragged her out the door. Leaving the stuffy room and stepping into the sharp chill of the arctic outdoor air restored my breath.

"You okay, Mira?"

"Fine," I gasped. Her eyes widened.

"You're not having a heart attack, are you?"

"Fine."

She fell silent as we walked across the parking lot, climbed into my Cadillac, and sat for a moment in the quiet. Snow had started to fall, weak flakes that melted the moment they touched the ground. Sarah let out a long breath.

"Well . . ."

My thoughts spun a thousand miles per second, whirling in a storm too heavy for me to track. I sat there, attempting to sort through the haze, until the first words I could conjure came out.

"He's acting like the hero, but he can't be. There *has* to be something behind all this. People don't just do this kind of thing. They can't buy the building, kick people out, and do whatever they want."

Sarah dug her teeth into her bottom lip. "Maybe?" she ventured carefully. "I mean, Tadd was really nice. I've heard good things about Platinum Developers."

"No one with that amount of money can have pure intentions."

Sarah quirked her lips and said nothing more. I jammed my keys into the ignition.

"Let's go home," I said. "I have three cats to feed, and two of them need insulin. Not to mention a litter box to scoop."

Spontaneous

Bitsy's text message burned a hole in my pocket.

I thought about it the next morning while listing all of the perfectly justifiable reasons to avoid church, then while taking twice as long to put my makeup on—which extended well past the beginning of the worship service—and finally while I fried bacon on the stovetop.

Church could wait another week.

Again.

Full-fat bacon, I thought. *Bitsy definitely wouldn't approve.*

I tossed another strip in the hot pan, enjoying the sizzle of the cold flesh against the hot bottom. Malcolm twined around my legs, purring obnoxiously. I glanced down. "You like bacon, do you? I knew you'd be my favorite."

On my way to the table with a plate of scrambled eggs, bacon, and a glass of whole milk, I dribbled a few drops of grease into Malcolm's food. His purr roared across the room when I sat down.

"Don't tell Sadie," I mumbled.

A familiar piece of white paper on the table caught my gaze. I glanced at it, looked away, then back. I didn't remember bringing it downstairs. Was it haunting me? Had it grown legs? Finally giving in, I spun it toward me.

The bucket list.

Lose 100 pounds.

"Twenty-five more to go," I said, tapping it with my finger. I chomped a piece of bacon and skimmed further.

Go without makeup for a month.
Drink at least one Coke.

My nose wrinkled. Drink a Coke? Not likely anytime soon. Pepsi had flowed in my veins since birth—Mom had become addicted once she got pregnant with me.

Learn how to tango.
Volunteer at an animal shelter.
See the Statue of Liberty.
Date someone really rich.

Intriguing, but the torture of dating again wasn't worth the cash flow. Besides, I had three geriatric cats to think about and still talked to my dead husband on occasion.

Not many people would understand.

Bake 100 cupcakes.

I grabbed a pencil off the tabletop and crossed that one off. "Definitely did that plenty of times for Sophia," I murmured, then paused. I stared at the paper, recalling Rachelle's news about my friend.

She wants to move back to her hometown, Rachelle had said. *Both of her parents are aging. She wants to be there to take care of them.*

Lucky girl. I'd give anything to have parents who still nagged me and needed help. Sophia would be very missed—she'd been a definite bright spot in my landscape, and that had nothing to do with the sheer amount of buttercream frosting she brought into my life.

My eyes trailed farther down the paper, stopping on one entry near the end.

Do something really spontaneous. Don't think. Just do it.

Without another thought, I shoved away from the table, tossed the last piece of bacon to Malcolm, and headed out the door.

After circling the Frosting Cottage bakery three times without seeing any sign of Rachelle, I finally headed inside.

Cheery winter light streamed into the store, illuminating the quaint eating space at the front. A wooden bar ran along one wall, chock full of miniature cookies. The infamous cookie bar—just one of Rachelle's ideas that had massively boosted sales. Across the room waited rows of cupcakes topped with fluffy swirls of buttercream.

Maybe this hadn't been the worst idea.

"Mira?"

Sophia's head popped up from the back. She beamed and waved at me. Flour coated her hands and smudged one of her cheeks. Heat poured out from the ovens, and the smell of warm bread enveloped me like a pillow.

Definitely not the worst idea.

"Come on back," she called.

I set my bag aside and stepped into the back with a smile. "Smells delicious."

She grinned. "I sure hope so. How've you been? Haven't seen you in a while."

"Busy."

The word felt like a lie, but *busy* was subjective.

"I totally understand," she said as she flipped a huge mixing bowl of dough onto the preparation table. "The holidays always catch up with me. Love your makeup, by the way. As usual."

My hand went to my face. I'd tried a new eye shadow today.

"Thanks. I heard some news from Rachelle."

Sophia paused, hands half buried in a ball of dough the size of my torso. She glanced up from underneath the brim of her black hat that said, *Frosting is in my Blood.*

"Oh?"

Panic infused me. I straightened. "Was I not supposed to know that you were leaving?"

Sophia's shoulders relaxed. "No, no. It's fine. I just . . . I guess I just realized I forgot to tell you everything that's going on. I knew you'd forgive me. You've always been incredibly understanding, Mira."

And giving, Bill said. *You didn't even get paid for all those hours you worked before Rachelle was hired.*

I let that slide.

"Tell me all about it," I said, infusing cheer in my voice. "Sounds like a fun new adventure."

Sophia prattled on while she worked with the dough, her wiry arms flexing with corded grace. Unable to help myself, I washed my hands, grabbed an apron, and set to work next to her. She sliced through the lump with a dough cutter and shoved it my direction.

Without thinking, I fell into the ritual movements of kneading and rolling out her dinner rolls. The rhythm was soothing.

"Anyway, Mom and Dad won't be able to live at home much longer, so I want to enjoy them while I can."

"I think it's a wonderful idea."

"I think I'll just do a wedding cake boutique and leave this stuff for other people. Anyway, do you have any extra boxes I could take? Do you think you could come help me pack one of these days? I need all the extra hands I can get."

"Sure."

She grinned. "Thanks."

"Can I ask you a question?"

"Of course."

She reached for a cookie sheet and plopped it on the counter between us. I grabbed a piece of dough between my fingers and rolled it between my palms.

"Would you have said goodbye if I hadn't come over?"

She paused, blinking, then looked up at me. "I would hope so."

"Hope so?"

"I mean . . . things are busy and . . . it's been kind of crazy with it coming up so fast . . ."

The temptation to rescue her, to tell her that *of course she's busy* and *don't even worry about it!* ran through my mind, but something stopped me. Hadn't I rescued her enough? Didn't she owe me something too?

Sophia stopped and swallowed. She set both hands on the counter.

"You know, Mira? To be honest . . . I don't know if I would have. I really don't, and that's the 100% honest truth. How horrible is that?"

"Thanks," I said with a smile. "I appreciate you being honest. Really."

"I guess I just . . . I would have thought you'd understand. You're always so forgiving and easygoing."

"Right."

Her gaze narrowed. "Are you okay, Mira? You seem a little . . . off."

The temptation to tell her I was *fine* and *just a little tired today* also ran through my head. Nice Mira would have done that. But I'd drawn a line in the sand. I'd separated from Nice Mira once I met Maude, Gladys, and Stella.

"No," I said, snatching another piece of dough and squishing it between my fingers. "I'm not."

"Really?"

I met her gaze without apology. "Really."

Something like admiration shone in her eyes. "Midlife crisis?"

"My brother died a few weeks ago. I think I'm still just . . . jumbled up from that."

Her eyes widened. Her hands flew to her face with a gasp. "Oh, Mira. That's right! Oh, I can't believe I forgot! I totally . . . I just . . . Rachelle took the time off, and I meant to send flowers but—"

"Don't worry about it."

"But . . ."

She trailed off, mouth bobbing open and closed like a fish. I set the finished roll on the cookie sheet, wishing that I hadn't noticed that she hadn't reached out. Wishing that it hadn't hurt. I reached across the table, unable to stop myself from comforting her.

"Listen, Sophia, you mean a lot to me, and our friendship has been a bright spot in my life," I said, meeting her stunned, guilty gaze. "I really don't want to part ways for who-knows-how-long with just a brief farewell. Can we schedule a time to go to dinner or something? I didn't come to make you feel guilty. I really didn't. I'm . . . just sorting through things right now."

"Of course, Mira. I'll make time for you."

"Thanks." A burdened awkwardness filled the air between us. Time would iron it out—and a little space. It wouldn't last forever, but right then, I needed to leave. "Listen, I better go."

"Yeah. Thanks for coming by. I—"

The thud of feet on the back stairs in the alley rang through the air. Sophia brightened.

"Rachelle is here!"

My blood turned to ice. I yanked the apron off and flung it onto the counter.

"Gotta go!"

"Wait, when do you—"

"I'll text you."

I jerked my bag off the counter and flew out of the kitchen just as Rachelle called into the preparation area, "Hello?"

With one last wave at the door, I darted outside, ran as quickly as I could down the stairs, and rushed to my car. When I peeled away, I didn't dare look back, too afraid I'd find a familiar face I couldn't bear to see.

So, I was at Chipotle the other day, and I thought of you. This is Lexie, by the way. Duh, I mean, who else goes to Chipotle? Anyway, it was right next to a MAC store, and I saw your favorite lip gloss that you can't find anymore. I grabbed you four of them and will bring them with me at Christmas. Anyway, wanted to see how you're doing. Isn't the anniversary of Bill's death coming up? Mom said you went to lunch the other day. Hope it was fun. Call me back when you get a second, I wanted to talk with you about possibly sewing me a few maternity clothes to save some money. Love you, bye!

Hello, Mira. It's Jackie. Just wanted to check in and see if you could start making a quilt for Lexie's baby. Like Kenzie's, maybe? I know it took you a long time and was pretty labor-intensive, so I wanted to bring it up early. I have some material, but we'll need to supplement. Give me a call when you get a second, thanks!

Hey Mira, it's Rachelle. Can you help me tailor a dress before the Christmas party? Also, I was wondering if you could meet up for lunch or something. I want to catch you up on the details for the Christmas party. And Sophia said you stopped by and she's worried about you. I still am, too, by the way. I stopped by your house a few days ago but no one was home. Did I see a cat in the window? Everything okay? Talk soon.

It's Bitsy. Are you alive? Did your phone die again? Sorry I haven't been communicating much. It's . . . busy. Listen, I want to talk. Things have been weird. Also, since you missed last week for some reason, can you be in charge this week? It would really help me out. Thanks.

Bitsy again. It's been a few days. Did you get my last voicemail? I'm starting to get worried. Rachelle said she hasn't heard from you either. Please call.

Shmoozing

Snow was falling in thick, fat flakes when James brought me lunch the next day. He sat in the chair across from mine and leaned back. The smell of fresh apricot chicken, veggies, and whole-wheat noodles filled my nostrils. I breathed deep.

"You're a doll."

He laughed. "You're an easy target. I came over to see how you're doing after the community meeting and see what your Christmas plans are."

He stared at me with a sharp gaze. I'd never been able to hide much from him, though I hadn't really tried. In truth, I'd been so focused on dodging my friends and navigating my new life with cats that I hadn't thought about Christmas. Maybe I didn't want to think about it.

I stabbed my fork into the bed of noodles, glazed with a thin, sweet apricot sauce.

"Not sure yet. You?"

"My daughter and granddaughter, as usual."

"Leaving town this time?"

"Nah. Celebrating at my place." He intertwined his long, thin fingers together. A greasy apron lay beneath his puffy coat, covering his old jeans and a plaid flannel shirt.

"You'll have to buy a Christmas tree," I sang. He snorted.

"Ridiculous traditions."

The door opened with a light jingle. I swallowed my first bite—enjoying every warm, tangy morsel—as Sarah stepped inside. A long, bright orange marshmallow jacket wrapped all the way around her, right to her ankles. It looked like something I would have worn in the 70s.

She could really use a thin layer of bronzer on those pale cheeks.

"Afternoon," James said with a nod. "You're looking colder than ever."

Her cheeks appeared pinched, a ruddy, splotchy color even though she'd only walked ten feet. Ice had been forming on the outside of my windows all morning. No one haunted the streets. What had once been slush on the roads had frozen into patches of black ice. Accident reports droned on the radio, along with school closures and road warnings.

Sarah shuddered and crossed the showroom toward us. James stood up to offer her his chair, but she waved him off.

"No, but thanks, James. I just . . ."

Her gaze briefly met mine, then dropped, hiding beneath eyelashes thick as evergreen boughs. I would have killed for lashes like that at *any* age. Pasting my eyelashes on was getting really old.

Something lurked in her gaze. Hesitation. Uncertainty.

I knew exactly what she was going to say. I set aside the fork and the knife and closed the to-go container lid.

"Everything okay?" I asked.

Her lips pressed into a thin line. "No. I mean . . . yes. But . . . I mean, I'm feeling fine."

James lifted one eyebrow while Sarah fidgeted with the end of her sleeve.

"Th-there's nothing wrong with me or my health, if that's what you mean. I, uh . . . I just thought I should tell you that Tadd came over this morning. Said he wanted to talk to me after the community meeting."

Although subtle, I could feel James shift.

"Oh?" I asked.

Sarah chewed on her bottom lip. Her cheeks had almost caught fire. No wonder she looked so cold—she was actually terrified. A slight tremor moved through her hands.

"Yeah," she said, tucking a piece of hair behind one ear.

"Was he following up?" I asked.

She blinked. "Sort of."

A long silence hovered between us. For some reason, I thought of Bitsy. Of the times I'd confessed my Pepsi splurges and secretly feared her judgment. The many, *many* times I had just wanted approval. I reached out and put a hand on Sarah's arm.

"Sarah?" I said quietly. "It's okay."

She closed her eyes. "I signed a contract with Tadd today to turn over my lease," she blurted out. "He increased his price, and I really couldn't say no anymore. Especially with business being so dry."

She spoke more quickly now, as if she just wanted to get the words out. Finally, our eyes connected. Terror, maybe even relief, lurked there. Signed a contract? James and I exchanged a quick glance.

Tadd must have bought it from Charles.

I gave her a smile.

"I understand."

Her eyes widened. "You aren't mad?"

"Not at all. You have to do what's best for you."

"But this means that Charles has sold. This means that . . . what about . . ."

"We'll figure it out," James said. "We always have."

Sarah nearly wilted. "Oh, thank you! I was so scared. With the price Tadd offered to buy out my lease, I just couldn't justify staying. You know, I wanted to move anyway. Traffic here has been decreasing the last year, and some of the new shops downtown are really cute. The leases aren't so long there. Obviously not as cheap as here, but I think I'd make more money from foot traffic alone. To be honest, though, it wasn't until I heard *why* they were doing this that I was really sold. I know you don't believe it, but—"

"When do you leave?" James asked. I almost thanked him for interrupting. The last thing I wanted was to hear Platinum Developers' advertised side of goodwill.

"I promised him I'd be out before Christmas."

My eyes nearly bulged out of my head. "What's the rush?"

She shrugged. "Dunno. I heard him talking on the phone outside before he came in, and he said something about meeting a Christmas deadline."

James and I exchanged uneasy glances. If Charles had sold—of course without telling us—and Sarah had fallen, others would give way soon. Especially if a deadline were involved. Sheila may have already agreed and made plans to sell out her stock of puppies over Christmas. Could we fight if the majority fell?

Why was Tadd in such a hurry?

"Listen," Sarah said, wringing her hands together like an old dish rag. "I'm really sorry about this. I didn't want to announce this so close to the holidays, but I'll be loading all my stuff up soon."

Her knuckles turned white. Sarah had only been here a year and wasn't even thirty years old. How could I expect her to understand the attachment that went into roots of twenty-five years?

She didn't see that twenty-five years ago, Bill and I put our hand prints in the wet cement even though we weren't supposed to. Years of parades, parties, community events. A packed parking lot. Constant foot traffic. Dogs that walked by every morning. Kids shrieking on the playground after school. Sometimes, I thought I could still hear their giggles on the wind.

This wasn't just a strip mall. And it wasn't just a store. It was the home Bill and I *really* created.

The one that actually worked.

I stood up and spread my arms. "C'mere, honey. Don't be worried about what James and I think. You need to take care of yourself first, and we'll take care of us. Do you need any help?"

Sarah slipped into my embrace like a lost little girl. Her hair smelled like lavender and patchouli. "Thank you," she breathed. "I've been worried that this would be the first domino for everyone else."

"Don't worry about it," I said to Sarah as I pulled away. "If you need any help packing up or loading boxes, let me know. I know a lot of young people who can help you haul stuff."

She smiled again. "Thanks."

"Got loads of boxes," James said, standing. "I'm happy to help anytime."

After one last round of farewells, Sarah left, nearly bouncing out the door. I slowly sank back to my chair. James did the same. Several minutes passed before James shot me a questioning glance. He didn't have to say anything, and I didn't have to ask.

"The others will fall soon," I said.

"Only a few."

"I guess I've known that from the beginning. Still, it seems anticlimactic."

He nodded. "Now, the question is whether we can hold back the tide," he said. "I'm all-in if you're still all-in."

A genuine grin slowly spread over my face. "Always. If there's anything I'm willing to fight for, it's the store. Besides, I still have seven years on my lease, and I've never breached contract before."

"I have three," James said. "I think yours is the longest in the whole mall. Think we can fight this?"

"Definitely. There must be a reason he's shmoozing us so much."

"You think?"

"I'll look into it."

With that, I opened my to-go container and forked a bite of chicken into my mouth. The tangy flavor of apricot sauce calmed my nerves.

With sauce like that, no one needed Pepsi.

"C'mon, Sadie," I muttered. "Where are you?"

Her bowl of food sat untouched when I returned home from the store, and Sadie had yet to miss a meal. In fact, she'd tried to gobble down Marilyn's more than once. The horrible feeling that I'd accidentally overdosed her on insulin and killed her streaked through me like fire, then disappeared.

No, I'd given her the right dose.

Malcolm rubbed against my arm with a purr, then twitched his tail under my nose. I batted him away.

"Yes, good kitty. Where's Sadie?"

He exited, tail lifted high and curled at the top. I rolled my eyes. Drama king. In the distance, my doorbell rang. I shoved off the floor—groaning at my creaky joints—and left the spare bedroom. The one that would have been our oldest child's room. Fitting that I should lose a cat inside it.

"Coming," I called, glancing in the bathroom, peeking into another room, and peeling away some drapes on my wall. "I'm coming."

The moment the door opened, my heart leapt into my throat.

Oops.

"Don't you dare shut that door in my face, or heaven help me, I *will* throw a fist through your window. Don't think I haven't done it before."

Rachelle stood there, arms folded across her chest, expression stony as a vengeful god. Flour dotted a black shirt beneath her coat. Her breath billowed in front of her in plumes.

"Hi," I said.

"Hi."

With a sigh, I opened the door wider. It could have been worse. Bitsy could have been standing there. "Come in."

Minutes later, she sat across the table from me in Bill's usual spot. A cup of chamomile tea steamed in front of her. I clung to a glass of Pepsi.

Rachelle leaned forward.

"You're avoiding us."

I shifted, uncomfortable with her direct gaze for the first time since meeting her years ago. Rachelle had never scared me. My own guilt, however, did.

"I'm trying to figure things out. Since Jerry died."

Her gaze softened. Outside, snowflakes drifted past the window, wetting the street and making the car tires hiss as they passed. Malcolm walked by, purring as loudly as an oil tanker.

Rachelle jumped. "Is that a *cat*?"

"Malcolm."

Her eyes widened. "You *do* have a cat?"

"Three."

"What?" she screeched.

"They're geriatric. Marilyn may not see the year out, and Sadie is missing and needs her insulin. She's pretty grumpy, but she reminds me of Bill, so I don't mind." I reached down to scratch Malcolm's back, as if it were the most natural movement in the world. "This guy's started to sleep on Bill's pillow at night. Kinda sweet."

Several seconds passed while she stared at me, blinking. "You okay?"

"Great!"

Her head tilted to the side. "Really?"

"Yep."

Another awkward silence passed. Rachelle shoved her tea aside.

"What the hell is going on? You're disappearing from meetings, won't answer calls, *definitely* wouldn't have answered the door if you knew it was me, and now you have three geriatric cats?"

My gaze dropped. How could I explain it to her without sounding like a spoiled brat? I was happy for everyone in the Health and Happiness Society. Truly. But I was also raw. Like fire had ravaged me from the inside out for too long, and now I stood as an empty, smoldering husk. I wasn't as strong as I used to be. Nothing had panned out the way it was supposed to, and I hated it. Walking away was the only viable option.

"I don't really know where my life is going now," I said, opting for the safest route. "Everyone else seems to have it together, but I . . . I'm . . ."

Drowning. Invisible. So lonely sometimes I think I could die from it.

Her brow smoothed. "It doesn't help that things *are* a little weird."

"You think so too?"

"Yeah. Not sure what's going on with Bitsy. Of course she's not going to tell us anything. She still rarely talks about herself, but it's certainly starting to affect . . . everything."

Was the Health and Happiness Society actually unraveling? I had already accepted this. So why did it haunt me?

Lexie would be distracted while pregnant, but it would be worse when she had a newborn. Megan was living in the bliss of newlywed happiness with a rich, adventurous husband. They'd probably save a third-world country together next year. With Rachelle's business venture, she'd spend more hours at work than ever—and she lived above the bakery.

The stricken look on her face told me she knew what I was thinking.

"You're frightened," she said.

"So are you," I shot back.

After a beat of hesitation, she nodded. "Yeah. I can see the writing on the wall."

"You really think there is?"

"Don't know. Everyone is taking new paths. Things are different. Unpredictable in weird ways. Can the Health and Happiness Society last through Lexie having a baby, Megan being married, me running a business, and . . ."

She trailed away, which was exactly what hurt the most.

What did Mira have?

What was Bitsy hiding?

"I get that you might need some distance from Bitsy right now," Rachelle said. "She's in a weird place, I think. I guess we'll figure out why eventually."

The burning snake that had been subdued since the poker game reared its hideous head again.

"Why do *we* have to figure it out?" I asked. "I don't feel like chasing her. Bitsy has always stayed above the rest of us, trying not to burden us with her problems or her needs. We're always saving her from her own twisted worldview."

I expected Rachelle to be angry, frustrated, or even a little defensive. Instead, she looked sad.

"Yeah," she said with a sigh. "I know. But Bitsy was there for me when I really needed her."

So was I.

I looked away.

"The Health and Happiness Society is a family," Rachelle said. "We can't . . . we can't *unravel.* So much is happening. Big changes are on the horizon, and we'll need each other. Family doesn't fall apart just because things are different."

But family leaves all the time, came the thought. There were no guarantees, even with blood ties.

Instead, I gazed out the window at the grumpy sky, which was so much easier to face than Rachelle's hopeful expression. She reminded me of Sarah. Too young to really know what was inevitable and what wasn't.

Or was I just jaded?

I didn't even know how to save myself, let alone Bitsy. Or Lexie. Or Megan. I was tired of trying. The Health and Happiness Society had needed me once, and I had been happy to help. Perhaps *too* happy. Right now, I just felt weary. Weak. Strung out like an old laundry line.

"It frightens me that you aren't saying much," Rachelle said after a sip of tea, "but I imagine you're going through a lot since Jerry's death. That's why, right?"

Until her compassion reached out and touched my heart, I hadn't realized how desperately I needed it. Jerry. Had I been unintentionally not thinking about him? I swallowed back tears.

"Probably."

"I'm sorry, Mira." Her voice caught.

I glanced up to see tears pooling in her eyes. "Sorry?" I whispered. "For what?"

"That you lost Jerry and seem so lost yourself."

Words failed me. I reached across the table and grabbed her hand. "Please, Rachelle, don't—"

"Just know that I understand. You need a break? Take it."

"Please don't say anything t—"

"I won't. I promise." Her voice was firm. "It's not mine to say, anyway. Just don't shut *me* out, okay? While you work through it, I mean. Until you come back."

"Of course."

Tears trickled out of the corner of her eyes, but she wiped them away with the back of her hand.

"Is it too much to ask for you to come to the Christmas party? It's . . ." She sucked in a sharp breath. "It's looking like that may be our last time together as . . ."

As a pseudo-family.

I hesitated too long again. The pain that rose into her eyes struck me deep, but not as deep as the pain of going back. Of seeing all I didn't have, hadn't done, might never get.

When I made no response, Rachelle simply nodded.

"It's okay. I get it."

Poker game next Tuesday night. See you there.

Bitsy again. Seriously, Mira, what's going on? I drove by the sewing shop and saw it was open, so I know you're alive. We missed you again. Lexie's worried. Rachelle is swamped and could use some more help with the Christmas party. I need . . . I mean . . . things are . . . anyway, call me back.

Hello again, Mira! Jackie here. Did you get my last voicemail? If not, no worries. I found the cutest material. You're just going to die when you piece this quilt together. Talk soon.

This is the assistant for Erasmus Flynn calling for Mira Montgomery. He would like to set up a time to speak with you before December 25th. Please reply at your earliest convenience to schedule a meeting.

A Safe Spot

The sound of church bells rang in the distance, waking me from a troubled sleep plagued by dreams of mascara tubes and candies with teeth.

"Oh, Mama," I muttered, running a hand through my hair. "I have to feel guilty about skipping church again."

But not so guilty I'd go back. Yet.

I threw off the covers and shuffled to the bathroom. The moment I accidentally glanced at my mirror, the bucket list caught my eye. I'd taped it there as an eternal reminder. My head tilted to the side. What better way to distract myself from missing yet another sermon—and avoiding another call from Pastor Burke afterward—than living my new life?

My eyes adjusted slowly to the morning light as I stood in front of it, blinking through my haze.

See the Statue of Liberty.
Go to California.
Ride a horse.
Milk a cow.

My nose wrinkled. Milking a cow didn't seem interesting at this point in the morning—and even for them I'd need to put more makeup on.

Learn how to play poker.
Learn how to play the ukulele.
Travel to a third-world country.

Gladys would be gratified that at one point I'd been interested in poker, apparently.

As if all the other options melted into nothing, my eyes honed in on one line. One single line written in a hasty moment as a naive young girl, never knowing the chilling effect it would have on me as a middle-aged woman.

Go without makeup for a month.

"That's insane," I muttered.

Imagine how much money you would save, Bill said.

"It has nothing to do with money. It's how I feel about myself when I go outside. Besides, it gives me something to get good at and enjoy. Makeup is a process."

I still think you look good without it.

In my mind's eye, he stood at the closet on the other side of the room, staring at his clothes. His stomach spilled over the belt of his pants, as if he'd given up on himself entirely.

In some ways, he had.

With steep apprehension, I stared at my bathroom counter.

My sleek black makeup bag, decorated with pinstripe pink, lay open on the marble counter. Everything inside it gleamed with promise and challenge and beauty. Something like dread welled up in my throat as I stared at it.

Just . . . *stop* wearing makeup?

My eyes darted to the mirror. How was I supposed to go without it now? After decades of crazy styles, would people even know me? No one would recognize me. My face would look pale. Age spots would show. My hazel eyes would be small, lackluster. Even my lips would seem invisible. What would I do with the extra time? Certainly not spend it cuddling with my new cats.

The renegades.

Malcolm wandered into the room and sat on the bathroom rug. I glanced at him.

"Hi."

He gazed into the distance, as if he couldn't be bothered.

"Where's Sadie?"

He licked his front paw, then fell to his side with a little *rutt* and rolled around. I sighed and opened the side drawer, glancing through my collection of compacts, tubes of lipstick, brushes, and eye shadow boxes. This was a safe spot. A place to go every morning. A ritual to complete with a cup of coffee and some soothing country music in the background, like Alan Jackson.

But that was the old Mira.

"I have to do it, Malcolm. I have to. Right? I mean, it's on the list. This thing is practically sacred now. It's my guide, right? The guide to the new Mira. The one who *made* the stuff that is supposed to happen, happen."

The sound of a bell tinkled. Ah, Sadie had come in. After searching for her for four hours after Rachelle left—and eventually finding her tucked under a bed, snoring away—I'd bought a bell for her collar. When I peeked around the wall, she'd curled up on the bed, glaring at me through shuttered eyes. Marilyn probably hadn't budged from the couch except to stretch.

She'd ended up being my favorite.

With the tip of my finger, I touched all the bits and pieces of makeup I'd assembled over the years. Most of them I went through within a year. The brushes were soft with use. The bronzer almost empty—powder clung only to the edges. Instead of a thrill, I felt empty. Even my specialty foundation, carefully chosen for my skin type and color, didn't strike a feeling of joy.

"I'm hiding," I whispered, staring at it. "That's all this is, isn't it?"

My hand paused, trembling over a neon pink compact mirror that I'd had since I was a teenager. Mama had given it to me on my sixteenth birthday. *Every girl needs a mirror in her purse,* she'd said. *Then you'll always remember your mama when you look at yourself.*

My fingers wrapped around the compact until it dug into my palm. I pressed a kiss into it, set it back in the bag, and pulled out my face wash to get the process started.

Later.

I'd do that one later.

Today, I'd go find a ukulele.

Only my favorite actress, Stephanie James, would compel me to accomplish number seventy-six on my bucket list after work the next day.

Go to a movie by myself.

Her romantic comedies always brought me out of slumps.

And if this wasn't a slump, nothing was.

The fact that Jim was her father only deepened my devotion—even though Bitsy still hadn't introduced me to her yet. I imagined she was as charming and adorable in person.

The idea of returning home, even to my cats, felt intolerable. Several voicemails that I didn't want to address sat heavy on my phone. The call to the adventure of being the new, friendless, selfish Mira was too strong. I swung by a burger joint, bought a Pepsi, cheeseburger, and fries, and sped across town to my favorite luxury movie theater.

When I had written the bucket list, I distinctly remembered how strange it sounded to go to a movie alone. Movies were a special occasion. A deeply social event where I giggled over boys with my friends. Why did it have to be weird now?

"Theater eleven, on your left."

While walking through the foyer, I toyed with the idea of buying an ice cream bar but settled for popcorn. The smell of butter reminded me of Jerry. The memories of late-night movies while growing up warmed me again. For that, I added an extra squirt of butter.

The lights dimmed when I settled into my seat. A handful of people littered the theater. Two teenage girls giggled in the corner, faces illuminated by their phones. A young couple sat near the front—misery already apparent on the man's face. Commercials flashed across the screen. Christmas deals. New releases.

I couldn't help but think about Bitsy's Christmas tree in the corner of her front room. The smell of the evergreen candle burning bright. It reminded me of home. Of Grandma, her "special" eggnog, and Jerry's habitual love for it—but only in season. Last year, Rachelle made delicious sugar cookies decorated like mini Santas with a sleigh and reindeer with red-hot candies for noses.

With a shake of my head, I turned my attention back to the movie screen. This wasn't the time to reminisce about what was lost.

Stephanie appeared just as the music swelled, a peppy, hip-hop beat that bounced along with her as she strolled down the street in New York City, her hair streaming behind her like flags.

Finally! An opportunity to forget Rachelle's sadness, Bitsy's voicemails, and the emptiness of my house.

Instead of sinking into the happily-ever-after, my thoughts circled back to Rachelle. She had a real eye for details and mistakes. The last movie we went to, the main character put cookies in an oven that wasn't turned on, then pulled them out freshly cooked ten minutes later. Bitsy always cleaned the seats and passed out baggies of snacks that, even while healthy, still tasted better than this popcorn, which had turned cold and stale.

Without Bitsy here to annoy me with her judgment, the whole experience felt a bit . . . bland.

My thoughts meandered to Gladys when the movie panned to a new, unfamiliar scene. Did Gladys have a Christmas tree? What were her Christmas plans? James had nagged me about celebrating with him and his daughter again. It wouldn't be the worst way to spend it. But still, a third wheel?

At Christmas time?

Maybe Gladys and I could make a date of it.

Despite my initial eagerness to see Stephanie in all her big-screen glory, I could barely keep my focus on the movie. By the time it ended, the middle remained a muddle to me. With romantic comedies these days, it hardly mattered. They were all the same—which was precisely why I loved them.

Or used to.

My nose wrinkled. How disappointing. I set aside my popcorn, which I'd only skimmed off the top of, as the lights popped on. For several moments, I sat and stared at the credits on the screen while the people in the theater shuffled out around me.

What was there to enjoy if not *this*? I felt such pride in my new life, without the Health and Happiness Society, but spent the whole time thinking about them. Maybe walking away wouldn't be as simple as I'd thought.

"Well," a voice said from behind me, "fancy seeing you here."

I whirled around to see Maude standing a few paces away. My initial prickle of fear subsided.

"Oh. Hello, Maude."

She wore a sable jacket that looked as soft as butter. A red-and-white cashmere scarf accented it, drawing out the curiosity in her gaze. She nodded toward the screen.

"Did you like it?" she asked.

"Ah . . . not sure."

Her nose wrinkled. "They're all the same."

"Kind of."

She glanced at the seat next to me. "You came alone."

"So did you."

"My son brought me. He insisted, even though I don't care for movies. Particularly not romantic comedies."

"How nice of him."

Maude's expression suggested otherwise—as if she'd come to tolerate his preferences instead of the other way around. I'd kill for a son that caring.

"He cares."

Something unsaid lingered in her tone. Normally, I would have let it slide. This time, I couldn't. How dare she take advantage of such a beautiful gift when women like me would have given an entire limb for such a blessing?

"You sound like *you* don't," I said.

"Let's just say he has different expectations for how my life should be lived as a widow and a grandmother than I do."

"It doesn't involve whiskey, take-out, and poker?"

A little smile flittered across her face. "Not exactly. Everyone has expectations, Mira. Some of them are harder to outlive and outrun than others. Some of them aren't worth it."

"You don't like your life?"

She sucked in a sharp breath. "Let's just say that this isn't how I thought my life would pan out."

Something in her tone tugged at my heart. How could *she* say that? She had everything I was *supposed* to have.

"For good or for ill?" I asked.

"That," she murmured, "depends on the day."

Silence stretched between us for several beats. Without Stella's naive, tipsy giggle and Gladys' intense, screwdriver stare to provide backup, Maude seemed far more intimidating than ever. And normal.

So normal it was almost frightening.

"Are you coming this week?" she asked. "Gladys will be furious if you don't, you know."

"I hate poker."

"So do I."

"What?"

The first sign of thawing appeared on her face. "The whiskey isn't so bad and the company is fine, but I hate cards."

"Then why go?"

"Because it's an out. Besides, Gladys is sort of an old friend, you could say. She needs us, even though she won't admit it."

"It's not your job to save her, you know."

"I never said anything about saving," she replied coolly. I had the impression she fought not to roll her eyes. Despite her annoyance, I detected a hint of approval beneath her manicured veneer.

"Thanks for the chat, but my son has returned. I don't like to keep him waiting."

Her gaze slipped to the side of the theater, where a man waited in the shadows while a group of teenagers passed by. He had broad shoulders and a strong chin. Although I couldn't make out his facial features, something about him seemed vaguely familiar. The theater was almost empty now, littered with popcorn kernels and discarded drink cups.

Maude stepped carefully out of the row, then turned around.

"We'll see you in a few days. She'd never tell you, and I would never admit to saying this, but it would mean a lot to Gladys to have you there. She's . . . she's lonely."

With that, Maude disappeared into the stairwell, accepted her son's arm, and left the theater, leaving me wondering.

After I'd taken a new vacuum order and helped a middle-aged man buy a sewing machine for his wife for Christmas, the phone rang.

Just as I reached for it, two women strolled into the store. Ah, my most dedicated regulars. I lifted a hand in greeting as I propped the phone against my shoulder. The *riiiip* of paper as I tore a receipt off the register sent a satisfying thrill through me.

I put the phone to my ear. "Hello?"

"Hey, Mira."

My breath caught in my throat.

Megan.

"Don't hang up! I just wanted to talk to you." She paused, as if holding her breath. "Are you still there?"

"Yes."

"Whoa. Sweet. Can't believe that worked. Anyway, I made sure to call your work from a phone here at the hospital because I didn't think you would answer if you saw it was me on your cell."

A feeling of sheepishness and the urge to apologize swept through me. I probably *wouldn't* have answered. Now that she was on the line and I could hear her voice, though, I wanted nothing more than to talk to her.

I needed to increase my defenses.

"Are you all right?" she asked. Real concern laced her voice. "Everyone is worried about you. Lexie has called Rachelle every single day this week, demanding she go to your house."

"Really?"

"Yeah. Trust me. She then calls *me* to vent about it."

"What does Rachelle say?"

"That you need space. Lexie isn't buying it."

I wasn't doing this for attention or with some weird reverse-psychology motive. One day, they'd see that the gradual, slow distancing had been the most compassionate way to put this to rest.

"Listen, Megan, I'm . . ."

The thought of lying made my throat nearly close up. Megan was extremely intelligent and would see through me in a second. Still . . . the truth seemed bitter.

"I'm unraveling," I blurted out.

"Oh?"

I'm lost at sea. I'm swimming but can't find the top.

"I mean . . . I just . . . after Jerry died, I-I've just been . . ."

"Lost?"

I closed my eyes. "Yes."

"Of course you're having a hard time. Mira, you've been through hell. And at this time of year? It's like someone upstairs is conspiring against you, or something."

A laugh bubbled in my chest, but I kept it there because it was too much to admit to. She was right. Although I hadn't put it into words myself, I felt like someone *was* working against me.

"I really appreciate the call," I said, glancing across the room. The two ladies had busied themselves at the patterns, sorting through them with critical eyes. "Honestly, I do. Right now I just need space."

"Is it easier if you're away from us?"

No.

"I-I'm not really sure."

"Is there something about the group that's stressing you out?"

Yes, I thought. *All your lives and the sheer amount of adoration I hold for you.*

But I wouldn't say that, either.

"All of you are wonderful, and I really do miss coming. *Really* miss it, actually. But right now, this is what feels best to me. And it's time for me to do what's best for me."

"Sure."

"Really?"

"Yep."

"That's . . . it?"

Megan sighed. "Yeah. Sometimes you just need a break from people. There have been weeks when I haven't come even though I could have."

The shock rendered me almost speechless. I couldn't even fathom missing a meeting for anything other than total mental breakdown. Like this one. Bitsy would . . . what *would* she have done? I never really gave her the chance to show me.

"I didn't expect you to say that," I murmured.

She laughed. "I love Bitsy, but sometimes I just can't handle her need for control. It's not so bad now, but before this summer? Preeeetty intense. And I adore Lexie, but she and I are so different. Sometimes it can just feel like a lot, and I need to step away to get some perspective."

"Have you ever felt that way about me?"

"No, actually."

The surprise in her voice reassured me—she meant it. Whether that was a good thing or a bad thing, I couldn't decide.

"How are *you* doing?" I asked, finally giving way to the questions that had burdened my mind. "Eloping so last-minute is very exciting! Probably a little stressful, too, I would imagine. Everything okay?"

Megan laughed. In the background, I thought I heard the beep of an IV machine and someone shouting.

"Not as stressful as trying to plan the holidays without my parents. Justin is wonderful. Married life so far is everything I had wanted it to be. But now my dad has a girlfriend, and my mom isn't taking it well. Which is stupid, because she's the one who initiated this whole divorce, but whatever. My brothers and Justin and I will spend Christmas with my family after I get back."

"Back?"

"From the party on Christmas Eve."

The truth smashed into me like a bolt of heavy wool. Megan would be here. *Everyone* would be here.

Megan sighed. "Yeah . . . I want to see everyone before . . . I mean . . . it's all kind of a time bomb anyway, don't you think?"

Her casual question almost took my breath away. Could she possibly mean what I thought she meant?

"What do you mean?" I asked, carefully controlling my tone. "The Christmas party?"

"No, just the whole Health and Happiness Society thing. Don't get me wrong. The Health and Happiness Society is wonderful. It's helped me and everyone else in so many ways. But it never was meant to last forever, right? How could it? We all have our own lives to live. Eventually, people grow apart. We were thirty minutes late starting this week because Bitsy was stuck at a client's house. If *that* isn't the end of the world, I don't know what is."

No sense of exultation filled me. No sense of being right, or justified, or not alone. Instead, the gap in my heart seemed to widen. The sound of beeping came from the background. I thought I heard someone call for her.

"Anyway, I gotta go. Just know that I'm here if you ever need anything, okay? Maybe I can be a soft spot for you to land if you need it."

"Thanks."

"Keep in touch, all right? You don't have to answer my calls, but at least answer my texts."

"I promise."

After hanging up with Megan, I stared out the front windows. Cold air had settled on the town like a bland gray fog. There wasn't even snow, just slushy roads and bitter cold. The bleak day was made even worse by the thought of the Christmas Eve party.

With a sigh, I collected the vacuum order, took it into the back, and left a note for the repair man. My thoughts whirled in what felt like every direction. When I returned to the front, the two women waved at me as they left without purchasing anything.

I grabbed my phone, pulled up Candy Killer, took a sip of Pepsi, and sank into the thoughtless, emotionless place I so often sought.

Insensitive

Christmas bells rang from a nearby church as I climbed out of my car and surveyed Gladys's street.

A chilly mist had fallen, filling the street with fog. Gladys's little shack loomed like a specter, a distant light flickering from somewhere inside. Every other house on the street seemed desolate. Nearly dead.

Did I really want to go back in?

With a sigh, I gave in. Yes. I really did. Why? I had *no* idea.

When I knocked on her door, my mind spun to Bitsy. It was Tuesday evening—the same night that the Health and Happiness Society was meeting. What were they talking about? What article had she chosen? I missed the way Rachelle always riled Bitsy up on purpose.

How far I'd fallen.

"Come in!"

The smell of evergreen overwhelmed me when I opened the door. Beneath it lay the less-than-subtle aroma of cigar smoke. I waved my hand as I stepped into the room, dispelling the worst of the lingering cloud.

"Gladys," I called, "you can't hide cigar smoke with a candle."

"Worth a shot," she said from around the corner. She appeared wearing a ratty old robe, tugging the tubing along behind her like a pet.

"Do you turn the oxygen off when you smoke?"

"Most of the time."

"That's terrifying."

I set a warm plate covered in tinfoil on the table, which was littered with orange prescription bottles, carefully cut coupons, and medical bills. The smell of honey-glazed ham emanated from the plate. Creamy mashed potatoes. Bright, delicious corn and a hearty scoop of gravy.

Even *I* wanted another plate.

"So, Gladys, how are you?"

Television droned in the background, some game show she

probably never watched. I understood the reasoning. Sometimes even television drivel was better than encompassing quiet.

"Come in here."

She led me to the front room, which was the only other room except a small bedroom and attached bathroom tucked into the corner. A rumpled, crocheted blanket covered her recliner. The poker table was already set up, although I suspected she never took it down.

"You look a little pale tonight, Gladys. You feeling okay?"

"Keep knocking on death's door, but the devil never answers."

"Do you want him to?"

"Hasn't he already?"

The serious tenor in her voice caught me by surprise.

"Can't even smoke when I want to," she muttered as she sank into her chair. "The doctor is after me for drinking too much, but honestly, at my age, why the hell not? I'm just going to go belly-up like everybody else."

Pastor Burke always had a startled expression on his face after he spoke with her at church. Now I understood why.

She peered at me through thick glasses. Her bent back gave her a shriveled appearance.

"Why are you here so early? The game isn't for another thirty minutes."

I motioned to the plate. "Thought you might like a homemade meal. It's not really homemade. I bought it at a restaurant."

"Give it to me, already."

I passed her the plate. She peeled the tinfoil off with trembling hands, the end of her tongue sticking out of the corner of her mouth. She sat back and stared at it. "Almost too pretty to eat."

"Almost," I said.

A pang of guilt streaked through me. How often did she get something warm *and* delicious? Her kitchen seemed bare enough—a small chunk of butter on a plate. An old bag of bread that looked stale. Her mini-fridge sat on the counter. I swam back to reality as she grabbed the waiting fork and dug in.

"You're regretting something, aren't you?" she asked.

I blinked. "What?"

"Something! What have you done?"

"What are you talking about?"

"Your life!" she cried, jabbing the fork at me. "That's why you came early. You wanted to talk to me about being old and alone, didn't you? You wanted me to tell you it wasn't so bad. That my fate wasn't the worst thing. Well, it's not! Trust me. Life is much easier when there's less to lose."

My mouth opened to stammer a reply, but I hesitated.

Was it why I'd come?

"Well?" She scowled. "What's wrong with you? Can't you speak?"

I sank into the chair across from her. I *did* need to talk to someone. Someone who knew exactly what I was facing.

"I don't know what's wrong with me, Gladys."

"You think too much," she mumbled. The smell of butter was thick on the air when she dove into the mashed potatoes. Her eyes fluttered closed as she savored each morsel. Her murmured exclamation of delight after she swallowed told me that she didn't get great food often.

"That was supposed to be a rhetorical question," I said.

"Nothing's rhetorical when you're my age. I know what's wrong with you. I think *you* know what's wrong with you too. You just don't want to face it."

"Face what?" I leaned forward. *This* is what I had been hoping for.

If she could have, I had a feeling she would have reached over and smacked my head. Instead, I withered under a glare.

"Don't be stupid." She scooped up a forkful of potatoes. "You're scared."

"Of course I'm scared."

"Life is too short for scared."

"I'm not *that* scared."

"You are, or else you wouldn't have come early."

The words burst out of me like a sledgehammer. "I've lost everyone and . . . so have you."

Gladys laughed. "So?"

"So?" I almost choked. "What's that supposed to mean?"

"We're alone. Big deal."

"It *is* a big deal."

She inspected a piece of gristle attached to the edge of the ham.

"A million other people have lost everyone too. You don't see them moping around."

"That's insensitive."

"Welcome to reality."

"Maybe this was a mistake."

"You're angry, Mira."

"I just adopted three cats! Angry people don't adopt cats."

"Don't take that bet. So what if you adopted cats? That's nothing."

"That's *something.*"

"That's you avoiding what you really need to be doing, which is probably something violent."

She peered at me from over the fork, a couple of green beans speared on the end. For several seconds, we stared at each other.

"What are you talking about?" I finally asked.

"Your rage. I can see it. I can practically *feel* it. You can do whatever you want to distract yourself from it, but it won't help. Whatever you're holding onto against the current of life, it's drowning you."

"I'm not . . ."

The words trailed away. *Rage,* she had said. Maybe I *was* angry. Livid. Enraged. Wasn't that the teeming river of liquid heat that bubbled in my chest so unexpectedly? The pain I felt every time I looked at my friends with their progress and lives and joy?

Wasn't *it* why I had to start again?

"Don't you ever get tired of being the victim?" she asked. "Sure, life sucked for a while. But now *you* are the one dragging the misery on. Get over it."

Her gaze drilled into mine. I wondered if she was talking to me or herself.

Did it matter?

"If I keep living, I'll just keep losing," I said. It didn't even sound like me. *Victim.* Hadn't I been? Hadn't life hit me while I was down? Not only did it take all my children, but my parents. My husband. My brother and best friend.

Possibly my store.

Everything.

"Yep." She reached for a butter knife. "You'll lose. That's the price you pay when you let people keep coming back. No ties, Mira. No loss."

"Is it . . . really worth it?"

"Isn't it? You and I are different than everyone else. We *know* what it's like to start over again and again. To lose constantly. To have the ground always shift. The people always leaving. The house always empty. No one else knows pain that exquisite. To bring it upon yourself again and again is foolish."

My breath stopped. She was right.

She glared at me, then set both utensils down. "You're a damn fool."

"I didn't—"

"You know what your problem is?" She jabbed a finger my direction. "You're so wrapped up in your bitterness you can't even see what you *have*. Maybe you don't have grandbabies, but you have a house. A store. You have plates of delicious food."

She reached for a tissue on a coffee table to her right and hacked into it. Her back bent forward like a dying flower petal. When she pulled the tissue away, blood came with it. She crumpled it and tossed it into a garbage can. Her body was broken, but her mind was still bright. And sassy. She didn't have the years ahead of her to fill, the way I did.

Perhaps there *were* worse fates than mine.

"A little gratitude wouldn't kill you. Besides," Gladys muttered after taking a sip from a water bottle. "Don't you hate it that everyone expects women in their fifties to be settled? It's a lie. This should be the happiest time of your life. Even if you didn't have kids, at least you have life experience. That's more than you had before. You can walk without oxygen, can't you? That's something to celebrate."

The question lingered in the air. Tears filled my eyes, but I blinked them back. Was *life experience* enough?

My fingertips tingled as I spun over her words. Doing something violent did have a certain appeal. I imagined smashing something with a baseball bat. The thrill it sent through me gave me a little shiver.

Next time.

A knock came at the door just as I started to answer. Stella stepped inside, a bottle of bourbon and four shot glasses in her hands. She kicked the door shut behind her.

"Five-card stud, ten dollars in tonight. I'm ready!" she cried, holding the alcohol high.

"Where's Maude?" Gladys asked.

"Can't make it. Her son had an award ceremony tonight."

"Another one?"

"Guess so. Leadership-in-Service award or something stupid like that. Not bad for a kid with a single mom and a prison record. You girls ready?"

Single mom? I thought. Picturing Maude as a single mom almost made my eyes cross. The two didn't mesh.

"He's always winning awards," Gladys mumbled. "Deal the cards out."

Stella settled into the chair across from mine with a gleam of anticipation in her eyes. "Ready for this, Mira?"

"Not if my life depended on it."

"You know five-card stud poker, right?"

"Nope."

The gleam intensified. "Excellent."

Dog hair littered her pants and shirt. I glanced down at my own. Clean from cat hair, so far. Maybe Stella had so many dogs she couldn't control the hair. Or maybe she didn't care anymore.

After Gladys's thorough scolding, the thought of picking up the playing cards and participating made me sick to my stomach. But if I left, they wouldn't be able to play.

My phone rang, fracturing my thoughts. I pulled it out of my pocket. *Lexie.* The Health and Happiness Society meeting had already started. The temptation to answer it and use it as an excuse to get out of *this* awkward meeting was almost overwhelming.

Instead, I silenced it and shoved it back into my pocket.

No ties. No loss.

"Well?" Gladys asked.

"Not—"

Important, I almost said. But that *was* a lie.

"Not a call I want to take."

"Why not?"

"Because some pain is better left in the past. Five-card stud," I said, rapping my knuckles on the folding table. Gladys nodded, as if she understood exactly what that call meant. "Let's get it going."

Long after I left Gladys's house—a hundred dollars poorer—my thoughts spun with reckless abandon. My own quiet house waited in my calm neighborhood, where the shadows weren't so dark or the bleakness so permeating.

Snow crunched under my feet as I walked up the porch, unlocked the door, and stepped inside. Dark rooms awaited me. I stood at my kitchen counter. Everything was immaculate. Warm from the furnace. I reached for the fridge, intent on another Pepsi. A beam of light broke through the darkness and illuminated the floor in front of me. Leftovers from the family-sized meal I'd purchased at the local restaurant were stacked on the shelves, right next to my newly purchased Pepsis.

You're so wrapped up in your bitterness you can't even see what you have. Maybe you don't have grandbabies, but you have a house. A store. You have plates of delicious food.

With a heavy sigh, I shut the fridge, trudged upstairs, dropped into bed without taking my makeup off, and closed my eyes.

You're a damn fool.

A restless sleep overcame me.

"Good morning, Mira."

Tadd stood in the doorway to the shop the next morning, brushing snowflakes off his shoulders with a bright smile. Seeing him there made my stomach twist. I couldn't stop thinking about Sarah, who had been lugging boxes out to her grandfather's truck for days now.

"Hi."

Invoices for vacuum repairs and sewing machine sales were scattered on my desk, but I turned away. After Bill died, I'd hired someone to do the repairs. Tadd stopped a few paces away, looking exhilarated.

"How have you been?" he asked, practically glowing with Christmas cheer. I fought off the urge to scowl. "It was great to see you at the community meeting."

"Is there something I can help you with? I have a feeling you're not here to buy a sewing machine."

His eyes darted around, taking the scene in. By sheer force of will, I kept my gaze on him and didn't let it wander to the drip stains spreading across the ceiling like yellow sewing hoops.

"No, but I think my wife would love a new vacuum."

"You're married?"

He grinned. "Guilty."

She must be one tolerant woman, I thought.

"How long?" I asked.

He held up his left hand. A silver wedding band glistened on his fourth finger. "A year. Much to the consternation of my family, we eloped."

"Brave."

"Is it? I always thought it was more desperate."

I fought back a laugh. "Well, if you're not here for a sewing machine or a vacuum, what can I really help you with?"

He held out his hands in an open gesture, as if to show his innocence. "Honestly, Mira, I just wanted to talk."

"Now that you've bought from Charles."

"I thought that might change the tide, a little."

"Sheila agreed to let you buy out her lease, didn't she?"

"Yesterday."

The pit of dread I'd expected never showed up. Now the pet store was down, leaving James, myself, and Tyler from *Nails, Nails, Nails.* I maintained a cool facade. Would that somehow give them more power if this went to court? *Could* this go to court? The missing piece of this puzzle still eluded me, and now we were only three stores strong against the opposition.

"Congratulations. I'm sure it's costing you a pretty penny to pay them out."

"Nothing we aren't happy to pay."

"So you came to see what you can do to persuade me to sell the rest of my ten-year lease?"

"Actually, I wanted to see if we could work together to make this easier for you."

"Easier?"

"Platinum Developers has never set a goal to help a community that we haven't made happen."

A subtle cord of something ran in his voice. I couldn't even call it arrogance—more like certainty. Tadd knew what he wanted and how to get it. I folded my arms across my chest.

"Is that a threat?"

"Not at all. More of a plea to understand your side of this. Businesses aren't attached to their real estate. You could still run your store from a different location."

"My husband chose *this* spot."

"He would have never chosen another?"

"No," I said with certainty. Bill had roots growing out of his toes.

"Is your resistance a money issue?" he asked. Before I could respond, he continued, "I've doubted it thus far, because you didn't even ask what I was willing to pay when I came the first time. Other shop owners did. But I hate assumptions. I wanted to hear from you what I can do to make your life better."

For a long time, we stared at each other. "Can you bring my family back? Because that *would* make my life better."

"If I could do that, I certainly wouldn't be in this business."

This time, I did smile. "You and me both."

"Listen, can I arrange a time for my boss, Troy, to stop by? I think if you could talk to him and find out the mission of the company, it might help change your mind."

I didn't want to change my mind. *What do you want?* Gladys had asked.

I didn't know anymore.

My brow furrowed. "Why would the owner of your company be willing to speak with me?"

"Pardon?"

I straightened, my thoughts whirring like a sewing machine gaining speed. "Because he needs us to give him the leases, of course. I know there's a way to fight . . . and he doesn't want us to go out ugly . . . but why? Because you don't want us to fight. Fight who?"

A flicker of uncertainty appeared in his gaze. I fought off my exultation to allow my thoughts room to expand. Residential *and* commercial.

So simple and elegant I couldn't believe it took me this long to realize it.

"Yes," I said quietly, "of course. Zoning."

"The negotiations between Charles and my boss are not part of my job," Tadd said. "I'm here to smooth the transition for everyone, so I have no official say on—"

"You want to add residential. *This* is zoned as commercial space. You have to change the zoning. And to do that . . ."

A thrill ran down my spine. Our eyes locked.

Tadd showed the first flicker of hesitation I'd seen in him yet.

"You have to go before the municipality," I said, grinning now. "The last thing you would want anyone to do is protest a big, bad developer taking over a small mom-and-pop store, isn't it? So you're schmoozing all of us to make your own life easier."

Tadd tucked a hand into his pocket and cleared his throat. "As I said—"

"Right, right." I waved a hand, my thoughts moving at manic speed now. I hadn't seen it before, but now I did. Their *angle*. They were sweet-talking the shop owners in order to buy the shops out before we could protest and ruin their plans.

So simple I'd never seen it coming.

"Listen, Tadd, I need to go." I reached for my purse and shoved my phone inside. "Sorry. Can we continue this later?"

"Ah . . . sure. Of course. Thanks for your time, Mira. I'd just like to reiterate that—"

"Sorry! Later!"

I rushed into the back, gathering my scattered lip gloss, compact, wallet, and romance novel. By the time I shoved them in my purse and grabbed my keys, Tadd had already left.

Good.

Right after locking the store behind me, I rushed over to James, breathless with relief and anticipation and the sheer joy of having a *plan*. The bistro lay empty.

"Hello?" James called from the bar. He lifted a hand. I hurried over.

"James, I think I know how we can call Tadd off and save our stores!"

"What?"

"Even though some have already signed their leases over. At least . . . I think I do. There's a lot of legal technicality we'd need to figure out with zoning laws and that kind of thing. But . . ."

His eyebrows lifted. "Really?"

"I need to do some research and talk to some people to make sure my assumption is correct. I'm closing the store now to do it. Are you still interested?"

A flicker of something passed through his eyes before he nodded once. "I want every option available before making a decision. What can we do?"

I grinned and pulled my bottom lip through my teeth. "I'll come back tomorrow with a plan. Right now I need to call the city, look into zoning laws, and figure out a few court system rules. Talk tomorrow?"

"I'll supply the food."

"Great. See you then."

The thoughts grew so frantically in my mind as I slipped out of the bistro that I almost couldn't sort through them. There was no doubt about it; Platinum Development was good.

But I was better.

Time to Fight

Snow drifted past the spires of my church as I sat in the parking lot. The gusty winds beat my car, shaking it. I thought of Gladys and her admonition to have more gratitude.

I shifted, trying to calm an internal itch I couldn't reach. Soft lights illuminated the building from different angles, highlighting the stained-glass windows and steep roof. The stone walls and wrought iron fence gave the grounds a medieval feel; the cemetery sitting off to the side didn't help. This place had once given me peace.

Now I just felt the familiar current of rage.

The one that, now that Gladys had mentioned it, I'd tapped into with sudden insight. In fact, it seemed to teem constantly below the surface, never more clear than in the moments when I won Candy Killer or stared at my ceiling late at night.

I kept my hands tight on the steering wheel.

"I'm not happy with you," I muttered, glancing at the cross. "I'm not happy with the path you put me on, the children you took from me, and the sheer number of deaths I've had to survive. This is not the way it's supposed to be, you know? There are supposed to be grandbabies and celebrations and people filling my house to the brim. Not . . . geriatric cats and empty Pepsi bottles." With a grudging sigh, I added, "Fine. There would always have been Pepsi bottles."

My car blocked out most sounds, leaving me in a strange silence once I finished speaking. Maybe that's all God was: a vacuum. A place to go. A person to blame.

A little gratitude wouldn't kill you, Gladys had said.

I closed my eyes.

Without opening them, I said, "But I guess I can't change what's happened, can I? You took everyone away. That will never change. And maybe Gladys is right. Maybe I *am* angry."

My grip on the steering wheel tightened until I thought I'd grind the leather to powder. I opened my eyes again. If possible, the world seemed darker, despite the blanket of snow to amplify the light.

"No," I whispered. "I'm not angry. I'm livid. You took everyone away. You took away my plan. My happily-ever-after. That's gone, and I couldn't stop it, no matter how hard I tried. And I tried *everything*."

The words sounded bitter and twisted, even to my own ears. My shoulders slumped.

"But I don't want to be the person I'm becoming anymore. I'm turning into a monster. Or, at least, someone I don't recognize. Someone who complains. A lot. That's not me, and Mama's probably relieved to hear me say that. So, this is me trying to change. This is . . . me . . ."

The words scattered like dropped needles. I tilted my head back and stared at the top of my Cadillac, blinking back hot tears.

"Can you just get me through this with Platinum Developers? That's all I'm asking. Help me save my store. I'll do all the rest. I'll deal with my anger. I'll even be more grateful. I already plan to start a gratitude journal like Megan and connect with myself the way Rachelle does. Maybe even self-care, like Bitsy. And fine," I muttered with a sigh. "I'll go back off Pepsi, like Lexie did with Dr Pepper."

No voice answered. No angel descended. Not even a whisper of wind interrupted the gentle drop of snowflakes from the murky clouds. But something in my chest had broken. A chain, perhaps. Something weighty. Whether God was there or not didn't matter right then. I had a plan.

No more anger.

No more blind rage.

No more ignoring Tadd.

It was time to fight—for myself and for my store.

"Can I help you with something?"

I glanced up to see a dollar-store employee peering at me, a bright yellow vest draped over her shoulders. Shocks of crimson hair tied into ponytails stuck out of either side of her head. Christmas music played in the background, ringing with a dull, lifeless sound. I picked up a glittery white plate. Jerry would have hated it.

"Are these breakable?"

She nodded eagerly. "Yup. When the shipment arrived last night, at least a third of them were broken. Can you even imagine? Definitely don't get those if you want something to last longer than a meal."

My eyes skimmed the selection. Black, pearlescent, and gray plates stood on the shelves like marching soldiers. A lovely turquoise set hid behind the black ones. I reached back and pulled it forward. Mama would have loved them. Flamboyancy was her battle cry.

"I'll take all the turquoise you have," I said. "How many plates is that?"

"In the back?"

"No, sorry. My fault. The broken ones, I mean."

She blinked twice. "Broken plates?"

"Yes."

"Ah . . . you want broken plates?"

"I'm assuming you can't do anything with them," I said, tucking a plate back into a slot after inspecting its thickness. "Unless you plan to glue them back together and hope they sell on clearance."

"Well, no."

"So, where are the broken plates now?"

"Still back there. My manager will deal with it when she gets back tomorrow."

"I'll give you twenty-five cents per broken plate."

"Seriously?"

Behind her, a collection of cheap wine glasses caught my eye. Paint peeled off the shelf beneath them in long lines.

"And I'll take every wine glass you have out here, too. Looks like that's what . . . thirty? That'll do. While you go get the broken plates, I'll carry these to the register. That work?"

"Uh, sure?"

"Great."

She stood there for another moment while I pulled the first box of wine glasses off the shelf. Then I stopped and looked over my shoulder. The glasses clinked when I pulled them down.

"Wait," I called as she started to walk away. She paused and turned around, eyebrows high on her freckled forehead.

"Yes?"

"Where are your baseball bats?"

Bing Crosby crooned through my house that evening.

A fluffy ball of fur lay on a pillow on the floral couch Bill and I had bought twenty years ago. Marilyn had been in that exact spot when I left in the morning. The only indication that she'd moved was her empty food bowl. Satisfied when a mirror fogged up underneath her nose, I picked up Malcolm, carried him to my bedroom, and set him inside. The door closed with a gentle *snick* behind him. He'd be safe in there with Sadie for the time being.

When I returned to the kitchen, I grabbed my ice-cold glass of unsweetened tea and took a sip. The cool tang slid down my throat. I closed my eyes, relishing the familiar zing that reminded me of Daddy. Every night, rain or shine, he had his glass of iced tea.

Ah, memories.

I picked up the bat that leaned against the counter, had one more sip of tea, and faced the glittering dishware that awaited me. A haphazard array of hastily glued plates sat in a stack off to the side—it had taken me an hour to patch them together.

Five different wine glasses lined my table on top of a white tablecloth. One my mother had given me a few months before she died. Jerry's old high-school blanket covered the chairs, while Daddy's favorite bedspread lined the floor. I'd moved everything except the table out of the dining room.

Don't you ever get tired of being the victim? Gladys had asked. *Sure, life sucked for a while. But now you are the one dragging the misery on. Why can't you get over it?*

"Yep," I said, tightening my grip on the bat. "Can't move on 'cause I'm pissed as hell, Gladys."

That's you avoiding what you really need to be doing, which is probably something violent.

"On my way."

I paused long enough to take a deep breath, process what I was about to do, and swing. The ear-piercing shatter of the bat connecting with the first wine glass rang through the air, drowning out Bing and the ghosts screaming in my head.

"That," I said, "was for my first miscarriage."

Mama's voice didn't speak from my past in a lecturing tone, reminding me that ladies didn't break glassware or drink iced tea on the rocks from a whisky tumbler. Bill didn't tell me I was losing my mind and remind me that it had started when I adopted three cats. I didn't even question my own sanity as I tightened my grip again and pulled the bat back.

If anything, Jerry would have approved.

"This," I whispered, "is for my first stillborn daughter lying in the ground near Bill."

Three wine glasses sprayed the wall at the same time, falling in chunks on the sheets that lined the ground. I reached back without looking, grabbed the tea, and had another swig.

"Now for my son."

The last of the five glasses representing my lost babies survived the bat, but not the wall. It collided with a *crash* and splintered into dozens of pieces. I reached over, placed five more wine glasses on the table, and stepped back.

"One more time for each."

Two more glasses down.

Three.

Five.

Bing continued to sing. I stared at the sparkling shards of glass. My nostrils flared. All the pain came rushing back. Those babies had been *mine.* I had been robbed of them. Of the opportunity to be a mother. To protect, snuggle, and raise them. That *hurt.* Negative pregnancy test after negative pregnancy test. The brutality of hope. The sudden plunge of despair month after month after month after month.

Unable to stop myself, I slammed my bat into the entire box of remaining wine glasses. They crumbled with a satisfying crunch. Then I hit it again and again and again.

"They were mine!" I yelled. "Mine, dammit!"

A stack of ten turquoise plates slid off the counter when I drove the bat into them. They fell, cracking on the ground. I slammed them again.

"For Bill!" I screamed.

The white ones hit the ground next under my assault. The bat shattered everything it touched. Splintering. Pummeling. Destroying. Tears ran down my cheeks.

"For Jerry! A-a-and Mama. And D-daddy."

I punctuated each word with a punishing blow, feeling satisfaction only when each piece crumbled to dust beneath my power. The bubbling current of rage that had lived within me now flowed out. I felt the heat in every part of my body. Fingers. Skin. The tears coursing down my face. A sob wrenched out of me as I grabbed another plate and threw it to the ground. It fractured. Then another.

Another.

Another.

By the time the stack had dwindled, my energy flagged.

"All of you left me," I shouted at the plates. "I'm mad at all of you! Why? Why did you leave?"

Finally, the last piece remained. A lone wine glass. I dropped the bat on the mound of cheap ceramic with a hideous crunch and wiped my cheeks off with my sleeve. Somewhere in the background, Bing had quieted into a low, depressing melody.

I picked up the tea, downed the rest of it in one swallow, and set the glass aside. I held the remaining wine glass up. It sparkled in the light. Scripted wording ran along one side of it. Our wedding glass. The one we both drank from the night we were married over thirty years before.

Forever, it said.

With a deep breath, I hurled it against the wall as hard as I could. Then I shut off the light, picked up Marilyn, and marched upstairs to bed.

Day 1.

Gratitude Journal

1. Cheap dishware
2.
3.
4.
5.

"That's it, Mira. I'm beyond worried. Now I'm just livid. You've missed three meetings. You haven't answered a single phone call or text message. Lizzy and Lana are worried about you, too, you know. No one will say what's going on, although I'm positive Megan and Rachelle know something. I'm more than annoyed. I'm hurt. I'm angry. I need to talk to you about something, and you're not here and . . . I can't even talk about this."

"Hello, Mira, it's Jackie again. Listen, Lexie said that you've been MIA in your meetings and she's been worried about you. I promised her I'd come by your place to check, but you never seem to be home. The store was closed early yesterday. Everything okay? I'll stop by tomorrow evening. Can't wait to show you the fabrics I bought for Lexie's baby! I know we don't know the gender yet, so I just bought enough for two quilts. Talk soon!"

"Hey, Mira. It's Rachelle. Just wanted you to know I'm thinking about you. Let me know if you want to catch up over coffee or stop by the bakery. We have some ridiculous Christmas cookies right now. So worth the splurge."

"This is Tara, Erasmus Flynn's assistant. I'm trying to connect with Mira Montgomery to set up an appointment before December 25th. Erasmus will be working up until 6:00 p.m. on Christmas Eve

but has limited availability. Please call back to claim one of those slots. Thank you."

"Mira, it's Lexie. I'm in town! I desperately need to see you. Where are you? I miss you, and I'm worried. I have a baby shower coming up, and I don't want you to miss it. Love you."

Revitalizing

Despite the frigid cold that nipped the end of my nose, I trudged through the nearest neighborhood, undaunted, rehearsing my script in my mind.

Do you want more traffic in this neighborhood? I'd been asking. *More crime?*

Platinum Developers are taking over the strip mall to turn it into a retail and residential complex. They're booting out people who have held legal leases there for decades just to make way for more money in their pocket. Sign the petition to save our neighborhood!

If at first you don't succeed, do it like your mother told you, Mama always said. In the same breath that she told me not to be a quitter.

Trooping through the neighborhoods with winter boots, a heavy parka, and a clipboard with papers on it wasn't my idea of a good time. But the fight against Tadd Williams had come to this, and I'd meet it where I had to. Even if that meant canvassing weary neighborhoods for signatures against rezoning a commercial space. I eyed the sky. The sun had started to sink low on the horizon. Soon, I'd need to head back to my car.

Just one more signature.

Occasional strings of Christmas lights decorated a few of the houses I'd visited. They glowed red, white, and green as I moved along the chain-link fences, some of which were trimmed with evergreen, mistletoe, and holly. A wreath adorned one gate that I pressed through, the tassels of a fat red bow drooping in the cold winter air. Every twenty minutes or so, the wail of a police siren or ambulance shrieked nearby.

A quick glance at my clipboard gave me a little motivation. "One more," I murmured under my breath. "Just one more."

One more signature would give me ten total—which didn't seem bad for two hours work and almost fifty doors knocked on. Considering most people acted like they weren't home or just didn't answer, anyway.

The next house I approached had kitty litter sprawled across the icy porch and bright pink cat toys littering the snow. I had this in the bag. Not only was I a kitty mama now, I had the hair on my coat to prove it. A woman with streaks of gray in a head of umber hair answered, wearing a ratty old robe and a pair of slippers. She glared at me through slitted eyes, a coffee cup in her hand.

"What do you want?"

"I'm here to talk about the recent developments that are going to take place in this neighborhood." The words rolled off my tongue like liquid silver now, after hours of rehearsing. "Platinum Developers have—"

She sniffled. "I already know all about it."

"Oh?"

"What do you want?"

"I'm gathering signatures to stop them from rezoning the strip mall into a housing complex that—"

"Why would you do that?"

I blinked. "Pardon?"

"What they're doing isn't a bad thing."

Not a single person that I'd spoken with had an opinion about it. Hers stopped me in my tracks.

She stared at me. "Well?" she asked. "Where's your defense?"

"Just that increasing the commercialization without proof that—"

"They're building apartments, bringing in a pharmacy, and providing jobs to the local community. Heaven knows we need it. How is that a bad thing?"

"I . . . well, with an already high crime rate and more housing comes—"

"Show me a study to prove it."

"A study?"

"Yes. A study. Do you have solid evidence to prove your case against Platinum Development working to better the community?"

"Well, I don't . . . that is . . ."

"Have you spoken directly with Platinum Developers about this?"

My chin tilted up. "Several times. We are in frequent communication. Do you mind me asking why you're in support of it?"

She rolled her eyes. "Oh, great. Another staunch conservative here. Listen, progress is good. This neighborhood needs a little revitalizing, and no one else has done it yet. I don't see the problem with Mr. Williams moving forward."

My heart squeezed into a fist. *Mr. Williams.* Of course Tadd had already come to them. Why hadn't I anticipated that already? She had probably attended the community meeting.

"It's not just a matter of revitalization," I said. "It's about supporting those who have been pillars of the community for a long time."

Her eyes tapered further. "You're that sewing shop owner, aren't you? I've seen you before. I've been into your store. You were here before I was. Are you sure this isn't personal? I firmly believe that business should never be personal."

"No, it's definitely not personal. Well . . ." I trailed off. Personal to everyone stuck in the crosshairs. Before I could open my mouth to explain it, she cut me off.

"Listen, I don't sign petitions, and I'm not interested in saving the people who have kept this neighborhood tired and old. If you want to talk to a raging liberal who's always against big business, check out that lady across the street. She'll sign anything that minimizes change in a free market."

I glanced back over my shoulder. She vaguely pointed to a small blue house with white trim and flower boxes that had long since been dead. When I turned around to thank her for her time, she shut the door in my face.

I dropped the clipboard to my side. The sun had faded, dropping low in the sky. Well, that hadn't gone the way I expected. I still had one last signature to gather.

I knew just where to get it.

Lucky's Irish Pub smelled like roast beef and wassail.

Patrons filled the tables that scattered the room, but no one sat at the bar. Pat bustled around getting drinks and sliding them to the waitress, who caught them as she walked by. He'd always run his pub like an orchestra.

A basketball game played on several TVs, the sharp voice of the announcer giving way to the occasional cheer from the crowd and the sound of the buzzer.

Once Pat saw me walk in, his face lit up.

"Mira! You're back."

"I came to see if you'd sign something for me."

The clipboard clattered when I slid it across the bar toward him. He glanced at it.

"Petition?"

"Just collecting signatures."

His eyes scanned the writing at the top of the page. "But I don't live near there."

The idea of explaining the petition and Platinum's goals—inasmuch as I knew them—made me queasy. I sighed.

"Sign it anyway?"

He scrawled on the line next to it, then motioned to a barstool with a tilt of his head. "Have a seat. I just made up some brussel sprouts. You gotta try them."

Minutes later, he returned with a plate of roast beef, brown gravy, hot mashed potatoes, and a leafy pile of brussel sprouts that looked as soft as pillows.

"Wow. Thanks."

"On the house." He paused right across from me, lifting one eyebrow. "How are you? Any better?"

"Are you afraid I'm in the middle of a midlife crisis?"

"I'm certain of it."

My lips twitched. Trust Pat to be boldly honest. I picked up a fork and dove first into the mashed potatoes, recalling the way Gladys had savored them. She certainly had some *gratitude* for that food.

I could afford to relish it a bit more.

"Maybe I am in the middle of something," I said, piling potatoes on the end of the fork. "But that's not really the worst thing, is it?"

"What're you thinking of now?"

The genuine curiosity in his eyes made me wonder if *he* wasn't having something of the same experience. I hesitated.

"A friend called me out the other night. Said I wasn't grateful enough for what I did have. Like I'm . . . hung up on the past, or something."

His expression never wavered. My eyes tapered. Pat could have coined the expression *wears his emotions on his sleeve*. If I couldn't tell his thoughts, he was hiding something.

"You must agree."

"I didn't say that." He held up both hands. "I didn't say those words."

"I wouldn't be angry if you did."

"Oh. Then, yes. I agree."

"You think?"

Had I been so absorbed in all I'd lost? Was *gratitude* really going to pull me out of my funk?

I had my doubts.

"We could all do with a bit more gratitude," Pat said, "especially around this time of year. Look, I'm not being judgmental. I'm just saying that sometimes, when we've lost a lot, we get . . . *stuck* in it. Maybe that's where you are. Thinking about what you do have—like a delicious plate of free food on a cold winter night—can snap you out of it a bit. Move you onto a different stage of grief, or something. I don't know."

"Aren't you supposed to be a professional counselor?" I teased. The mashed potatoes melted on my tongue. Pat snorted.

"It's requisite for any bartender."

I gestured to the greens. "They're delicious, by the way. Is that a hint of vinegar, I detect?"

"Definitely. Good. New recipe." He tossed a towel over his left shoulder. "I've been getting creative in the kitchen."

"How very bold of you."

He shrugged. "It passes the time."

I understood the sentiment. Whether emboldened by his honesty with me, or the years of flirting around the edges of something undefined, or being tired of everything being *something undefined*, I motioned between us with the fork.

"Pat, are we dancing around something here? Is there something that we aren't telling each other?"

Pat blinked, tilting his head to the side to regard me. "What do you mean?"

"Both of us are widows, right? You had a crush on me for a while, and I've had one on you at various times. We've been on dates, and we talk often, but it never seemed to click at the same time. What do you think?"

Several seconds passed in thoughtful silence. "Just because we're widows doesn't mean we have to marry each other," he said.

"I never said anything about getting married."

His meaty shoulders relaxed. A new customer walked inside, jingling the bell on the door. Pat lifted a hand to greet them. When the customer asked him a question, he sidestepped me. The pause in conversation gave me a chance to scrutinize him. I certainly had opened up a side order of awkwardness.

There was something truly down-to-earth about Pat. Something a little bit refreshing and . . . unintentional. The idea of marrying anyone but Bill was too overwhelming but a bulldog puppy like Pat would be a good choice. Or maybe my life hadn't changed enough since Bill died, so it felt like cheating to even think of someone else. But even as I stared at him, I realized that another husband wasn't what I wanted.

Plenty of people asked me all the time when I would get remarried, whether I'd gotten over Bill yet, what was next for me. The questions felt as loaded as twice-baked potatoes.

Even the new Mira didn't want marriage.

I didn't know *what* I wanted.

In fact, that moment, turning over memories of both Pat's friendship and Bill's life, felt better than wondering. Than chasing. I stared at the pool of gravy around the roast beef. I complained about Bill's death all the time—and I would give anything to have him back—but I had him once. No one could take that away from me. I thought of my too-big house. The empty fridge. The quiet halls that creaked when I walked down them.

I did have a lot.

The customer moved down the bar while Pat filled his drink order. "Bossy in a bowl with an all hot and a sleigh-ride special."

"Listen, Mira, I know what you're getting at here. The truth is, I'm really not interested in getting remarried since Darla died. I'm feeling pretty good, and I'd like to just enjoy that."

With relief, I smiled. "Me too."

"I didn't expect you'd be at my bar, proposing marriage."

I laughed. "No proposal. Just . . . defining."

He let out a long breath. "Good."

"Though, with roast like this? I thought about it."

His brow had grown heavy over his eyes. "You sorting things out for the first time, you think? You've had a rough go the last ten years. Seems like everything's been hitting you all at once."

"Sorting through it," I murmured. The phrase had a certain appeal but didn't quite fit. The grief had been real. I'd moved through the stages many times now. This was different. "Perhaps. It feels more like I'm just . . . finally moving forward again, maybe? Figuring out the new normal instead of staying in the old one. I guess I've just been tired of being alone."

"What's your definition of alone?"

"Um . . ."

He gestured around. "You're not alone here on a cold winter night. Lexie's been calling *me* to see if you're doing okay, by the way, so I know you still have friends. You have customers."

"I guess I never . . . I'm not . . ."

"Does alone mean an empty house?"

"Probably?"

"You could change that."

I blinked, stunned by the simplicity of his response. I'd never thought of it that way before. To *define* what I felt was . . . empowering.

"I guess it's the lack of someone to talk to at the end of the day."

"You can change that, too, right?"

My mind flashed back to the Health and Happiness Society. In some ways, I could. In other ways? I couldn't.

"I never thought about it that way." I leaned forward. "Does any of this sound crazy to you?"

"Not crazy. Almost everyone our age talks about the same thing. Finding purpose again. Grieving something. Being pissed off that they lost a chance at something. It's all normal, I think."

A rush of relief overwhelmed me; finally, I had been heard. *Actually* heard. Not Gladys barking at me, Bitsy coaching me, or Lexie trying and failing to understand.

"Thanks, Pat."

"Anytime. We gotta stick together, you know? Even if we don't get married."

"Agreed."

A rowdy group of men stormed into the pub. Pat nodded once to me.

"See you soon, Mira. Always good to talk."

Twenty minutes later, I stood just inside my house with a styrofoam to-go box in hand. After the chaos of people yelling at me as I walked up and down the street, the basketball game at Pat's, and all the sounds of the day, the silence felt like a warm, soothing poultice.

I had never appreciated the silence before.

Marilyn slept on the couch. Malcolm stood at the window, tail twitching as he watched snowflakes cascade from the sky. Sadie's bell rustled as she darted by, ignoring me.

My eyes trailed over my belongings. Mom's old grandfather clock. Dad's favorite painting of a moose drinking out of a river. Memories of Bill were strewn through the room. His recliner. A few pictures of us—admittedly, not many—and a framed one-hundred dollar bill. The first time he'd won blackjack against Jerry, who'd famously never lost before. A picture of Jerry and me, standing on a pier with a line of trout in hand.

I smiled.

The floors were swept—mostly thanks to my tizzy—and the counters clean. The sink sparkled, still shiny from a coat of cleaner and a good washing. Nothing had messed it up while I was gone. There were no loud noises. If I would actually go to the store, there would have been fresh food in the bare cupboards.

It really *wasn't* so bad here.

Ever since Bill died, and that part of my heart shriveled like a raisin, everything had a dark tint to it. But it didn't have to. Living the single life could, in some ways, be really . . . advantageous.

Even with three geriatric cats.

"I guess I do have someone to talk to at the end of the day," I said, scratching Marilyn softly behind one ear. She glanced up at me with wide eyes, then leaned into my palm with a little purr. Malcolm stepped off the back of the couch, winding his body around my arm. I smile as Sadie slipped over and rubbed against my ankle.

"Several someones," I murmured, and reveled in the quiet.

Day 2
Gratitude Journal

1. Pat talked to me
2. No one threw tomatoes at me while I was asking for petitions
3. I have a warm coat
4. . . .
5. . . .

Day 3
Gratitude Journal

1. Malcolm hacked up a hairball on the tile, not the carpet
2. Didn't have to clean my house
3. My heater is working
4. This morning, the gym hadn't canceled my account despite lack of use the past month
5. . . .

Invisible

Thanks to a tail under my nose and the warm *rutt* of Malcolm in my ear, Sunday started at four a.m.

Despite every effort to settle back into the dark, warm place of sleep, my body and mind fought it off. Finally giving in, I trudged into the bathroom, cranked on the shower, and stood beneath the hot steam until I started to fall asleep again. Then I shut off the water, toweled off, and slipped into my favorite robe. The steam cleared when I wiped it off the mirror with my hand. For several long seconds, I stared at my own reflection, hardly recognizing it.

Church, I thought. *It's Sunday. I can do this. I can go to church.*

Only ten days stretched between now and Christmas, and I still didn't have plans. Maybe Pastor Burke had something planned for the widows in the congregation.

The thought of conjuring up the energy to brush my hair, blow dry it straight the way Rachelle had convinced me to start doing this summer, and put on all my makeup was overwhelming. My gaze drifted to the bucket list, taped again to my bathroom mirror. As if I knew where they'd land, my eyes dropped to the line I least wanted to see.

Go without makeup for a month.

My thoughts spiraled in a thousand directions. Why did I wear makeup so faithfully, anyway? Why so *much* of it? The progression of my daily routine had been subtle through the years. As I stared at my pond-water eyes, I realized I almost didn't know myself without the paint.

What would happen if I just walked away?

Did that apply to *all* parts of my previous life?

Before my thoughts ran too deep and thick to stop, I reached for the second drawer—my *face* drawer, as Bill called it. Inside, compacts abounded. Eyeshadow in shades as extensive and numerous as the thread I sold. Bronzer. Blush. Eyeliner in five different colors and three different types—inkwell, pen, pencil. At least four mascaras: one for plumping, one for color, one for length, one for fullness. Foundations? Five experimental ones I used rarely, because I found one I loved and stuck with it for the past seven years. With all that came creams, face washes, towelettes, cotton swabs, and more.

There was no real end to the madness.

"What would happen if I walked away?" I murmured, staring at it.

You'd be invisible, came the thought. *Who would see you if not for the forced brightness? When your soul is dim from grief and pain, how else can you be known?*

The bag of makeup where I kept the essentials—which wasn't even part of the stockpile—sat on top of the counter. I glanced at it and back at the drawer. The more my babies died, the more my family left, the greater my obsession had become. Why? Because they were leaving.

I wasn't.

Like I was standing there, waving my arms, screaming for help, and no one could see me.

Invisible.

Frantic, I ran into my bedroom, fumbled for my bottom dresser drawer, and yanked it open. Photos lay scattered among other paperwork and journals that I shoved aside. I snatched any picture I could find, sorted through the ones with me in them, and tossed them onto the carpet by the handful. Once I snagged each photo, I crawled across the carpet and laid out each picture by year.

Two hours later, I sat back on aching knees and hips. Sunlight streamed through my muted curtains with a dim glow. Sadie stretched, staring at me upside down from the top of the bed.

A timeline of photos stretched across my entire bedroom floor in rows. Almost as if I had planned it, each successive year—especially the ones punctuated by loss—showed a significant change in *something.*

After my first stillborn? A perm.

Mom and Dad's unexpected death? I'd signed up with a makeup company and sold their products on the side. My eyeliner was sharper, bolder.

Bill's death? I gained fifty pounds. Switched to elaborate, bright muumuus so I didn't have to see my own body, but I couldn't go unnoticed. My eye shadow was more electric than ever after that.

No pictures from this year lay on the floor. A damning truth.

I didn't need the pictures to prove that my makeup collection had expanded. My blush grown bolder. An occasional stroke of glitter, in fact, despite my age.

"I *was* trying not to be invisible," I murmured, touching each picture with a gentle hand.

You've never been invisible to me, Bill said.

"Yes, I was," I said, thinking of the nights he spent watching football with his friends. The days I cried alone in bed after another miscarriage. The hours spent in counseling, hashing out our grief in different ways. I'd forgotten. "Sometimes, I felt like I always had been."

He said nothing.

If my family didn't hear me screaming as they died, someone would have to see me in person. And if they didn't see me?

Then I had to save them.

Quilts for Jackie. Dragging Lexie to the dieting group and paying for her gym membership. Babysitting for Bitsy. Driving Rachelle. Trying out recipes. Working free for Sophia. As if the makeup hadn't been enough, I'd tried to be indispensable. They'd never be able to forget me, because I was always there. Always waiting.

For . . . something.

Until I couldn't stand it anymore.

A tear trickled down my face. No anger rushed up with it. No rage. Just a tight rock of sadness that burrowed into my chest—no. Not sadness. My heart. All this time, I thought I'd been lonely, but I hadn't been. Not really. People had surrounded me all the time. I made sure of it.

I'd been scared.

Scared that I'd fade into the background. Scared I'd disappear into the folds of life and lose yet another loved one. Scared the Health and Happiness Society would leave me behind.

My thoughts spun, too heavy to peg down. The implications sprawled into avenues I wasn't ready to face. Bill. Sophia. *Bitsy.* Looking at the progression of photos over the last ten years was a sobering experience. I'd been searching, all that time, but looking in dark corners.

Was I still doing that?

I stood up, marched into the bathroom, and yanked the entire second drawer free. Then I chucked my makeup bag into it and took it outside, ignoring the layer of snow on the bottom of my feet. Compacts, blush, brushes, cotton swabs, and more spilled into the garbage can in a landslide. The lid slammed shut when I spun back into the house.

"One month," I said, throwing open the door, "starts now."

Erasmus Flynn wasn't a typical lawyer.

When Erasmus first started working for us back in our thirties, Bill had already accepted that our family wouldn't happen the way I planned, even though I hadn't. Erasmus helped us put together a few basic odds and ends through the years—living will, durable power of attorney, and some other conglomeration I didn't care about until Bill died and I desperately needed it. He'd mainly been a visitor we welcomed over every Christmas Eve. With no family and no desire for one, he rarely left his office.

Where he happily resided.

When Erasmus walked into the store later that morning with a bright red flower in his pocket, the hair on the back of my neck stood up. I'd blatantly ignored his assistant's messages.

This wouldn't be good.

Shocks of white hair sprouted from either side of his head in a fuzzy halo. He looked as if he'd shaved with a dull razor. Although it was eight in the morning, a five o'clock shadow graced his weepy cheeks. He was a compact man, with a deep sense of pride in the way he dressed, and a love of all things bourbon.

"Erasmus," I said, straightening. A bolt of blood-red silk slipped from my fingers and onto the counter. "What an unexpected surprise."

He strode over without acknowledgment. His gleaming briefcase slid onto the counter between us. He studied my face. A more perfect first person to see me makeup free didn't exist. Erasmus couldn't have said the word *makeup* without extensive coaching.

"Good morning, Mrs. Montgomery," he said.

"Erasmus, we've been friends for decades. You can call me Mira."

He gave no response.

"Everything okay?" I asked.

"Fine."

"It's Sunday. Do you work all week long?" I asked.

My cheeks heated a little. I *should* be at church, but the idea made me sick to my stomach. Erasmus knew how dedicated I'd been through the years, when at times it seemed like the only stable thing I had.

"I don't recognize weekends," Erasmus said. Dull, hazel eyes met mine as he studied me. "As you also don't, apparently. Silly construct of a modern life. I'm here to talk to you about the store."

I scowled. "Don't tell me that Tadd Williams has gotten to you, too."

"Don't flatter yourself." He clicked the locks on his briefcase. It popped open, revealing a perfectly organized interior lined with silk. "He doesn't care that much about you."

"Wait, he *has* contacted you?"

"Platinum Developers and I have worked together, but it has nothing to do with you. A bit high-handed today, are we?"

My nose wrinkled. I didn't like this at all. "Then why are you here?"

"You're a fool, Mira."

"Please tell me you aren't charging for this."

"Billable hours start at nine. When Platinum Developers officially offer to buy out your lease," Erasmus said, sliding a paper over the counter toward me, "you should take it."

I glanced at it, but seeing tables, graphs, and numbers, pushed it to the side. "Not interested."

"Mira—"

"It's not going to happen. I already have information on when Platinum Developers is going before the municipality to attempt to officially rezone this area. If they don't get approval, they'll have to honor my lease."

Take that, I wanted to say, feeling smug.

"Losing this real estate is the least of your worries."

My throat caught. He said it with perfect equanimity, not a ruffle in his voice.

"What?"

"Your finances are a mess, Mira."

"I've been careful!"

Two white fuzzy eyebrows lifted. "Perhaps not." Enough alacrity remained in his expression that I couldn't help but wonder what he knew. Attorney-client privilege, in his world, was more solid than diamonds.

"I know your company, Mira. While I don't work with real estate law, I do know Platinum Developers. They're a solid company. I've never seen them lose when they stand up for a fight."

My chin lifted. "I'm not afraid."

"It's not *them* you should fear. You're fighting a giant that you don't need to fight. Business isn't good since Bill died, and it wasn't doing great before then. Your giants lie in other places."

"Like what?"

"Your financial situation."

"How do you—"

"You pay me to know."

The same surge of indignation and disbelief swelled in my chest. I let it go, swallowed it back, and stared hard at him. Erasmus and I had enough history that I wasn't afraid to be honest. He feared nothing except emotion.

"I am doing just fine, thanks," I muttered.

"You may think you're fine now, but you'll be a swamp within a year at this rate." He tapped a finger on the paper he'd given me. "Projections of what you have left of Bill's life insurance. Take a look at it. It isn't pretty. And it's probably time you knew that Bill and I spoke more often than you knew. His insurance covered expenses you weren't aware of."

"What?" I hissed.

"His will stipulated that I take care of all of that without telling you the entirety of it until a certain time frame had passed."

"You didn't tell me?"

"At the time, I felt that it was a worthy task considering the size of your grief and how much loss you had recently faced."

"That was seven years ago!"

"It's also stipulated in my agreement with Bill that I could tell you after five years had passed."

"It's been *seven*," I ground out.

"And this seemed the most advantageous time for a hearty dose of the truth."

"Bill didn't want me to know?"

"Let's just say he didn't want you to mourn more than one thing at a time."

The same surge of rage threatened to swell, but it died halfway through the attempt. I didn't have the energy to encourage it along, and I realized I hadn't felt it in several days. Now it felt weak. Too hot. There was nothing buoying about it.

"I always follow through on my clients' wishes, Mira. But now it's time to face the truth. Mira's Sewing and Vac had been failing for many months before Bill died. In fact, I believe stress was one of the reasons he succumbed to his heart attack in the first place, although I have no backing of a medical professional on that, so take it for what it's worth. You've done very well on your own, but you cannot sustain the store without dipping substantially into your retirement, something that I would never advise."

I thought I would succumb to a heart attack as well. Instead, I stared at him with a sense of numb disbelief. Bill had, effectively, lied to me.

For years beyond the grave.

"I see," I whispered.

"You don't. The finances had been ugly for a while. He didn't want to tell you and make you worry."

"So he told *you*?"

Erasmus sniffed. "I'm his estate lawyer. Of course he told me. Also, arguably, I was one of his only friends."

"That went both ways, I imagine," I muttered.

He nodded toward the document on the counter. "That's a list of all the accounts and debts that I settled with a portion of his life insurance policy immediately after his death. The rest of it I put into the savings account that you having been using to run the store."

I shifted uneasily. His eyes tapered with intense scrutiny.

"What?" he asked.

"N-nothing."

"Is there something wrong with the account?"

"In theory? No."

Except for the uneasy truth that I had used up most of it. Business really *had* been rough since Bill died. Lease payments. Paying off the second mortgage he'd taken out to keep us floating. Basic living expenses.

Geriatric cats.

In other words, Bill had done me no favors by protecting me. Things had still been as ugly as an eight-year-old with a tube of mascara.

"That's disappointing to hear," he said. "Also damning. In that case, I would like to triple my concern for you."

"Try it from my side," I said.

He fought not to roll his eyes, I could tell. "Even with a good offer on this place, you probably won't get enough to live off of. You're going to need to find a different job. A steady income to put away money. Trust me, Mira, you don't want to be stranded in your eighties because you didn't let go today."

"But—"

He held up a hand, silencing me.

"I know that Bill told you he had a plan. An IRA with money set aside for your retirement."

"It was a lie?"

"Not exactly. He had the account, put money in it for a long time, but then used it to keep the shop afloat the last six months of his life."

My nostrils flared. "What?"

"Listen, Mira, I came as a friend. I couldn't care less about Platinum Developers, but it just so happens that I honor the memory of my friends after they pass. I couldn't sit back and let you destroy yourself."

"This store is my home and Bill's *dream*."

He snapped the briefcase shut, lifted it by the handle, and jerked his shoulders back. It gave his squat little body the appearance of a well-dressed gargoyle.

"Was," he said. "Turned into a nightmare at the end. And you've been living it for him long enough. Do the right thing, Mira. Don't fall into this trap. Don't regret holding on to something you can't have just because you think it's all you have left of him."

The papers trembled in my hands as I watched him stride out the door, hearing the crisp staccato of his shoes on the hardwood. I didn't want to see the numbers, the graphs, the proof that my husband wasn't the man I remembered.

"You're a rat," I said to the quiet air.

Bill remained silent.

Day 4
Gratitude Journal

1. I'm not married to a man like Erasmus
2. Garbage cans that smell so bad it prevents me from diving into them to get things back I may have regretted getting rid of but need to keep in there
3. Marilyn is still breathing
4. Bill
5. The pastor hasn't called to check on me yet

Mira, this is Tadd. I hope it's all right that I called you on your cell phone. Listen, I've been discussing things with my boss, and he'd like to make an official offer to you on the lease. Can I come by sometime to talk to you about the price? And possibly a few other things that may help you see our side. Thanks.

Hey Mira, it's Megan. Thinking of you. I'll be flying in soon and want to see you, even if it's not at the Christmas party.

Mira, it's Jackie. I'm officially worried. Let's forget the quilts and just go to lunch again, okay? Lexie said she hasn't heard from you, either, and Pat said something about you figuring life out. What does that mean? Please call.

Pastor Burke here. Just wanted to call and see how you were. We really miss you at church. The choir hasn't been the same without you up there, and the prayer circle is mourning your loss. Please let me know how you are. I know the holidays are hard to navigate alone.

Not Real

The rapid approach of the Christmas season—combined with the devastating revelation from Erasmus—drove me back to the attic.

I could have been avoiding the carolers that patrolled my street, or the possibility that Bitsy could stop by at any moment and I might not have the strength to keep the door shut. Either way, I found myself in the cold air again, wondering why.

I wasn't sure what to do next.

What was I looking for?

The open box I'd left scattered when I found the bucket list lay in front of me. Papers sprawled on the floor around it, petaled in white sheets like discarded snowflakes. I approached carefully, choosing my steps as if the papers were glass orbs. Several small books sat on the floor. Most were a deep sapphire, with uneven paper edges, worn with time. Stains littered the front and back flaps.

My throat tightened. I knew exactly what I had come up here for. These. My old journals.

I had known they were up here, lost amid the mess. In the past, I'd tried several times to throw them away. Something always propelled me to pull them back out of the trash can. Bill's ghost, maybe. Sometimes I thought it was myself.

I was never really sure.

Most of the entries chronicled my twenties and early thirties, when I kept losing the babies. Back when I still wanted to know what my thoughts were. Once I had accepted that the family I had dreamed of was never going to be here, I stopped writing about it.

The numbness was easier.

With trembling hands, I bent over and picked one up. It fell open to the middle of the book. This particular entry was written hastily, as if I'd been frantic, almost manic, in my attempt to spill my thoughts. My eyes pulled out individual words, even though I tried not to read full sentences. Nothing was as scary as the emotions *behind* these memories.

April 2nd, 1991

The doctor told us today that pregnancy was probably just a matter of a couple more tries.

"As coldhearted as it sounds, many couples miscarry their first child," he said. "One day we'll be able to prevent 99% of miscarriages, I would imagine. Science is always changing. For now, we have to move on. Can you do that, Mira?"

Science. I never thought of conception as a science. Felt like even he couldn't believe, keep up with, or imagine this would ever happen in his lifetime. He is an older man, so I can't help but wonder what he was taught.

"Your children will come," he said. "I will see to it that we do everything possible."

I confess, it had been one of the lowest moments of my life. Why did my body fail me on the first try? If the babies never come, and my worst fear is realized, then what? Can a couple survive without the unifying experience of a baby?

I'm getting ahead of myself. It was just one pregnancy, my first, and there will be more. I'm twenty-four, healthy, and so is Bill.

But . . . it was my pregnancy. And I desperately wanted it.

That's why it hurts.

The writing on the page ended, but I couldn't bring myself to turn it. I swallowed hard, remembering the exact day I sat down to pen that entry. The day after my first miscarriage at eleven weeks pregnant. My joy in the four weeks that I had known had been utterly blissful despite the nausea, then the cramps, then the blood.

I could still remember the way the air in our house seemed so quiet that night, as if it could be broken. With a shake of my head to clear my thoughts, I thumbed several pages over. In the new entry, nine months had passed. Tear splotches blurred several words into inky smears.

January 15th, 1992

Another baby lost.

This time at sixteen weeks. I can barely speak. The surgery is over, but I feel as if I'm still sedated, even though it's been three days now. My limbs are heavy. "A girl," the doctor said. "I'm so sorry, Mira."

Not as sorry as me.

I can barely think straight, or write. Two in a row? And they don't know why? They've taken almost a gallon of blood out of me. "Testing. Let's figure out if something else is going on."

But what if there's nothing to find?

What if my body just keeps failing? Or what if there's no discoverable reason except bad luck?

And why is it so easy for some and so hard for others? I can't help but wonder . . . will Bill hold this against me? Eventually, I mean. Not yet, I would imagine. Two losses, for some, is only the beginning. But they still hurt. So much. Especially this one. Sixteen weeks was long enough to move on from the first one. To hope. To get through the awful first trimester and dream of the day I felt her move.

Bill says he won't hold it against me, but I can't help but wonder. How could he not? I hold it against me.

Does Bill even know his own mind?

He's so distant. At least he has been lately. Every time I'm pregnant (which has only been twice but feels like so much more), he feels more gone than ever. The man can barely decide what we're going to get for dinner on the way home. I have a hard time imagining that he actually puts a lot of thought into what his response will be if we never have children. He's so distracted by the store lately. Sales have been low this month, and we spent money on an ad that didn't pay out.

Sometimes I fear–

A lump rose in my throat. I slammed the journal shut, then set it aside and grabbed one with a lime-green cover. Beneath it lay a black one. I kicked that one under the box so I couldn't see it and opened the green one to the first entry. For a long moment, I stood there and stared at the writing. Then I sucked in a deep breath.

November 4th, 1996

I brought up adoption again. We're three pregnancies down and no closer to holding a baby in our arms. Not one that we can keep, anyway. I must have a child. I don't know if I can stand it. What is the purpose for empty arms?

Why not me?

I think losing his son at 24 weeks—after getting to hold the tiny little body in his palm—has deeply affected Bill. Inconclusive tests. More doctors. This whole thing is exhausting.

Even my mention of adoption was met with the usual stonewalled silence. I've never met a man who can avoid a topic as surely as he can. Like always, it brought me to tears. By the end, we fought. Again. It always ends this way, doesn't it?

Perhaps my greatest fear is happening. Perhaps our lack of children really is going to drive us apart. Maybe it's something that neither one of us can work through. Shouldn't this be the time we pull closer together than ever? I've never felt so far from my husband before. He's gone. If he's not at the store, he's at his games.

It's like he doesn't want to see me.

Unable to handle it, I moved to the next entry. A year later.

October 30th, 1997

Bill and I started counseling. He's not happy about it, but I can't live like this anymore. I can't accept that our dream family is never going to happen, that we bought this massive house for nothing, unless I feel like he's along for the ride with me.

Right now, I feel like we're on two different trajectories, except we can't really get there alone. I don't even know what his trajectory is. I know mine.

At least there's hope, right? He's there at counseling. Grudgingly, but nothing the therapist can't handle, I'm sure.

Here's to hope. That thing I hate the most.

I knew what I would find on the next entry, and the next entry. I had read and reread these entries many, many times since Bill's death. Until I finally stashed the journals away in the attic where I didn't have to face them anymore. Good moments, dark moments, and the spectrum between. Therapy had stirred up all the ghosts that neither one of us wanted to face but knew we had to. No one had told me that marriage counseling got harder before it got better.

Life with Bill was always taking me by surprise.

I skimmed through the rest of the green journal, snatching snippets of my old life as I went.

Big fat negative this month. Thought it was a positive but was just late.

Another lab draw. Another appointment coming up. Can I really take this?

Decided to take another six-month break. Sex is becoming tedious, and that's not fair to Bill.

Sold thirty compacts this month, so that felt better. Love the new fuchsia they came out with.

Mom came to visit. I cried on her shoulder for hours.

Bill held me when I got another negative tonight.

My heart sank deeper and deeper into my chest. The problems had seemed so big then, as if I couldn't survive the pain of infertility and marriage issues and loneliness. But I hadn't known what was coming. If I had, I would have lived that life so much more gracefully.

Like I was trying now.

When I set the green journal on top of the sapphire one, my eyes went right to the hidden black journal under the box. Oh, *that* journal. Tears filled my eyes when I bent over to pick it up. My fingers had turned cold in the winter air, but I appreciated the numbness.

I hadn't finished the green journal when I switched to the black. At least thirty pages remained. But I hadn't been able to write my dark thoughts in that journal after my parents were killed.

As if I had to separate the two distinct forms of grief in my life.

February 21st, 2002

They're gone.

Mama and Daddy just . . . gone. How can death happen so fast? How can such a fatal decision be made in split seconds? The drunk woman that killed them with her car was a total stranger. Somehow, she walked away from the car wreck.

My parents didn't.

Why does that happen? How does that happen? What kind of God would allow such pain? I feel that my body cannot tolerate anymore.

The handwriting was shaky, and scattered. As raw and difficult to read as my own thoughts had been to think.

Everything in my head right now feels so cliché. I've known loss before. I've mourned five children. I've struggled through a marriage that has almost failed so many times I've lost track. But this? Losing them at the same moment?

This will overcome me.

It feels like it already has.

The black journal contained the deepest shadows of my heart to that point. Sheer disbelief. Inability to discern reality and my nightmares. Jerry appeared more in those pages than any of my other journals. The superhero older brother. Next to Bill, he'd been my stable point. He knew my dark days better than anyone.

Until he couldn't.

Unable to bear it anymore, I shut the book, stacked it top of the others, and gathered them in my arms. I left the mess of papers behind me a second time as I headed back downstairs. The cold followed me, driven into my bones like it intended to stay. Not even the sound of the heat whirring in the background brought me comfort. I left the journals on the table and slipped into the kitchen, my slippers gliding along the wooden floor.

For the longest time, I stared at the open fridge. Like always, there wasn't much in there.

I shut it.

I stared at the floor. One thought circled in my mind over and over again.

Life with Bill hadn't been perfect. The life I always dreamed of living again wasn't really that . . . happy.

In fact, it had been *hard*.

The happily-ever-after I'd always thought I'd been promised had faded as reality sank in. I had forgotten. In the haze of grief, my mind had glazed over how difficult things had been for Bill and me to maintain. The fighting. The stress over the store. The heartbreak of infertility. His gambling addiction. We had constantly been at odds over how to run Mira's Sewing and Vac.

Infertility had been hell.

Losing my parents was even worse. I wanted to sell the house many times. *Let's move on,* I remember saying. *Let's get a smaller place and put this behind us and not live with the ghosts of children we will never have.*

But he couldn't let it go.

So why was *I* still here?

Overwhelmed with the weight of memories, I turned off the lights, locked the door, and settled into bed. Then I stared at the ceiling.

"It wasn't easy, Bill. It's wasn't magical, except for little moments that were. It's like . . . like I've been holding onto only the good things. And that's not real."

He said nothing. I dreamed of nothing.

Day 7
Gratitude Journal

1. For memories
2. For truth
3. For new beginnings
4. For Bill
5. For the purr of a cat in my ear
6. For the healing power of tears

Alone

The local homeless shelter smelled like bleach.

I swallowed hard as I walked inside, taking in the bleak, utilitarian tables and chairs that lined a clean cement floor. A crowd of people waited on the other side of the room, talking among themselves. Most wore shabby coats in muted shades of brown and gray, with cut-off gloves and tattered shoes.

What was I doing here?

A gaunt woman with yellowed skin and sallow eyes glanced at me, then looked away. I stuffed aside my discomfort.

I needed to do this.

Christmas approached. An empty holiday loomed ahead—something I wouldn't stand for. Even if that meant celebrating with my three geriatric cats and volunteering to help at the homeless shelter that day. Helping other people was probably just what I needed to spawn the much-needed gratitude.

Why don't you call Jackie back? whispered a little voice.

I banished it.

"I've met a lot of people who come here, but I never expected to see you."

I whirled around. Maude stood behind me, arms folded across her chest, staring at me through narrowed eyes. Behind her steamed dishes in the food line. Green beans, it looked like, swimming in a pool of broth. Workers bustled around wearing plastic aprons and throwing out a wave here and there to the congregants.

"What are *you* doing here?" I asked. Why did she keep popping up in the most unexpected places?

"I was just about to ask you the same thing," Maude said, studying me. "Where's your makeup?"

My cheeks heated. "On its way to a new home."

She tilted her head to the side. "I like this look better. Listen, I knew that things were rough for you, but I didn't think they were this rough."

"I'm not here for the food. I signed up for a volunteer spot for tonight."

Her lips rounded into a silent *O*.

"I called the office this morning, and they said they could use a few people." I fidgeted with the bottom of my coat. Somehow, Maude seemed far more terrifying than the new landscape.

"We're always desperate for volunteers." Maude waved to a thin, blonde woman carrying a carton full of milk containers.

A wretched feeling of guilt swept through me. For a fleeting moment, I had thought of calling the Health and Happiness Society to let them know positions were open, but I realized my mistake before I picked up the phone. It was the kind of goodwill that Bitsy would have loved. In fact, she probably would have found an article about why it burned calories to volunteer, or something ridiculous like that.

Maude stared at me as if she expected something, and I realized that she was waiting for me to reply.

"Gladys told me to get over myself when I saw her last," I said. A hint of amusement flittered across her face.

"She's one to talk."

"I guess, after looking at my life, I realized maybe she had a point. I was getting sort of wrapped up in . . ."

Everything.

". . . what I didn't have."

"Sometimes she does have a point," Maude said. "And then sometimes she doesn't." She gestured behind her with a quick jerk of her head. "Come on back. I can get you suited up for the food line. Unless you feel like washing dishes or prepping food?"

"I have no preference. Wherever you need hands, I'm happy to help."

It felt good to mean it.

She led me into the back, through a metallic kitchen with bland tile and cupboards to spare. Five other volunteers mingled, murmuring quietly, warming food on the stovetop or stirring it on the counters. Soup bubbled over a large stove on the far wall. What appeared to be biscuits rose in the oven, filling the kitchen with the smell of fresh-baked bread. Another familiar face popped into view.

"Hey! What are you doing here?"

I reared back, startled. "Stella!" I cried, a hand over my heart. "You scared me."

She grinned in the naive, happy way of a toddler. Today she wore a bright purple visor, fluffing the gray-and-white hair above her head. Her thick glasses were fogged up from the soup she was stirring.

Her brow furrowed. "You're not homeless."

"Volunteering."

"Me too!"

I glanced around, half expecting to see Gladys walk out of the nearest closet. Probably with a cigar in hand, dragging her oxygen tank behind her while barking obscene jokes at the volunteers.

"Don't tell me Gladys is here as well," I said.

Stella snorted. "Not even if it saved her life. No one risqué enough here. I've been volunteering here for thirteen years now." She motioned to Maude. "When she recruited me."

"Good people are always in short supply," Maude said, with just a hint of disdain. "Come on, Mira. You can be on biscuit duty. We had a local supermarket donate ten pounds of butter."

"It'll be a real treat to get their biscuits buttered," Stella said, then cackled to herself as we walked by.

Gladys wasn't the only strange one.

Within minutes, I stood at a counter by myself. While another volunteer slid hot trays of steaming biscuits my way, I grabbed a stick of butter and slathered it on top of the hot rolls. It melted down the sides in long rivulets. Despite how yummy they looked, an occasional glance into the hall to see the desperate faces that stood out there robbed my appetite. I had known instinctively that Gladys was right. But it wasn't until then that I realized just how much I really *did* have.

I took a tray out, passing a man asleep beneath one of the tables. Life in my drafty, empty house wasn't so bad at all.

Five minutes before dinner officially began, Stella sidled up to me and grabbed an extra wooden spoon. She pulled a pot of instant mashed potatoes toward her, dumped a stick of butter inside, and began to stir.

"So," she said, "it's fun to see you outside of the embarrassment of a poker game."

"Thanks."

"Why *did* you come?"

"Why not?"

"Good reason."

"I'm not all that surprised to see you here," I said, looking at her from the corner of my eyes. "But I am a little surprised to see Maude. She's so refined and . . ."

"Hoity-toity?"

"She doesn't exactly strike me as the homeless-shelter type."

Stella's gaze crossed the room with a half-wistful glance. "Then maybe it'll surprise you to know she lived in one."

"What?"

"Maude has always liked taking people by surprise," she said wryly. "Besides, her son Troy owns this place. He runs it. His whole family comes to help on the holidays to give the rest of the volunteer staff time with their families. These young kids wandering around? They're Troy's. Maude's grandchildren."

Three or four late teenage, early twenty-something volunteers bustled in the kitchen, taking orders from a woman with blonde hair in a high bun and grungy old Levi's. She barked commands like an officer.

"That's Tracey, Troy's wife and Maude's daughter-in-law."

"Seems like a great family."

Stella shrugged. "They are, of course. I think Troy feels like it's his duty, considering their past."

"Past?" I asked.

Stella paused, mouth halfway open as she stared at me, as if she couldn't decide whether she trusted me. She must have decided she could, because she continued.

"Maude's second husband was extremely wealthy . . . and extremely abusive. Three months after she had Troy, she fled to save her own life. No one believed her when she tried to get help, which meant she ended up on the streets."

"No family?"

"Not that she felt she could turn to, I guess. For a long time, Maude was eating out of soup kitchens with her son. At least, until she was able to get her own apartment while working as a maid. Troy was three by then, I think."

I stopped measuring potato flakes to look across the kitchen. Maude stood next to a handsome man with a strong chin and a head full of thick black hair. He wobbled on a ladder underneath a window. A pile of tinsel dangled from one hand and a colorful pair of Christmas lights from the other. He draped the lights and tinsel around a window over one of the two sinks. When one of the teenagers walked by and quipped something, he laughed. A full, steady, happy sound. Even Maude smiled back, quiet adoration in her eyes.

This time, I wasn't consumed with jealousy. I didn't think about the sons I'd lost. Or the opportunities I'd missed. Because my heart had nearly stopped.

I knew that man.

The same man I'd seen in the shadows with Maude at the movie theater. A face I remembered from somewhere else.

Like the community meeting for Platinum Developers.

I swallowed hard, my throat tight. My mind drifted back to the second poker club meeting, when Stella and Gladys talked about Maude's son winning another award. Community service, or something equally honorable like that.

"Her son the businessman?" I whispered. "The one who's won all those awards?"

"Yep."

"He runs his own company, I presume?" I asked.

"Some sort of real-estate something."

"Platinum Developers?"

Stella snapped her fingers. "That's the one. How did you know?"

The desert in my mouth prevented me from answering. A hundred voices spoke to me from different parts of my mind. Tadd telling me about the natural goodwill of his company. Trying to get me to meet his boss so I would sign my lease over to a better cause. Considering the neat, sprawling expanse of this homeless shelter, his words seemed a lot more credible.

A bell rang near the food line. Stella stirred faster. I snapped back into motion, dumping the loose flakes into the closest pot while my thoughts spun.

"Have you heard from Gladys lately?" Stella asked.

"Not since both of you cleaned out all my cash."

Stella giggled, then motioned around her with a sweep of her arm. "Behold, your sacrifice. I always donate my winnings to the shelter."

"Gladys?"

She snorted. "Hardly. She's barely eking by as it is. Troy is planning on opening a weekly Medical Clinic here, and they want to start construction soon. They've been doing fundraising for several months now."

If possible, I sank even deeper into a quagmire of guilt.

"Doesn't surprise me that Gladys doesn't donate. She doesn't strike me as the charitable type," I said, just to turn the subject.

"She's not. She definitely creates her own problems."

"What do you mean?"

"Gladys," she said, as if that explained everything. "She's brought a lot of her own misery upon herself, hasn't she?"

"I don't know . . . I just . . ."

"Gladys hides away in her little house all the time," Stella said, eyebrows high. "Can you imagine a life so isolated? Living only for yourself just to avoid feeling pain again?" Stella shook her head, as if, even after all these years, she still couldn't believe it.

My mouth stalled, half open.

"But . . ."

"She's tried to rope you into it, too, hasn't she?"

"Well, not necessarily like that."

"There's being safe about who you love, and then there's just running away." Stella's gentle gaze caught mine. Dog hair still graced her shoulders, softening the intensity of her expression. "Gladys is running away."

My throat tightened. "Right. Sure."

Stella turned back to the potatoes. "Life hurts. But that much? What about joy? What about happiness? How can you have the highs without the lows?"

The words echoed through my chest like an empty chamber. I straightened up, filled with panic.

"I should probably go."

Stella's eyes widened. She gestured across the room. "But we haven't even served the cake yet. Troy always gets extra around the holidays and lets us have the leftovers. It might be from a homeless shelter, but it's tasty!"

Before I could scuttle away like a dog with its tail tucked between its legs, a body moved into my path. I skidded to a stop and glanced up in time to see Troy standing there, hand extended toward me, as if our conversation had summoned him.

"Merry Christmas," he said. "Sorry for the delay, but I always try to meet new volunteers. We can't tell you how much your time here means to us." He slanted his head toward the cafeteria. "And to them. How did you find us? We're always looking for more good people."

Dust covered the woolen plaid of his long-sleeve shirt. At one point, I thought I'd seen him crawling behind a large refrigerator with a mousetrap. The smell of tomatoes drifted off of him. Much of the food in here had clearly been donated as surplus from various places, but that didn't account for everything. No doubt he made up the rest.

"Mira," I said, accepting his hand. "I'm always happy to help where I can."

He smiled, reminding me of his mother.

"We'll always take it. Most of this is family run, meaning that the volunteers tend to be more like family members to each other than not. Just let us know if we can ever do anything for you."

Someone called for him. He stepped away with a murmured apology and a promise to talk again soon.

I didn't even glance back at Stella. I snatched my keys out of my back pocket, made sure I had my cell phone, twirled my coat onto my shoulders, and headed out the back door as fast as my legs would carry me.

Day 9
Gratitude Journal

1. For food. Even when it's been too much. Even when it's stale. Even when I don't want to go to the grocery store, but I can because I have money.

2. Gas in my car
3. Warm clothes
4 A big house
5. Three geriatric cats
6. A working furnace
7. Diet Pepsi in my cup
8. My brand-new coat
9. Boots that keep my feet warm
10. Friends
11. Walking on the treadmill because I choose to—not walking because I have to—to stay alive

"There," I said, stepping back. "All ready for the Christmas Eve sale."

Ribbons, streamers, Christmas lights, ornaments, and garland lay scattered on the counter by the register—which was now laden with red tinsel and jingle bells. *National Lampoon's Christmas Vacation* played in the background. Although not my favorite Christmas film, the familiar voices reminded me of Jerry and brought some comfort. A cup of eggnog sat next to the register, just to drive it home.

My head tilted to the side as I studied the decorations. The legendary Christmas Eve sale would give me the boost I needed to get through the quiet holiday. Not only did I have a stockpile of Diet Pepsi in my fridge at home, as well as a ridiculous number of romantic comedies that I'd checked out from the library to help the day pass, but I'd even ordered food. It would be delivered tomorrow night before I left to hole up at home on Christmas Eve.

And possibly feel a little sorry for myself for a while.

Thoughts of the homeless shelter flickered through my mind, but I let them pass. No need to see Troy again this soon.

The bell tinkled on the front door, startling me from my thoughts. James shuffled inside, shoulders slumped. A frosty jacket covered his shoulders, partially obscuring a dirty apron. With both hands in his pockets, he stared at the floor.

"Hey, James."

Shreds of tinsel clung to my shirt and sleeves when I turned to face him. I brushed them off. He nodded once.

"You don't look like you're feeling very well," I said, studying his grave expression. "Everything okay?"

"Not . . . I mean . . . I'm fine."

An awkward pause caught me by surprise. I blinked.

"But?"

"But . . . not so good, either."

For half a beat, we stared at each other. I saw it, then. The truth. The brutal, ugly truth.

"You're selling to Tadd."

The words rushed out of me, feeling like a bog in my mouth. I silently prayed he'd rear back, act shocked, even offended that I'd *suggest* such a thing. Instead, he met my gaze with an expression that was without remorse but filled with compassion.

He nodded.

Tortured guilt lingered in his gaze. Self-inflicted, no doubt. I didn't want to hear the words. Not now. Not tonight, when I'd settled into the idea of a lonely Christmas after all. My already-weakened armor would shatter under this blow.

"Mira . . ."

I attempted to say something, but my lips went slack. What was there to say?

"Oh," I finally managed.

"Do you want to know why?"

Why you're telling me right before Christmas? Why you gave up after less than a month? The plans I'd had to beat Tadd wilted in my hands like play sand. How could I do this alone?

"Of course," I said, but it came out hoarse. I couldn't meet his gaze. A fathomless chasm of darkness reared its ugly head. Rage tinged the edges. Fear. Pain.

All the things I'd been avoiding.

"It's more about me than them," he said. "I can promise you that much. This has nothing to do with money or Tadd or—"

"Are you sick? You okay?"

"Not sick . . . I just . . . Mira, I'm getting old. I can't run the restaurant by myself anymore. I'm not making enough to hire more employees, and my daughter has her own life. Besides, she said . . . she said the neighborhood was just too rough to be safe for my granddaughter. She doesn't want her spending time here. But this is where I spend all *my* time."

The idea of James's granddaughter falling victim to any number of crimes common to the area made me sick to my stomach. James lowered his head a little.

"Tadd made me a good offer. A *really* good offer. Better than I could get otherwise. It'll help seal a few holes in my retirement that have popped up the last few years, once business declined."

My heart shrank several sizes. I felt as if someone had hit me right in the throat. Just like the night the police officer called me about my parents. The ICU doctor telling me Bill wouldn't make it. Charlotte calling to say that Jerry had died.

Rage would have been convenient right then, so much easier than the pain of knowing I had lost. But it wouldn't come. As if it didn't exist in me anymore. Instead, there was just fear.

I opened my mouth to congratulate him, but stopped. I stared at him, helpless, wishing I could do more. He seemed to understand. His gaze softened.

"I know, Mira. I understand. And I'm so sorry."

A shaky breath finally broke my paralysis. "Don't apologize, James. I understand. You have to take care of yourself first."

"But—"

"Don't. Don't beat yourself up about this."

The tension in his face relaxed. "What about you? What are you going to do now?"

"I don't know."

My gaze traveled around the store, lingering on the newly placed decorations glittering in crimson and evergreen and silver. Ornaments hung from a petite Christmas tree on the desk. Shiny vacuums. Brand-new sewing machines. Even the color-coordinated spools of thread seemed dismal. I tried to picture the store empty but couldn't. There had always been supply.

Even without much demand.

"Will you sell to Tadd?" he asked.

They could drag me to court, find a loophole, bribe me, do whatever they could. But I wouldn't give up.

Would I?

My first attempt to smile failed, but the second one managed a faltering success. "When are you leaving?" I asked.

"Right after Christmas."

"Have you told your employees?"

"They saw the writing on the wall. They knew what was coming before I'd accepted it, and a few of them have already been looking for other jobs."

"What are you going to do without the restaurant?"

Picturing James without an arm or leg was easier than imagining him restaurant-free.

He shrugged.

"Don't know. Guess I'll have to figure out how to be retired, or start cooking for my daughter. I'll probably end up opening a catering business from my house."

A laugh bubbled out of me. "Sounds like an easy retirement."

He smiled, displaying pearly-white teeth. "You know I can't give up cooking for other people entirely. It's my love language."

"You can always feed me."

"I will."

His voice rang with promise. I walked around the desk and stood in front of him. James would be gone from my everyday routine, and that felt like losing my sturdiest friend. Of course, this didn't mean the end. We knew where the other lived. He probably *would* bring me food when the silence of freedom became too much. Until then, however, I would miss his kind eyes, soft hands, and the gentle way he spoke. Tears misted my eyes when I held out my arms.

"Good luck, James."

Deep in my chest, I felt the eternal chasm that came with every loss I'd ever had.

He held me tight for several seconds. When I stepped away, a tear dripped onto my cheek. I didn't bother wiping it away.

"Have a Merry Christmas," I said, meaning every word. "I'm happy that you're happy."

He gave me a crooked smile and squeezed my hand. "You, too, Mira. I'll plan on cooking you dinner for New Years."

I laughed through the tears. "I'll take it. Make it apricot chicken."

"Nah-uh." He ticked a finger back and forth. "No way. This man is going global. Indian food, I'm looking at you!"

The bell rang again as he pushed his way out the door, singing in his deep baritone. After he disappeared to the left, I followed his steps to the front of the store and stared down the street. Snow fell in a thick blanket. I removed the bell from the door and silenced it against my palm.

If it never rang again, maybe that would mean something.

For a long time, I stared out the window at the falling snow, lost in thought. Could I fight Tadd alone?

Was courage knowing when to fight, or when to back down?

Finally, too exhausted to continue, I let out a sigh, stuffed the bell in my pocket, and turned around to gather my things. This time, several tears fell. I let them go, too tired to wipe them away.

When I drove home, my thoughts had wandered so far and so long that I didn't realize I wasn't in my own neighborhood at first. Startled, I looked around, barely registering the familiar street.

A crowded road packed with sardine-can townhouses encircled me. They had quaint fronts, with shuttered windows, flower boxes filled with snow, and wrought iron fences intermittently decorated with Christmas lights. In the summer, the sprawling trees created a lovely green drive. In the heart of winter, however, the ghostly skeletons of the trees appeared wretchedly thin and lonely.

Halfway down the lane, I stopped the car in the middle of the quiet road. Blinked. My eyes grew misty again.

In front of a familiar mauve townhouse—with darkened windows and no sign of life inside—hung a SOLD sign. Based on the piles of snow on the stairs and the utter lack of life within, I knew exactly what that meant.

Sophia was gone.

Without saying goodbye.

On autopilot, I wound back through the roads and through downtown. Near Lucky's Irish Pub, I slowed. The lights were off inside except for one over the bar that cast a gentle glow on the sidewalk outside. Pat must be home with his family, of course. Nephew, if I remembered right. A sign hung on the window.

Nollaig Shona.

Merry Christmas in Irish Gaelic. He said it often this time of year. With a sinking heart, I drove home to face my Christmas-free house, with nothing more than three cats and bottles of Diet Pepsi.

Alone.

Just as I had feared.

Space

My feet ached when I stepped onto my porch, as if even *they* were dreading the days ahead. Just as I reached for the doorknob, the door opened. From the inside.

Bitsy stood there, glaring at me. One hand rested on her hip. She wore a pair of jeans and a black t-shirt. Fire filled her eyes. Fire . . . and something else. My mouth dropped open.

"Bitsy?"

"I thought you wouldn't let me in if I showed up after you got home," she said. "I parked down the road three hours ago and let myself in just to make sure I beat you here. When did you get *cats*?"

My pounding heart didn't settle. I wasn't sure what frightened me more—coming home to someone in my house unexpectedly, or knowing there was no way of avoiding her now.

"A few weeks ago," I said. "After Jerry's death."

"Three of them?"

"They're old," I muttered.

She tilted her head to the side, regarding me with narrow-eyed scrutiny. "Are you . . . did you not . . ."

"I stopped wearing makeup."

She pushed the door open wider and stepped back. "We need to talk."

My thoughts rankled at the idea of her entering my house without my permission, but she had done it a few times before. Regardless—it felt different now. Everything felt different now. Especially when I walked past *her* and into my own house, as if she had invited me into my own space.

Neither of us spoke as I shrugged my jacket off and hung it on the rack behind the door. She stood there, looking as awkward as I felt, until I headed for the kitchen. The urge for Pepsi danced on the back of my tongue. Resignation filled me. I certainly couldn't avoid this confrontation any longer.

"C'mon," I said. "Let's talk in here."

A teacup and a book sat on the table, and I felt a little relieved she'd at least brought something to do while she waited. At least she hadn't cleaned my house—not that there was much to clean—and stumbled onto my bucket list upstairs. The speechless quiet remained until I opened the fridge and rooted around inside.

"So," I said from behind the door, finding it easier to talk when I couldn't see her. "What's up?"

"You've been dodging text messages, meetings, events, chats. Everything, basically. From me *and* from the group. We've been planning the Christmas party without you. I mean . . . what is going on?"

I winced but forced myself to back away from the fridge, Pepsi bottle in hand. Her gaze dropped to it for half a second before returning to mine. I stalked to the cupboard and yanked out a glass.

Let her think what she wanted.

"I just . . . needed some space."

Bitsy lifted her hands. "You have plenty of space."

"Not *physical* space." Although there was that. "I needed emotional space. I couldn't . . ." My mind trailed back to the last Health and Happiness Society meeting I had attended. "I couldn't find it there after Jerry's death."

Her voice softened. "Why?"

"After Jerry died, everything was different," I said, twisting the top off the Pepsi bottle with savage strength. "I . . . I felt like no one could understand. Like I was so . . ."

"Lost?"

"Scared."

Tears pooled in my eyes. The build-up of fear after learning that James was leaving—and that Sophia had already left—spilled out despite my attempts to restrain it.

"Why didn't you say something?"

"I tried to. But things kept getting in the way, and . . . I sort of just . . . I couldn't do it."

"What are you afraid of?" she whispered. She stared at me, stunned, with her usual piercing gaze. In it, I saw surprise. Utter shock.

"All of you."

"Us?"

I nodded.

She blinked. "I-I-I didn't know."

"I know. Everything was changing. Megan married. Rachelle a small-business owner. Lexie pregnant." I hesitated, then waved a hand toward her. "You were . . . holding something back. What did I have? Nothing."

"Mira, that was . . . I . . ."

She trailed away.

"When everyone else had such wonderful things to report, I couldn't deal with it," I said. "I needed a break. I needed . . . to find people who *could* understand. How could I expect that of any of you?"

"Oh."

A burdened silence fell between us. Bitsy rubbed her lips together and dropped her gaze. Neither of us knew what to say.

"So, what now?" she asked. "Will you ever come back? Megan thinks you aren't going to come to the Christmas party. Rachelle has no opinion on it, but I think she's just afraid to agree with Megan."

"I'm not," I whispered.

Bitsy stared at me, wide-eyed.

My voice wavered, and I wished it hadn't. I wished I could tap into the steel fire that burned like brimstone in my chest. If I could have, I would have brought it out of my heart and wielded it like a burning sword. Instead, I drew in another steadying breath.

She swallowed hard. "I . . . that is . . . things have been really difficult lately and—"

"I assumed, but I never knew because you wouldn't say."

She shoved a hand through her hair. "Mira, it wasn't . . . it wasn't like that. It was never personal. I just . . . I was scared too."

"What was it?"

She stumbled for words. A flash of something came into her eyes. Irritation, perhaps? Annoyance? Bitsy had never liked being vulnerable. It soon faded into something like resignation, maybe even sadness. She reached for her purse, tucked it under her arm, paused, then started for the front door.

Say something, my brain said. *Stop her before she's gone.*

The words wouldn't come.

If I had the courage, maybe even more emotional reserves to draw on, I would have told her how much I had missed them. How incomplete I felt without the meeting every week. How scary venturing out without them had been. Allowing the Health and Happiness Society to go the natural way of these things didn't have to be bitter—just matter-of-fact.

Halfway to the front door, she stopped. For a long pause, I didn't breathe while she stood there, back to me. Then she spun around.

"My landlord gave me two months left to stay at my house before I have to move. They're going to let their newlywed daughter use it instead of renting it out."

The sentence felt odd in the strange, still air. My brow wrinkled. She continued.

"Just as I was about to tell Jim, he started talking about marriage."

My insides froze.

Marriage.

The word spun. *Bitsy* talk about marriage? The two of them had only known each other since this spring. No one—and literally *no one*—was more guarded than Bitsy, which meant she was likely just barely lowering her guard with Jim in the first place.

"What?" I whispered.

"To my utter surprise, the idea didn't frighten me the way I expected. I've been thinking about it. But I don't . . . I can't . . ."

No. This couldn't be right.

"Oh."

She fidgeted with the strap on her purse. "That's what I wasn't saying because I hadn't sorted through it myself. Maybe you're right. I shouldn't have been so closed off, but I didn't know how to say it without feeling . . . crazy. Listen, the Christmas party is coming up, and we all really miss you. I'd love to see you there, even if it's the last time. With all the changes that are coming, there's no guarantee we'll ever get together again."

She headed out my front door. I didn't move for what felt like five minutes. I slumped onto the counter.

Marriage?

The first of many tears slid down my face. Now everyone was gone.

No Christmas tree. No celebration. No presents. No plans. The very ending I had feared the most had come about. Bitsy's voice echoed through my head.

With all the changes that are coming, there's no guarantee we'll ever get together again.

Isn't that what I thought I wanted?

To never have to face the possibility of losing them? To let go before they let go of me?

If it *was* what I wanted, why did I feel so empty?

Less than twenty minutes later, my purse slammed on the counter near the register at the store. I jerked my coat off my shoulders and flung it into the chair at the desk.

"All of this is your fault," I cried. "Everything is falling apart because of you!"

What are you talking about? Bill asked. I knew he would. It was why I came. Tears still streamed down my cheeks.

"Bitsy. Platinum. All of it."

My fault? Bill said. *Have you lost your mind? I didn't bring Platinum Developers over here. I didn't ask them to take over my legacy. I didn't ask Bitsy to get selfish with you.*

"She wasn't being selfish," I snapped, shoving a hand through my hair. "She was . . ."

Making you invisible.

"*I* made me invisible!" I shouted. "I did it. I didn't tell them what I needed or set any . . . boundaries with them. I could have tried harder!"

Silence rang in my ears.

"No thanks to you who left. Who *lied.* You're still in my head. Reminding me that you aren't here, talking to me, inserting your opinions into my life. I can't get rid of you."

You are rid of me.

The words burned all the way down my body, as if they wanted to light me on fire. Any response I could have made slowly died, falling away from my tongue like smoke. Tears filled my eyes, but I blinked them back. This wasn't the time for tears.

This was the time for rage.

"You have to just . . . you have to go already. Just *go*."

I've been gone, Mira. It's you who keeps me here.

"You're here because you love the store! It's your legacy, remember? The thing you poured our retirement money into. The thing you almost ran into the ground."

No. I loved you. *The store was a means to provide for you in the only way I could, because I failed in so many other ways. Like giving you the life you always dreamed of.*

A suppressed sob made me hiccup, then it wrenched free, taking my heart with it. That couldn't be true. Among all the other things I'd gotten wrong, it couldn't be true that he loved the store as a way to love *me*.

"You are the reason I've held on to the store for too long," I said. Shadows clung to the walls. I hadn't even turned the lights on when I stormed inside, filled with wrathful vengeance.

Not the only one.

"The one that mattered!"

Why have you held on?

"Because if I got rid of the store, I got rid of you. You were supposed to be the one who stayed. The one who never left me. Didn't we make vows? Didn't we make promises?"

I was only a man, Mira.

"A man I loved! Possibly more than I ever loved myself. How was I supposed to cope when everyone else was gone? No baby stayed. My parents were lost. How was I supposed to let you go?"

My heart thundered in my chest. I ran a trembling hand through my hair. The words had filled my mouth on the way over here. So many that I could barely keep them in. Now that I stood here in the store, gazing around at the four walls that had been my entire life, all the words fled.

What was the store, anyway?

Besides brick and mortar. Besides something to care about? It was memories. Triumph, in a way. A link to Bill. Possibly the only link really left. It was broken and lost and filled with things that didn't bring me happiness.

It was . . . me.

Now I stood in it, alone, the way I had most feared. The way I had *made* happen. Everyone was gone now. My fight with Bitsy sealed that fate. The break with the Health and Happiness Society was as official as it could get without me signing a resignation letter.

Safety hurt so much more than I'd thought it would.

Tears filled my eyes, making my view of the store swim. Bolts of fabric. Piles of discount thread. Sewing needles. Serger blades. Hook and eye crafts for children. I still hadn't figured out what I wanted, but I knew what I didn't want.

I didn't want this anymore.

The peal of the phone broke through my thoughts. I fumbled for it in my pocket, desperate for it to be Bitsy. Lexie. Rachelle. Any of them. My thirst for human connection drove me like a dying woman. I'd give up my cell phone and all the Candy Killer lives the world had to offer for one more chance with my friends.

"Hello?"

"It's Gladys," said a strained, raspy voice. "I . . . need you. Now."

Click.

I grabbed my keys, snatched my purse, and rushed out the door again, heart in my throat.

Indifference

"Gladys?"

When I rushed into her house, the smell of holly berries was overwhelming. Since when did Gladys attempt festivity? I shut the door on a howling gust of wind. Hordes of snowflakes fluttered by, swirling around the icicles on the porch. The television droned in the background. I hurried inside, propelled by a sense that all was not right.

"Gladys? Are you all right? You sounded—"

When I emerged through the front room—still set with the card table—and into her living space, I found her on the couch. Her skin was pale, breath shallow and raspy. She blinked once, then twice. Horror flooded my body.

Gladys was dying.

"Oh, honey," I murmured. "You aren't looking good."

She shook her head in a sharp back-and-forth. A shaky hand lifted, pointing to something on the other side of the room.

"I-I need . . . help."

Her words came slow, in between the punctuation of short, shallow breaths.

"You need an ambulance. Right now." I snatched my cell phone from my pocket. Of *course*. Of course Gladys, of all people, would die right around Christmas. Because why not?

Who *hadn't* left me?

"No ambulance," she snapped. "I would have . . . called them myself. Get me . . . the damn oxygen."

I paused. "What?"

"Oxygen," she muttered. "I . . . need help opening . . . the canister."

"Oxygen?"

"The regulator's broken!" she cried, gasping. "I need . . . the spare until they arrive . . . to fix it."

The shift from terror, to confusion, to disbelief rolled through me like a wave. Gladys wasn't *dying*. She couldn't fumble with the top of the reservoir canister. I bit my bottom lip to keep from laughing—and then crying—and then throwing up.

"Right," I said. "I can do that. I had to help my brother with his oxygen tanks before he died."

"The green key . . ." she panted. "On the shelf."

Within three minutes, I had the spare canister cranked high, the tubing strapped to her face, and Gladys lying back, catching her breath. She pulled in shallow breaths—that I suspected were as deep as she could manage—with her eyes closed and hands on her chest. Slowly, color infused her cheeks again. The raspy quality of her breath faded.

"Do you need me to call your home-health company?" I asked, sitting down on the edge of the couch. She had no other chair in the room, just scattered tissues crumbled in balls on the floor.

She shook her head. "On their way."

A moment of silence fell over us while I glanced around. "Horrible timing, isn't it? Why do things always go wrong around the holidays?"

One of her eyes cranked open. "What are you talking about?"

"It's Christmas Eve tomorrow. Hopefully they can have it fixed in time so you're not living on oxygen cans."

Her eyes closed again. "Oh. That."

The emptiness of her words echoed in the room. *Oh. That.* Such indifference.

Then again . . . had I been any different?

"Thanks," she said, poking a finger toward the front door. "I can take it from here. Goodbye."

I glanced around her quiet house, steeped in shadows, junk, and dust. Only a small Christmas tree decorated the far corner. An old rerun of a crime thriller ran across the television, where she lay with a blanket over her legs. The utter lack of *any* kind of cheer, not just Christmas, settled deep in my heart. Perhaps my emotions were riled from the argument with Bitsy, or James selling to Tadd, or the confrontation with myself. Something in my mind flittered just out of reach. Lurking like a wraith.

Or maybe . . .

Gladys's breathing evened out, drawing my attention. The troubled expression on her face smoothed itself. She'd fallen asleep.

Breathing that hard must have worn her out. I wondered how long she'd fumbled with it before calling me.

Probably a long time.

I watched her for several minutes, my mind spinning to Bitsy and the Health and Happiness Society. From there it wandered to Candy Killer and Pepsi and Bill and Jerry and a bucket list taped on my bathroom mirror and a home where three geriatric cats stared at me in judgment all day from a very undecorated house.

Unable to bear the thoughts, I stood up.

While Gladys rested, I quietly cleaned up, straightening items, throwing others away. She didn't even stir when I changed the channel to a Christmas movie. Amid the paperwork on her table, I found the name and number of a hospice nurse, but one quick glance verified that Gladys's color had started to return and her breathing had evened out.

"Hospice," I murmured, setting the paperwork aside. She must have been on the downward spiral for a while. Also nestled on the chaotic tabletop were old photos. Receipts. Pieces of paper with scrawls on them. Life stuff. I found a picture of her and what must have been her husband. Gladys had been petite, with a bright smile and short hair.

I set it back down.

She thought she wanted a different life than what had been laid out for her. No doubt she didn't *want* to lose her husband and parents. No doubt she didn't want to spend holidays alone. Knowing her, she'd probably die alone as well. Stubborn to the end.

But she didn't have to.

She didn't have to be cranky or off-putting or isolated. She chose it. She'd sculpted her own ending, as lackluster and lonely as it would be. I thought of her dying on the couch, no one there to hold her hand. A familiar pang struck me, so quickly it took my breath away.

"Loneliness is a kind of pain too," I murmured.

Gladys had been swapping one agony for another. The ache of losing loved ones for the misery of having none. With suffering came joy of some form, even if it didn't happen right away. Wasn't that life?

Wasn't that *my* life?

I sucked in a sharp breath.

"Oh," I whispered. A thousand glittering shards—that I imagined had once been my heart—vibrated, pulling together like a magnet beckoned them. They clinked into place along with my thoughts.

Then I saw.

Among the horrors had been beautiful moments.

The day Bill made me laugh so hard I snorted root beer out my nose. The feeling of his warm arms around me when yet another pregnancy test came back negative. His hand clutching mine at the graveside of our stillborn. The warm days in the shop together. Cuddling at home in front of our Christmas tree.

He had loved me amid the stress, the shame, the failure, the junk food, and the torture of infertility. Even though he wasn't here, he had been once.

No one could take that away.

We hadn't been perfect. At our low points, we hadn't even been *good*. His antagonism pitted against my bitterness had been a dangerous combination. But we'd had good times.

That meant something.

"It's been me," I whispered to Bill. "All this time I wasn't really talking to you. You're not here. You haven't been for years. It was me trying to keep you here. Just as I've been trying to keep you here by keeping the store, even when I hated it. I want more. I've wanted more for a damn long time. And I've always thought it was you who kept me back from it. Your memory. Your insistence that the store was ours. But it's not you. It's been me."

No sweet release of emotion accompanied the realization. Understanding that I had been holding myself back all this time was a bitter and prickly pill to swallow. It was more than that. I'd cut myself off from the people I needed most.

I had self-sabotaged my way into my own nightmare. Here I was.

Alone.

With no one to blame but myself.

Bitsy, with her imperfect meddling and attempts to live her best life, loved me. Lexie too. Rachelle, Megan, Jackie, Sophia. All of them cared in their own ways—just as they were selfish in their own ways. I cared. I had also been selfish. Life with them, though imperfect, had been far more rewarding than without them.

An empty life, filled with nothing but television and oxygen tubing and long nights, seemed far more terrifying than bumps along the way.

"You're wrong, Gladys," I said with conviction. "Playing it safe is far more painful than losing again. I'd much rather love and lose then never love at all."

Eager to escape the suffocating confines of her house, I grabbed my purse and looped it over my shoulder. It settled on my hip as I walked over to Gladys's side.

I had a lot of mistakes to correct.

"Thank you, my friend," I whispered as I pressed a kiss to the back of her hand. "You have given me a great gift. Whenever I play poker, I'll think of you."

Her eyes shot open. "What are you doing?" she barked. "Get out of here already, you creep. I'm not dead!"

Stifling a laugh, I strode to the front door, cell phone in hand, a new plan whirling through my mind. I knew what I had to do.

I prayed it wasn't too late.

When I rapped on the door, the knocker rattled.

A lush wreath made of evergreen boughs trembled under my knocks, sounding like my heart. Uncertain, jittery, and terrified.

The sounds of a Merry Christmas celebration rang inside the sprawling, elegant house. Christmas music. Hot chocolate. Was that a hint of brownies I detected on the air? I hardly had the presence of mind to tell. Words filled my mouth like sand, and I couldn't think around them.

A pair of boots walked to the door, reverberating with dull thuds. My heart clenched like a fist when the door swung open, revealing me on the porch. No doubt my makeup was smeared beyond oblivion.

No, it couldn't be.

I immediately recognized Troy.

"Merry Christmas," Troy said. His brow wrinkled slightly, as if he recognized me but couldn't remember from where. "Can I help you?"

"I came to apologize."

His eyebrows shot straight up.

"What?"

"Hey, Troy, did you want to join the Canasta competition?" asked a familiar voice. Tadd appeared over Troy's left shoulder. He wore a green sweater with a hideous reindeer jumping across the front. The nose glowed with a bright light. He must have married Troy's daughter or something because they didn't look alike. Tadd's eyes widened like extra-large spools of thread.

"Mira?" he asked.

"I should probably apologize to you too," I said. I wasn't even sure *I* knew what I was talking about, but I couldn't stop now. Troy opened the door and glanced between me and Tadd with a shrewd gaze. In what seemed like seconds, something clicked.

"Mira Montgomery?" he asked quietly.

"I swear I'm not a stalker," I said, then added with a mumble, "Can't even figure out Google Maps. I got this address from Gladys's house. I had just hoped that someone would be here." I glanced at Troy. "Namely . . . you."

Troy and Tadd exchanged a glance. Tadd gave a little nod. Troy swept an arm back. "Come inside, Mira. I've been wanting to talk to you for quite a while, I believe."

Christmas lights glowed along a tall banister running along a decadent entryway. A plethora of Christmas decoration and the smell of fresh-baked ham filled the inside. Not only did I *not* intend to stay, but I had my own decorating to do.

Besides, I didn't want to see Maude.

I shook my head. "No, but thank you. What I came to say can be said very quickly. Listen, I've been holding off on selling you my lease. We all know that. I was planning to speak at the municipality against you next week because of . . . well, because of a lot of reasons. Most of them were about me."

Tadd's expression softened into a mixture of curiosity and astonishment.

"Look, I didn't really believe that you wanted to improve the community," I continued. "I thought you wanted money and maybe to destroy my life. In reality, I've been holding on to something that isn't real."

Tears filled my eyes. I sniffled and blinked them back.

"My husband and I have been leasing that store since Charles built it. My husband died seven years ago. Giving up the store felt like losing him all over again. When my brother died last month, I thought the store was my last tie to what my life *should* have been. But now I see that's kind of silly."

Troy didn't say a word. His expression didn't waver. No sign of pity or compassion appeared on his face. Nothing but raw curiosity, and perhaps understanding. It gave me the courage to press on.

"I've looked over all of the information, and I agree that the community will be better off with your plan. So I came to sell you my lease. After Christmas, come by. I'll sign."

Tadd grinned. "Perhaps we should seal that right now, just in case. You've been known to be stubborn."

This time, I did laugh and it felt wonderful. "Touché," I said. "I deserve that."

"Mira, I appreciate you coming over here to say that tonight," Troy said. Even in such an awkward, strange situation, he was still sublimely kind and confident. "I can tell you that your generous offer will certainly add a level of sweetness to our Christmas holiday that hadn't been there before. Thank you. We're always striving to make a difference because that's what someone did for me and my mother a long time ago. I've been paying it back ever since."

He looked over his shoulder, and I caught a glimpse of Maude in the background. She sat at a kitchen table, wine glass in hand, a quiet smile on her face as she spoke with her family.

"There was once a time when my mother and I survived because of the help of others," Troy said. "After rough teenage years and a stint in prison, I decided I'd never go back to that life and didn't want others to suffer it as well. Creating more affordable housing is one way we try to help the community. Then I can do for someone else what others have done for me. That's the purpose of Platinum Developers."

"Then I look forward to our negotiation," I said. It came out more confident than I expected.

Tadd clapped his father-in-law on the shoulder. "Don't worry, Mira. I'll be seeing you shortly after Christmas. Only during Mira's Sewing and Vac open hours, of course."

"Are you sure you don't want to stay?" Troy asked. "We're prepping for the big Christmas Eve party tomorrow."

I grinned and shuffled back a step. "Thank you for the invitation. Forgive me for declining, but I have some phone calls to make. I hope all of you have a very happy Christmas. I know I will."

Day 9
Gratitude Journal

1. Everything

Delightful

Mannheim Steamroller played in the background of my Cadillac as I dialed a familiar number.

"Frosting Cottage, this is Rachelle," came the dulcet sounds of a very missed voice.

"It's me."

My voice cracked, and it was all I could do to get those two words out. Rachelle didn't even pause.

"Hey, Mira."

She said it as if it hadn't been ages since we last spoke. As if I hadn't been ignoring them, and putting them off, and trying my best to get them out of my life. I cleared my throat and picked at a loose thread that spiraled out of my steering wheel.

"I called to grovel. And to apologize. And to see—"

"Stop."

"What?"

"No apologies necessary. You needed some space. You got to do what you got to do, Mira. I knew you'd be back eventually. This *is* you coming back, right?"

I almost choked on my own sob. "I want to be back. I really do. And I don't want to miss the party tomorrow."

"Then come."

She said it so simply, as if forgiving me for abandoning them was a simple matter. I wiped a tear off my cheek.

"Are you having it at the Frosting Cottage?"

"Yeah. It'll be pinched, but we'll be fine. If we have to, we can eat in the kitchen. Or we can go upstairs to my studio, even though it's definitely smaller."

There was a wry, amused tone in her voice, but I detected a spark of something underneath. Maybe regret.

"Or," I drawled. "We could have it at my store."

"But I thought that—"

"I did too. I was wrong. I'm sorry I was so wrong."

"Well," she said, brightening considerably. "You have yourself a deal! What if we make it a surprise for everyone else?"

I sucked in a sharp breath.

"Well . . ."

"I know you had a . . . *thing* with Bitsy tonight."

"You do?"

"She called."

"Oh."

"She'll be fine, Mira."

"Do you think Bitsy will come if she knows I'm involved? I wouldn't blame her if she didn't want to talk to me ever again."

"Yes."

She couldn't hide a blip of hesitation. I'd never given up on Bill, no matter how much he had hurt me and I had hurt him. Why would I give up on Bitsy?

"I plan on dealing with that situation," I said firmly. "I just need to get her in the same room as me. I'm not sure she'll be up for it."

"She wants to as well. Listen, what about your Christmas Eve sale? Isn't it the biggest one that you do every year?"

"Not this year."

"You're sure?"

"Trust me."

"All right, then. I'm just finishing up a batch of sugar cookies, putting the finishing touches on some cupcakes, and finalizing the peanut brittle. How about I come over tomorrow morning and we can talk more?"

I grinned all the way to my toes.

"That," I said, "sounds delightful."

The next morning, I woke up after the best sleep of my life.

A crisp, winter morning greeted me. The bright blue sky was sharp with the chilly tang of winter. Not a cloud lingered in the sky from the late storm, which had left a layer of snow on the ground at least six inches high.

A gentle purr and a bright meow came from right next to my ear as I stared at the ceiling, reviewing what the day would bring. Or *should* bring, if my plans panned out.

Marilyn stared at me for a few seconds before butting her head against mine. I gently reached over and scratched behind her ears with a little laugh.

"Well, well. Christmas *does* spawn miracles. You left the couch. Good morning to you too."

Another purr answered me before she jumped onto the floor and strolled away.

I sat up. Bill didn't speak to me. No rush of anxiety overcame me about filling the hours in the day. Today—and hopefully forevermore—there would be a lot to occupy my time.

After pulling on warm clothes, snatching my purse, keys, and a granola bar for breakfast, I snagged the last Pepsi from the garage and slipped into my car. It chugged to life, then groaned through the snow on the driveway as I hurried away.

The store lay dark and empty. Instead of flipping my sign to *open*, I ripped down the papers declaring the giant Christmas Eve sale and lowered the blinds.

Then I went to work.

Dust billowed through the air as I carried, pushed, swept, wiped, and rearranged inventory. Rows of threads disappeared, and all the vacuums along the wall found a new home in the back. Signs came down. Tinsel went up. Christmas lights brightened my windows and the desk and the register. Cleaning occupied me so intensely that I didn't hear the door open.

"Wow. Who knew you had so much space?"

I whipped around to find Rachelle walking toward me, a scarf with skeletons riding motorcycles wrapped around her neck. She carried two boxes from the Frosting Cottage—delicious goodies for tonight, no doubt—and beamed.

The moment she set them aside, I threw my arms around her. "I've missed you!" I cried. "Oh, how I missed you."

She tightened her arms around me. "We've really missed you, too, Mira."

For what felt like an eternity, I clung to her. Finally, when she tapped my shoulder and said she couldn't breathe, I pulled away. Tears streamed down both our cheeks. She wiped hers away with a laugh.

"It's good to have you back," she said.

"Not as good as it is to be back. Are you ready to get set up?"

"More than ready." She nodded to the two boxes. "I brought fresh cinnamon rolls and sugar cookies to fuel our work. You ready?"

I grinned.

"For cinnamon rolls? Anytime. Break out the sugar, and let's get to work, sister. We have a party to plan and a group to reunite!"

Darkness descended early that day.

Mariah Carey played in the background while I stood at the front and stared out the windows. I fidgeted with the bottom of my hideous red sweater, the one Bill had given me as a Christmas present. It was knobby, three sizes too large, and had a rosy-cheeked Santa slapped across the front. Rachelle praised it for being the best ugly sweater she had ever seen.

I couldn't help but agree.

Streams of silver tinsel and bright Christmas lights illuminated the store inside and out. The parking lot was almost empty, except for a few cars pulling through the drive-thru of a fast-food restaurant across the way. Gray clouds piled up in the sky again. I hoped for more snow while butterflies plagued my stomach.

Rachelle and William had been working all afternoon to prepare before they left to pick everyone up. We had organized, decorated, and arranged an entire army of food for the last several hours. Not even the Christmas music had seemed trite or corny. It stirred my heart with new strength. I remembered Bill even better now. The red velvet of his Santa suit. The rough texture of his fake white beard. As if I could hear him ho-ho-hoing from the background of my sweeter memories.

With one last glance around the practically empty store, I took in all that had changed. It looked like a whole new world. The thought of putting everything back where it had always been made something hot rise in the back of my throat.

Could it be the same when I felt so different?

No. This was the time to move forward.

Two cars pulled up. Their bright headlights shone in my eyes before turning off. I scrambled outside. What felt like mere seconds later, several bodies approached me.

At first, I didn't recognize any of them. Then I realized that Rachelle was leading them, arms hooked through theirs. Blindfolds shielded their eyes. William was on one side, leading several others. Jim was the only one without a blindfold.

A lump rose in my throat when they all stopped a few feet away. A young man with short-cropped hair and wiry shoulders strode next to Megan, one arm around her strong shoulders. They laughed quietly about something. I recognized Bradley's burly, broad figure right away. He held onto Lexie, whose blonde hair spilled onto her shoulders in corkscrew curls. This *was* a big occasion if Lexie had prepped to such an extent.

We hadn't all met together in the same room since Lexie married Bradley. We were back together.

Not for the last time, if I had anything to say about it.

Bitsy held onto Jim's hand, muttering something under her breath. Jim smiled at me as they approached. Did I imagine relief in his gaze? Rachelle had a wide, sparkling grin on her face.

"Everybody ready?" she asked. The murmur of voices died down. The same nervous feeling rose all the way in my throat, threatening to choke me.

"Take 'em off!" Rachelle called.

A quick row of gasps followed. Tears filled my makeup-free eyes. I had no illusions of making it through this without crying, but I had hoped to get one word out. They all stared at me, eyes wide, for a solid seven seconds.

"Surprise," Rachelle said, but it came out in an awkward squeak.

The silence became more deafening. I opened my mouth, but words choked me again. Finally, with a calming breath, I cleared my throat.

"I messed up."

Breath billowed in front of me. My voice cracked.

"After my brother died, I was scared. I've lost so many people, and it's like they all . . . just compounded and merged together when Jerry was gone. I sort of . . . I don't know . . . had a midlife crisis or something. I-I-I was afraid because all of your lives were moving forward, and mine wasn't. I felt like I was in the same old rut, and that I would stay there, probably for the rest of my life. Knowing that all of you would keep moving and I would stay behind was too much to bear. So . . . I thought . . . I guess . . . I thought I would leave you before you could leave me."

Megan's expression was the first to soften. The corners of her lips turned up in a slight smile when I paused.

"I'm sorry," I whispered. "I'm so, so sorry."

A definite shade of hurt lingered in Lexie's bright blue eyes. There was no backing out now. I had to be all in.

"I'm so much older than all of you," I said, "and I just needed people who could be a mirror for me, show me what I was going through and how to get through it. And then . . ."

Gladys ran through my mind. The loneliness in her eyes. The poor attempt at hiding her desperation. I didn't want that for myself, but maybe they wouldn't find room for forgiveness. Perhaps our lives *were* too far apart.

"I realized how stupid I've been. That just because my blood family is gone doesn't mean I'm an orphan. Because I do have a family." My gaze traveled to Bitsy, who stared at me with an unreadable expression. "I just have to *let* you be my family."

Lexie opened her mouth, then closed it again. There was still so much more to say, but I couldn't summon the words.

"Anyway," I said, hoping to combat the still-awkward air. "I guess I just needed to step back and reconfigure."

The word trailed away into the winter air. This time, instead of waiting for someone else to snap the thread of silence, I turned to Lexie.

"I'm so sorry that I haven't really celebrated your news and that I missed your baby shower. I want to talk to you about the baby and your plans and the pregnancy. There's not a lot of advice I can offer beyond five months, but I can at least commiserate."

Then I turned to Bitsy, and it was possibly the hardest moment of the entire night.

"I took a lot of my anger out on you. That wasn't fair. Instead of communicating, I just let go. I'm sorry. For what I said, and for not giving you a chance to work it out with me first."

Tears welled up in my eyes again, but before they could spill down my face, a pair of warm, strong arms wrapped around my shoulders.

Megan.

"We all have to step back sometimes." She pulled away to look me in the eye. "It's okay. If there's anything I've learned in the last couple of years, it's that family forgives. We stick together, no matter what. Blood ties notwithstanding."

My throat was too thick to speak when I hugged her back. Before I could utter another word, Rachelle wrapped her arms around both of us.

"We're all a bloody mess," she said. "Welcome to the club, Mira."

"Can I join?"

The timid voice belonged to Lexie. Megan and Rachelle stepped back, allowing me to see Lexie face-to-face.

"Do you hate me?" I asked.

"Hate you?" Her voice was raspy with tears. "I hate nausea, Mira. I hate how many calories are in my favorite brownies and how weight goes *right* to the hips. But I could never hate you. It's okay. You've been through a lot, and we haven't exactly taken care of you. I understand." She reached into her pocket, eyes swimming. In her hand, she held four brand-new sticks of my favorite lip gloss. "Look! I even brought these just in case."

She threw her arms around me. Pieces of my heart clicked back together. If I had just found the courage to tell them, maybe this all could have turned out differently.

Then again . . . maybe it wasn't supposed to.

"I was wrong."

All four of us looked up to see Bitsy standing a few steps away. Megan's eyes widened. Rachelle's jaw dropped.

"What?" Lexie screeched.

Bitsy shot her a quick glare. "Yes, I am *sometimes* wrong. But this time, I was really wrong. I got so used to Mira taking care of me that I forgot to take care of her. Mira has always been doing things for me. Babysitting the girls. Buying my haircut this summer. Listening when I needed a friend. I forgot to be honest with you, Mira, and give you the friendship back that you deserved. Will you . . . ah . . . can you . . ."

"Forgive you?" I asked, lips twitching. Bitsy sighed.

"*Please* forgive me," she said.

Rachelle snorted. Megan pretended to pass out. I yanked Bitsy into a hug that felt a lot like . . . home. They wouldn't leave me to die alone. Not if I let them stay.

Jim stepped closer to Bitsy, putting both of his hands on her shoulders. "We all love you, Mira," he said. "It will be good to have you back."

"The girls need you," Bitsy said. "They've desperately missed you, you know."

"They're the only granddaughters I have!" I cried, laughing.

While we all cleared our tears, Bradley glanced around the strip mall. His brow grew heavy over his eyes when he asked, "Is this place closing?"

"I read about the plans for redevelopment in the paper," William said. "Does it include your store?"

The sheer swamp of information I had to catch them up on nearly overwhelmed me. But that would have to come at a later time. Instead, I said, "Yes. It includes mine."

Rachelle's head snapped up. "What?"

Lexie gasped. "No! It's not possible. Bill's ghost would never allow it!"

My gaze traveled up the shop, then to the buildings that surrounded it. Cracks snaked through the sidewalk. Shadows—not entirely made of darkness—haunted the space. The strip mall had been falling apart for a while. I just hadn't seen it.

The time for change had come, and that meant big things. Big things that should have happened years ago. This time, I wouldn't be afraid.

"It's a long story," I said. "I'll tell you about it later. For tonight, let's celebrate! The entire Health and Happiness Society is back together again. Megan is married, Rachelle owns a store, Bitsy is moving, and Lexie is pregnant."

"What?" Bradley cried, then dodged a punch from Lexie.

"And this is *not* for the last time," Rachelle added.

"Hear, hear!" Bitsy called.

"Health and Happiness Society power!" Megan cried, fist raised.

"Everyone inside!" Rachelle said. "I have Lexie's favorite brownies and homemade oatmeal cookies and cinnamon rolls and everything she's been drooling over for the last two months."

Lexie dove into the store first, yanking Bradley behind her. Everyone followed, leaving me, Bitsy, and Jim behind, as if by unspoken agreement.

Bitsy reached out to hold my hands. "I wanted you to know that I've been really scared too. I'm sorry I wasn't more open with you."

"No apologies. Have you decided?" I asked, glancing between them. She drew in a deep breath that lifted her shoulders.

"Sort of. We're going to move into Jim's house."

My eyes widened. Bitsy held up a hand.

"Cora bought a house not far away that she plans on using whenever she comes to see her dad. He's going to move in there for the time being. That way we don't have to move far, the girls don't have to change schools yet, and we're still close to Daniel and Jade."

"So no marriage?"

When she glanced back at Jim, he squeezed her shoulders. "Not yet," she said, turning back to me. Her eyes sparkled. "But let's just say that it's not too far away, either."

A wave of happiness rippled through me. There was no jealousy or fear or anger, just joy.

For all of us.

"Well?" I asked, "Shall we go inside?"

The sound of an approaching car made me pause. A silver Honda drove past, parking only a few stalls away. Bitsy grinned. Jim muttered something like *always late, the weirdo.* My breath stopped in the back of my throat as I caught sight of a familiar head of blonde hair and a quick smile.

"Is that . . ."

The breathless words faded. Jim called over Bitsy's shoulder. "About time!"

"I was stuck in traffic!" a young woman called back.

"You know it's rude to be late!" he said.

"My father taught me to be fashionably late because he can't figure it out himself."

"Must be a stud of a man," Jim said. Bitsy snorted, then turned to me, grinning from ear to ear.

"Cora is here for Christmas," she said. "I realized that I still hadn't introduced you to the infamous Stephanie James, so I invited her for the party."

All the blood drained from my face, leaving a loud ringing in my ears. "Really?" I whispered as Cora shut the car door and started toward us. She wore an adorable black coat with a pair of bright pink heels. Her straight hair spilled over her shoulders in undulating waves as she walked. She looked like she'd walked right out of the movies.

"Trouble," Jim muttered, tsking under his breath as she approached. She crashed into his side with a lopsided smile. He tucked her in close, dropping a quick kiss on top of her head. She turned to me with a beaming smile.

"You must be Mira," she said. "I've heard so many wonderful things about you from Bitsy and the girls. I feel like I'm meeting a celebrity."

"It's so good to finally meet you," I said, holding out a hand. "Th-thank you for coming. I really am your biggest fan!"

"Impossible," Bitsy said. "Jim has already claimed that."

"I don't even like her," he muttered. Cora laughed. Rachelle poked her head outside the store.

"Hello? Can we get this party started already? The cinnamon rolls are getting cold!"

I hooked my arm around Bitsy.

"C'mon, Bits. We pulled this dieting group together, didn't we? Let's make sure it doesn't crash."

Forever

"What's your plan from here?" Rachelle asked an hour later while studying a cupcake with a tower of frosting, as if planning her attack. "I mean, now that you won't have the store. If you're missing small-business life, you know, you can always come run the Frosting Cottage."

William stood next to her, holding a glass of slushy lemonade and his usual quiet smile. His grandmother sat in a chair near the television, content with watching the party while Rachelle pampered her with offers of cookies, slush, and hot chocolate.

"I don't know," I drawled. "I haven't really thought this out yet. Maybe something with sewing again. Doing custom orders could be fun. I'll have to call Erasmus. I have some retirement issues to clean up."

In the background, Megan and Lexie sang a karaoke song, while Justin and Bradley attempted to figure out how to fix my broken television set. Bitsy and Jim had pulled out a couple of the vacuums from my stock and were admiring them. I thought I heard the words *Christmas present* and *wedding gift* float through the air.

Only Bitsy would want a vacuum for a Christmas present.

"William and I would be happy to start a propaganda campaign against Tadd at any time, you know. Seriously."

William nodded. "I love any reason to do a concert for a cause."

I laughed. "I don't think that will be necessary. In fact, if all goes according to plan, Tadd will contribute in a big way to my retirement fund."

"I think it sounds awesome," Lexie called from where she stood at the microphone. "You get to start over. You can do anything you want from here on out. You won't be tied to the store. You won't be worried about marketing and income and taxes and all that stuff that always went right over my head."

"Very true," I called back.

"Will there be time for you to babysit my child when I need a break?" Lexie asked. "I have a few editing firms that want to hire me, so I'll need someone to keep the baby alive while I edit and find my sanity again."

"Always. And I've already texted your mom," I shot back with a knowing smile. "We're meeting up next week to discuss quilts."

Lexie applauded, then fumbled with the microphone.

"Will there be room for me and Justin to stay when we come back to visit once a year?" Megan asked, sending a wink to her husband, who winked back.

"Are you going to take me to Honduras with you in February?" I asked.

"All are welcome," Justin said, "but it's not going to be fun building and running a hospital for a month in the heat and the bugs."

My nose wrinkled. "I think I'll just donate to the cause."

"Hey!" Megan cried, jumping on his back. "Speak for yourself, buddy."

"There's always room for you," I said to Megan. "Always."

Not for the first time that night, I thought of Gladys. What was lost in her life was found in mine. Possible pain notwithstanding, I was right where I belonged.

With all my friends.

My family.

"All right!" Bitsy called, tapping a plastic fork against her glass. "Everyone, pay attention. This week's meeting is now called to order." She looked over at me with a sly grin. "And Mira is in charge."

"No calorie counting, and free food for everyone!" I cried, thrusting my slushy drink higher. "Here's to delicious grub and even better company! The Health and Happiness Society will live forever—you can bet I'll make sure of that."

A raucous cry of agreement echoed my words.

The empty store loomed around me.

I couldn't believe nothing remained except for the built-in counter. Not even the cash register that had practically become an antique.

In fact, I'd sold it for almost a thousand dollars on eBay. A thousand dollars that tucked nicely into my new retirement fund.

Erasmus had been pleased.

The keys to the store jangled in my hand as I waited for Tadd. I paused in the silence.

"Bill?" I whispered.

Something shifted in the air, as if the store knew my change of heart. As if it understood what I was trying to say but couldn't find the words. My nostrils flared as I drew in a deep breath, lifting my shoulders with the effort.

"I love you."

The quiet air answered. No snarky whisper in my mind. No brush of a memory acting out in front of me.

Just the quiet store and me in it.

With December firmly in the rearview mirror and the beginning of a brand-new year only hours ahead, I couldn't believe how much had changed. Everything. It seems like too much and not enough at the same time. How could one comprehend selling their house, offloading their small business, and starting over?

Or maybe I never would, and it would just be a matter of working through things as they came. The way I always had.

The door opened behind me. I turned to find Tadd standing there.

"Welcome."

He grinned. "I'm not going to lie, those are words I never thought I'd hear from you."

I laughed. "Those are words I never expected to say. But here we are. Both of us on the cusp of something great."

I extended the keys to him without a beat of hesitation.

"These are for you now."

He accepted them, his smile widening. "You posed a pretty decent opposition, you know. But I never underestimated you. I could tell from the first moment we met that there was fire in your eyes."

"I had a few ghosts I needed to confront first."

Literally.

He shrugged. "We all do. Oh, you may be happy to know that the municipality approved the rezoning. Construction begins in a week."

"That is good news indeed."

"I have a few papers for you."

Tadd set a briefcase on the counter and opened it up. He handed me a manila folder with the words *Mira's Sewing and Vac* written across the front in sharpie. My hands didn't even tremble as I accepted the packet.

"Thanks," I said.

"All the paperwork is there. You've already signed everything, and now we've signed everything, so we're final. Those are your copies to keep. The money was wired over this morning."

I tucked the folder under my arm. "The bank called with confirmation. Thank you."

"Good. Oh, and Maude told me to tell you not to run away. Apparently, they still want you at the tea club she goes to every month."

I stifled a laugh. Tea club? She'd pulled a fast one over their eyes with that lie. But really—I couldn't blame her.

"Thanks. I plan on being there next week. Gladys has been calling me with death threats if I don't come. Stella bribed me with takeout, so I can't miss it."

Tadd smiled, looking for a moment like a young kid. "I wish you the best in whatever you pursue after this."

"Thanks."

I didn't know exactly what that would be. The beautiful thing was I didn't need to know. I had a meeting with my realtor in thirty minutes at the coffee shop down the street. Shortly after that, I'd stop at Sophia's to help her with the last of the cleaning before she left for the final time.

Sometime in the near future, I'd sell the house and buy one of those adorable townhouses Sophia had loved so much.

In for a penny, in for a pound.

Or so Mama used to say.

"Good luck, Tadd. Make this place into something great."

"It always has been."

When I walked out of the store for the final time, I knew I'd never be back. Not even to reminisce or see what became of it. The bittersweet feeling had passed days ago. I was no longer lost in the ghosts of the past.

What was lost was now found.

Acknowledgments

Mira's book posed a daunting and significant challenge for me.

Not only am I a thirty-something woman who hasn't lived Mira's life experiences, but I was wrapping up a five-book series that I was deeply in love with. (It's almost tragic at some point.) While I knew the series would have to end eventually, and this really was the best spot, I didn't want it to.

Most important, however, was making sure it wrapped up *right*.

For this, I owe a huge debt of gratitude to my beta team for not only reading the book and giving me feedback on early drafts, but doing it on a very tight timeline! Tara, Jennifer, Darcee, Amanda, and Kathy rushed to my rescue to help me make the best Mira book possible.

My team, as always, came through beautifully. Huge thanks to Kella, Jennifer Jenkins, Catherine, Stephanie, Jenny, Gemma, Kelly, Steve and my entire chick lit launch team, who are literally a group of supportive rock stars that I look forward to interacting with every day.

Most all: the biggest thanks to my readers. The *Health and Happiness Society* wouldn't be what it is without you. Thank you for the emails, for the connection, for the funny food memes you send me, and the comments on Facebook. Keep them coming, because there is more fantastic chick lit coming your way.

Trust me, friends. This is not the end, but just the beginning.

glitter bomb

—KC

About the Author

Katie Cross grew up in the mountains of Idaho, where she still loves to play when she gets the chance.

If she's not writing, you can find her traveling, working as a nurse, trail running with her husband and two dogs, or curled up with a book and a cup of chai.

To learn more about Katie, visit katiecrosschicklit.com.

Manufactured by Amazon.ca
Bolton, ON

12858394R00129